GW01003695

The Obsidian Mask

Caroline Ludovici

INFINITY
PUBLISHING

ISBN 978-0-7414-7064-5 Paperback
ISBN 978-0-7414-7065-2 Hardcover
ISBN 978-0-7414-7066-9 eBook

Printed in the United States of America

Published July 2014

INFINITY PUBLISHING
1094 New DeHaven Street, Suite 100
West Conshohocken, PA 19428-2713
Toll-free (877) BUY BOOK
Local Phone (610) 941-9999
Fax (610) 941-9959
Info@buybooksontheweb.com
www.buybooksontheweb.com

To the teacher who would read my stories out loud,
but laugh with the class at my spelling mistakes.

But more deservedly, to the creators of Spell-Check,
who will probably never realize how they have changed
some people's lives, giving them the ability to write
with confidence, conviction and ease.

PROLOGUE

THE ATTACK

3,000 BC

"I'll wear her out sooner or later," the General muttered bitterly. He looked out across the hot, dusty plain that separated him from the long ridge that rose out of the desert sands like a monument to his problems.

"She'll soon see who she's messing with; her water supply will be quenching my thirst before long, mark my words, Samek."

The General was camped with his army of six hundred on the south side of the shrinking river. He was preparing to attack the city of Ashook once again. He had been there a month and had attacked five times, taking heavy losses, but to his exasperation, with very little effect on the enemy. This infuriating delay in taking the small, scarcely fortified city nestled in the shade of the ridge, was partly due to Queen Sorrea's mounted archers, who, with their incredibly long bows could shoot with devastating accuracy while on the gallop. Yet it was the high, cliff-like ridge rising directly behind the city that had been the main obstacle to his victory, as it offered the Queen's lookouts a perfect panoramic surveillance of the whole Kingdom of Ashook, making a surprise attack from any direction virtually impossible.

In the early days of the siege, the General's aging King, King Arshir of Tamur, had received a proposal from an equally parched neighboring Kingdom to the north of Tamur. In return for a share of Ashook's water, the King was offered fresh reinforcements to help secure the siege. The General had first rebuffed the offer, taking it as an insult. He could take the city without anyone's help. There was no need to share the precious water with anyone. But now, as the exceptionally hot, dry days dragged on without a victory, and with his men on the verge of serious dehydration with no sign of even a cloud on the horizon, he had reluctantly swallowed his pride and sent word that he would accept the deal.

This supply of reinforcements was now seen as a windfall, and the General had little remorse in using the new arrivals as a cushion between his own men and Ashook's archers, especially as they had arrived exhausted, parched and undernourished. There was nothing 'fresh' about the reinforcements at all.

"Look at them," the General mused with distaste to Samek, his second in command. He glanced over at a group of the newly arrived foot soldiers a few yards away, who were trying to filter the mud from an almost empty water barrel. "Look! They're half dying of thirst anyway! Whether I decide to keep to this presumptuous water deal or not, is irrelevant. It would actually be a waste *not* to use them," he smirked. "They're such a scrawny, young bunch, they wouldn't survive the march home even if they survived the siege! Right, Samek?" he laughed.

Samek looked at him, but said nothing.

The General licked his dry lips, and his attention returned to the distant city walls beneath the ridge across the plain.

"How much longer do you think she can hold, General?" Samek eventually asked. "This campaign is a lot tougher than you originally anticipated, is it not, with the look-outs up there watching our every move, and the river drying up so quickly, and this heat…?"

The old warrior's eyes flashed at the young man, and Samek worried that he had spoken out of place. The General kicked his horse hard, yanking so violently at the reins that its neck bent far back and its eyes bulged in pain. He moved in close, pressing his horse's flank hard against Samek's, almost crushing his leg with the pressure. Samek immediately knew that he had spoken out of place. The General leant into him, looking him in the eye, breathing heavily. He slowly broke into a half smile, and wagged his finger in Samek's face.

"You should do well to remember, Samek, my boy that time is irrelevant," he said dryly, his breath in his face. "Humiliation and defeat are not in my vocabulary; never have been, nor will they ever be."

He held his gaze and the crushing pressure against Samek's leg with it.

Samek nodded at him, trying not to show the pain, and taking in the lesson. But still, he thought, it was not an answer, and the General knew it.

Releasing the pressure, the General steered his horse a couple of paces away, and stared back across the plain towards Ashook. The smile he had used to hide his irritation had disappeared, and he clenched his teeth. Inwardly, he was frustrated. He should have made a dent in the dusty walls by now, let alone penetrated them completely. The heat was getting to him, his eyes were sore and his throat was dry. This was a first for him. Samek was right, the Queen was holding fast. Never before had a campaign taken this long, it was unheard of in his long career. This could damage his reputation. Not only that, the thought of being on the banks of this cesspit of a river, even for another day, was almost unbearable.

"The woman is beginning to bore me," he said quietly to himself. "I need to draw her out."

He thought for a while, and then broke into a half-smile. He reached into his saddlebag for his canteen of water, poured himself a large cup and took a mouthful, feeling confident of his new plan. But before he could swallow he spat it out in disgust. He coughed violently and threw the cup away in temper. He wiped his mouth with the back of his hand, cursing the Queen.

"BOY!" he bellowed. "BOY! Get me some fresh water from the river. NOW!"

But when the young servant tried to explain that the water was foul however far upstream he went, the General leant over the side of his horse and kicked him in the backside, making him yelp in pain and fall over. Another servant boy rushed to his friend's rescue and scrambled to help him pick up the General's cup from the mud.

"Well go further up then, idiot!" he shouted at him. "And then when you've got the water, make sure you squeeze some pomegranate juice in it. Go!"

He watched the two boys scuttle away up stream through the camp, muttering that he'd have them whipped when they returned. He then turned his attention towards the city again.

Now he was seething. He took some deep breaths and refocused. He would lure her out, and he would do it tonight. He would send word that he wanted to talk. He would say the King had a proposal for her and wanted to negotiate after all. He would say he wanted to discuss the digging of the wells. She would like that!

But then, as if a gift from heaven above, the gods saved him the trouble.

A lone messenger from Ashook was cantering towards him. The General signaled to his men to hold their fire, and to let the rider approach. The young man dismounted in front of the General and Samek, bowed, and conveyed the news that the Queen and her entourage would be coming within the hour to discuss a truce. He wanted to know if the General would be willing to receive her.

"Oh, yes," he said dryly. "Tell your Queen we will receive her. We will receive her with pleasure."

Queen Sorrea knew that the stubborn General might again refuse her offer of help. But she had to try one last time, especially now that he would be feeling the ill effects first hand of the shrinking river. Twice before she had offered him the loan of her brilliant chief engineer, Hashamet. The proposal had been to start the digging and get their new wells operational in Tamur as soon as possible. But twice she had been spurned.

Ashook's water was stored in two massive underground reservoirs in the western quarter of the city, which fed the canals, irrigating her land for as far as the eye could see. These subterranean reservoirs had taken four years to chisel out of the bedrock and had been a necessity after the last two droughts. Queen Sorrea's people knew that Hashamet's water works were an engineering marvel.

Although there was an envious amount of water stored in the reservoirs, they still needed rain to sustain the levels. The water table was slowly shrinking, and despite cutting the flow to the outermost fields, the level still continued to shrink. Even the daily prayers and offerings month after month to the sacred black rock housed deep within the inner chamber of the Temple, the High Priests of Ashook found they could do nothing to please the gods; it seemed that no amount of incense or ritual purification could bring on the rains. Each day the sky seemed bluer than the day before, pounding the whole region with never ending, relentless, blistering heat. Even the harbor on the coast directly to the south was almost dry, and the ships were having to be anchored further out to sea to prevent them from becoming stuck in the sand, which was slowly encroaching the shoreline, and it seemed, no amount of praying could stop it.

Because of the shortsightedness of the desperate King of Tamur and his General to secure their own city's water storage units, despite the attacks on her city, the Queen decided to make one final attempt to stop the pointless bloodshed and ride out to the General's camp herself, with

Hashamet, the wiry, white-haired engineer. Perhaps talking to the General face to face, and having the plans explained by the engineer himself, would persuade the General to see sense.

She took with her a small bodyguard of ten chariots to show the General that she came in peace. It was risky, but she knew his reputation as a strategic planner in battle was as important to him as the victories themselves, and it would be very unlikely and out of character if he were to do anything cowardly to tarnish his heroic reputation.

However, to cover the odds, she had made sure her mounted archers were at the ready by the city walls, far enough away so as not be seen by the General. If there was trouble, one of the charioteers would shoot a flag into the air and the lookouts on the ridge behind them would sound the alarm for the archers to respond with lightning speed.

So with this precaution in place, Queen Sorrea approached the General, and they greeted each other cordially on the near side of the muddy river. The Queen introduced Hashamet and his assistant to the General, and he in return introduced Samek, who bowed his head respectfully at the famous warrior Queen.

The Queen asked Hashamet the Engineer to explain to the General what he could do for the King and the parched city of Tamur.

Blinking his eyes in bouts of rapid succession, as he did when he was under stress, the little engineer started to explain to the General, with the aid of detailed diagrams on his clay tablets and in as simple terms as he could, how fresh, drinkable water could still be brought to the surface in Tamur within the week.

"General, I can still, even at this stage of the drought, guarantee a good supply of water for your King and his thirsty citizens if we act immediately."

He received no response. He looked at the General, not quite understanding why he hadn't jumped at the offer.

"…The longer we delay the breaking of new ground, General, the deeper we will have to dig, which of course will delay the project further. I did explain this with the last correspondence to your noble King…"

The General said nothing and shifted uncomfortably in his saddle.

"Believe me General; I *know* the lay of the land," Hashamet continued, almost pleading. "I understand the rocks and the earth. I have this circular drilling mechanism that can cut through extremely dry earth…"

Still, no response.

"...I can estimate within nine or ten paces where the best place would be to strike for the new wells, I can read the land and with my testing probes, and see what lies beneath as if it was as clear as sky, my Lord. I have even designed holding tanks similar to ours for your noble city for when the rains do arrive; your rocks on the west of the city are perfectly suitable for them…"

He went on to explain about the filter he had developed, that removed many of the impurities in the water, which would also cut down on the sickness that occurred when water tables were so low, as at times such as these. He offered the detailed tablets for the General to examine, but the General wouldn't even look at them. He ignored the little white haired genius as if he was invisible.

Instead, the General stared at the Queen and slowly shook his head in defiance.

"No," he said under his breath, almost grinning at her, enjoying her frustration.

The Queen sighed. It was as if his ignorance was a virtue, she thought.

The General glanced back at Samek mounted on his agitated, black stallion a couple of paces behind him. He was gripping the horse tightly between his knees on an even tighter rein to keep the animal under control. The two men smirked at each other, as if sharing an inside joke. Though in truth, Samek was unsure of his General's plan. He wondered why he hadn't jumped upon the chance to have wells and holding tanks built; a truce was surely better than bloodshed. He was confused too, as until now he had been unaware of any previous correspondence between the two cities in regards to the digging of wells and holding tanks that the engineer had just mentioned.

"So be it, this was your final chance," the Queen said, demanding the General's attention. "Can you not see that it is all pointless? Tamur and Ashook have been neighbors and traded peacefully for over fifteen generations. My father and King Arshir hunted together as boys. There has never been a bad word between us, ever!"

She was unable to hide her frustration.

"We have never been enemies, General, are you sure this is King Arshir's wish?" she asked. "Is all this bloodshed, this death, really what your King wants? Or is it what *you* want, General?"

She had her suspicions that the frail old King was being pushed into action; this was so out of character. But she couldn't be sure. Desperate men take desperate measures.

Not a word of response was uttered by the General. The Queen sighed, and composed herself.

"We have offered peace, and a solution. At this rate there will be no one left alive to drink the water," she said. "Who knows when the rains will come?"

The General stared back at the Queen with contempt, but still said nothing.

She looked him in the eye and spoke slowly and surely, so that it would penetrate his thick skin.

"General, I will not surrender my water tanks, my livestock or my fertile lands to you. King Arshir knows we have little enough water for ourselves; we cannot support your people too. These are desperate times for everyone, and you repeatedly refuse my offer to help you dig your own new wells. Until now we have been on the defense. From this day forward we will be on the attack. And, may I point out to you General that not only do we have the water, and the longbows, but we also have the high ground. I do not think you understand the gravity of your situation."

No response. Only his face changed color.

Queen Sorrea knew she that was renowned across the land for her kindness and diplomacy, but she wondered if her thirsty neighbors had now mistaken this as a sign of weakness. She held her ground, hoping the bloodthirsty General had begun to question his actions and misjudged her strength.

But, it seemed, this was not the case.

The General, seething, glared at the Queen, using all his self-control not to strike her off her chariot and drive a spear through her arrogant heart. His eyes narrowed and his knuckles turned white as he clenched his reins.

"May the gods be with you, General," she said softly, and she looked into his cold, unflinching eyes. Tomorrow morning, before first light, she would send her scouts and archers to surround his camp while they slept. She would put an end to the attacks once and for all.

They turned their chariots and the Queen and her small entourage started their way back across the plain towards the safety of the city walls of Ashook. But it was a journey they would never finish.

Before they were half way across the dry plain the deep roar of four hundred hooves thundering behind them made their stomachs churn in utter disbelief. The hard ground shuddered and trembled beneath the wheels like a tremendous earthquake. They whipped their horses harder and yelled at the top of their voices urging them to gallop on faster and faster, shouting them on, willing them on. But their yells were drowned out over the thundering roar gaining on them, and their swift, lightweight chariots were no match for the charging men on horseback.

The deep rumble became louder as the enemy gained on them, closer and closer, and before they could turn their chariots and face them, the enemy was upon them.

The Queen's guards put up a wall between their Queen and the enemy, and fought a heroic fight before they were hacked down. Only minutes later their mounted archers had flown like the wind to get to their Queen, but too late. The archer whose job had been to shoot the signal into the air had misfired due to the speed of his retreating chariot, and he had to waste seconds in firing a second. But every second counted. In horror, the people of Ashook watched the massacre from the top of the ridge; The General had attacked so far from the city walls and so close to his camp by the river, that it was over by the time the archers could reach their Queen.

There was a hush. The Queen's bodyguards lay in pieces, their blood soaking into the thirsty ground, their limbs sliced from their bodies and scattered like branches of a tree after a storm.

The triumphant General quickly retreated back across the muddy river, leaving behind his own two dozen or so slaughtered and dying men to blister in the sun. He couldn't believe his luck.

"It was almost too easy," he said to Samek, smirking to himself. "I should have done this weeks ago!"

And it wasn't quite over yet; it was to get even better for him. The Queen's furious mounted archers charged after the General towards the river, but the General had anticipated this by having his men lie in ambush on the riverbanks in the reeds, with long ropes laid just below the surface across the line of attack. As the charging horses passed over them, they pulled at the ropes, causing the horses to rear and stumble. There was utter confusion and mayhem. It didn't take long before the Queen's archers were lying lifeless on the ground.

"What a victory, Samek!" the General laughed, drunk in his own triumph. "Soon we will be bathing in their water tanks! One last wave on the city and we will be in!"

Hashamet, the brilliant engineer, who had made the city of Ashook the envy of all cities with his pumps and ingenious methods of supplying clean, running water to every household, was dead. His clay tablets lay trampled and smashed on the ground around him, along with his brilliant designs, which would be lost for centuries to come. His assistant's body lay next to him, lifeless and limp; his severed head a few yards away by an overturned chariot.

Face down in the sand, only a few yards from her dying horse, lay Queen Sorrea. She was horrifically wounded. But despite the arrows in her back and the blood red sand beneath her, she was still breathing. And unlike those around her, she was in one piece.

THE QUEEN

"My Lady, the Queen is stirring. Come quickly, your Highness, she is opening her eyes!"

The physician beckoned the young Princess Afsineh over to her mother's bedside. She had been sitting by the window of the vast, airy bedchamber for the last twelve hours, praying for a sign that would show some glimpse of hope, of recovery.

She wiped her eyes and ran over to the physician, who was bent over her mother's bed.

He too had been anxiously waiting for a response from the Queen. After recovering her from the scene of the massacre, it had taken them several hours to stabilize her, to clean and suture the wounds. Given time, her prognosis could have been promising, but for one major setback.

"Princess," the chief physician said softly, "you must prepare yourself, My Lady. Of the two arrowheads lodged in her Majesty's back, it is the one nearest her neck that is the most dangerous. The one which had entered the lower left side by her pelvis we have removed with relative ease, but after examining this one, I regret that the options facing us are..." he hesitated, "...are as we feared. Because of its position, My Lady, removing it would cause paralysis and certain..." he looked down, "certain..."

The Princess's eyes widened as she tried to take in what he was saying.

"Leaving the arrowhead where it is," the younger physician quickly stepped in, "might give the Queen a day or two if we keep her still and relatively pain free."

Although she knew her mother's injuries were bad, it was distressing for Princess Afsineh to have the situation confirmed by the only men that could save her. Devastated, her head was spinning. She was weak at the knees, as she tried to come to terms with the inevitable.

Her mother had at her disposal all the latest medicines available to the civilized world, including medicines from Egypt that reduced infection and relieved pain. Her surgeons had learned advanced surgical techniques from the Indian team of physicians who had stayed for two months teaching their revolutionary methods of reconstructive surgery, especially how to overcome the problems of skin graft rejection, which had always been a problem for soldiers with facial injuries, particularly to the nose.

But it wasn't any use to the Queen. What the physicians needed now was a miracle.

However, for the first time since the attack, the Queen was stirring. She was trying to speak. The Princess leant over her mother's bed.

"Mother, it's me, Afsineh..."

Queen Sorrea opened her eyes and looked at her only surviving daughter. She smiled at her, and closed her eyes again. She could see her little girl as a three-year-old, red faced, screaming and kicking as she was lifted up into her father's lap into the saddle for the first time. The child had hated it, she was terrified of the horse, but the King had persevered, as he had done with all their children.

That was a long time ago, long before the droughts. Long before these attacks; a lifetime ago.

"Tell Sima to come back and play her harp. Quickly! Please hurry!" Afsineh whispered the order over her shoulder to the maid standing behind her.

The two guards at the far side of the room lifted the massive bolt and heaved open the ornate double doors for the maid, as she ran across the polished floor to find the girl. A breeze swept through the chamber and stirred the silk curtains at the window and around her bed.

Within seconds, the young harpist was there, red eyed and blotchy faced. She was sixteen, slightly built, with jet-black hair down to her waist. Her black eyeliner was smudged, and she had given up caring.

The young girl sat at her harp a few feet away from the foot of the bed, and played a lullaby to the best of her ability through her silent tears.

"Afsinehhhh," the Queen whispered to her daughter. "Afsineh, the kingdom is now yours. I leave Ashook in your care. Lead us into battle, my child. He will attack soon, when he has regrouped. Be ready…"

She coughed quietly, and gathered the strength to ask for her maid.

"But mother, don't leave me here alone, I cannot do this without you..." She felt helpless, terrified.

The Queen's breathing became heavy and labored.

"Mother, don't go. Don't leave me. *Please.*"

Afsineh looked desperately to the physician standing on the other side of the bed. He felt the Queen's pulse, and then slowly shook his bald head. He backed away to give the Princess more privacy.

Afsineh looked at her mother. She had closed her eyes again, but had still managed a smile when she heard the harp playing one of her favorite melodies. The Princess gently shook her mother's shoulder, as if keeping her awake and focused would make her well again. The older physician tried to comfort the Princess, taking her hand from her mother's shoulder.

"It will soon be her time, my Lady," he said softly. "She has been great Queen, my Lady, truly, a great Queen." Because of her foresight, we all prospered, while other Kingdoms struggled and suffered in this time of drought. Our lands are still green and fertile while elsewhere is parched. She is a Queen who will be remembered for many generations, and with much, much honor."

"Thank you, Doctor," Afsineh sniffed. "Your kind words are comforting. But how can she be honored if we are all to die in battle? Who will be left to remember her?"

He bowed, and walked around to the base of the bed to replace the pot of frankincense with a new one, and lit it.

"It is in the hands of the gods. You will find a way to honor the Queen, My Lady," he said bowing his head. "The gods will help you. And afterwards, your grief will no longer be painful, but a joy in the thought of the reunion, as it will be for all of us, for we shall all be with the Queen in the afterlife." He smiled, bowed again and left Afsineh with her mother.

In her sixteen years, Afsineh had lost everyone close to her. Her husband had died in battle; her father, her uncle and younger brother were gone too. There was no one left to advise her. Her mother's trusted advisor had gone to Tamur six days ago to negotiate directly with the King, and he hadn't returned. They fear he never even reached the city. Afsineh felt desperate.

"Mother, you must get well, please."

The Queen whispered something. Afsineh immediately told the harpist to stop playing. She knelt down closer to hear. The Queen was asking for her maid.

The maid quickly came over and bent over the Queen, putting her ear close to the Queens lips. She then hurriedly left the room.

She returned with a small, bulging leather bag and placed it beside the Queen's hand. She then bowed and withdrew to the corner of the room.

The Queen nestled the bag, and then pushed it with the back of her weak hand the small distance across the sheet towards her daughter. Afsineh knew what the bag contained. The Queen looked at her daughter and nodded. She reached out and stroked her daughter's damp cheek and smiled. She closed her eyes, and then was gone.

The Mask

Afsineh climbed the steep path that wound its way up the side of the cliff to the top of the ridge. It was a tough climb, but she knew the path well. She had climbed it secretly since she was a young girl, usually covering her head and face with a veil so as not to be recognized. Watching the sun set over the land was something that had always given her delight. But it was without pleasure this night.

Looking out across the plains she could just see through her tears, the edge of the cultivated land on the horizon. Caravans used to appear from the east, sometimes hundreds of traders at a time, bringing all kinds of goods and luxuries to Ashook, Tamur, and Ur and other cities along their path. But they hadn't come this year or the last. Not since the rains stopped. The once-green pastures were turning a pale, sandy color and the desert was encroaching. It was frightening to see it so clearly. What was she going to do with the city on the brink of disaster? How could she cope without her mother?

She needed to stop crying. She needed to think. Crying had weakened her, exhausted her, and she found the preparations for her mother's burial ceremony too much to take. The all too familiar sickly smell of incense in the air everywhere she went seemed to stick in her throat. It made her feel ill; it was the smell of mourning, it was the smell of death. At least at the top of the ridge where there was a light breeze, she could escape from it all.

Afsineh looked down at her sad city below her. Everyone had had their share of grief; many families had lost a young son or a husband in the recent attacks. They were tired of war, of fighting, and of visualizing the inevitable disaster that would follow.

And now their Queen was dead, and it was the next attack that could overpower them completely. What would become of her city, of the survivors? Had the gods abandoned them? She wept again and looked to the heavens for help.

Across Ashook, the evening lights were coming on one by one. To the left, behind the curve of the ridge, Afsineh could see a straight, white plume of smoke rising up from the temple complex. The high priests would be busy through the night, she thought.

The sprawling palace below her was in darkness. Its two hundred rooms were lifeless and hushed. This really was the end, she thought. No more family gatherings, entertainment or ceremonies; it was over. Just empty rooms. She wished she could stay up on the ridge all night.

Beyond the twinkling lights of the outer city walls, across the fertile plain that was now the source of all their problems, there, in the distance, on the other side of the diminished river, Afsineh could just make out in the fading light, a large grey smudge. This was the General's encampment. He was now part of the landscape, like an ugly infection that wouldn't respond to treatment. He wasn't going anywhere, she thought, he was here to the end.

Afsineh knew the General would be reveling in the death of her mother and gathering strength for his next onslaught. The attack would come soon. Perhaps tomorrow or the day after, he would be back for the final push.

The eerie silence over the mourning city was broken by a lone falcon, soaring and circling a hundred feet above Afsineh, its screech reaching far across the plain. She thought how lucky the falcon was, to be free to soar the skies. When they were all gone and the city had turned to dust, she thought, the falcon's offspring would still be here, flying above her ridge to the end of time.

She sighed, wanting to close her swollen eyes, to make today go away. But she had to think. She slowly followed the path along the perimeter of the cliff-top to the first of the lookout guards. He stood by his torch that danced and lit up the sky around him. He straightened his body and bowed his head in respect as he recognized the Princess approaching. To his side was a large stone with a flat, smooth surface, and the guard took a couple of steps away from it in case the Princess wished to sit there.

She took up the silent offer and rested her exhausted body.

She sat for a few minutes, and watched the sun sink behind the horizon, as it had done since time began.

She wiped her eyes, and untied the strap over her shoulder that held the leather pouch. She studied it. It was soft and well worn, and she saw that had been recently re-lined in turquoise silk. Perhaps, she thought, her mother had done that in the knowledge that she would soon be passing it on to her.

She tried to hold back the tears, but couldn't. She sniffed in a very unladylike manner but she didn't care. She wiped her nose defiantly with the back of her hand.

The guard stepped a few paces further away from her to give her more privacy, his own moist eyes catching the flicker of the torchlight.

Opening the golden threaded drawstring and gently tipping the contents of the pouch into her lap, she let the weight of about thirty precious stones form a well in the soft folds of her tunic between her knees. In the faint light, she examined them through her tears. Each stone represented a child born to the Royal family. With each newborn child, a stone had been blessed by the high priests in the special 'naming ceremony'. This ceremony was a tradition as old as time, and the birthstones were passed down through the family, from generation to generation. No one had ever seen what the High priests did in the naming ceremony with the babies, as it took place deep in the inner chamber of the temple. This was where the sacred black rock lay; the exact spot where it had been pushed up from the depths of the earth by the gods when the world was on fire at the beginning of time.

Afsineh gently rolled the stones between her hands. She asked the guard if he could bring the torch closer.

He detached the top section of the torch from its pole, and stepped towards her, lowering the flame nearer her side. He stood stiffly beside her.

"Come and see," she offered him with a smile. She needed to talk to someone. "These pieces of polished alabaster are from Egypt, the land where the great river flows northwards instead of southwards; they look almost transparent, don't they? And these, these are lapis lazuli, which was my father's favorite stone."

The guard looked at them politely and nodded, not quite sure if he should converse with the Princess.

"These little round pink and white pearls come from India," she offered. "The traveling physicians who stayed with us when I was a child, told me that where they came from small boys, some as young as six years old, make a living by diving into the deep sea and prise the shells apart to find these precious pearls inside."

She looked up at the soldier, who said nothing. "It is dangerous work," she continued. "Boys have to hold their breath for very long periods. The physicians told me that they are often eaten whole by white sea-monsters, with sharp jagged teeth and jaws as big as a house. Can you imagine?"

The guard's eyes widened in horror. He leant over her shoulder, still keeping his distance, and looked closer at the pearls.

"If I may, my Lady, it seems to me," he said softly, "that your family's birthstones are very precious. They must not be lost or dispersed, or their efforts and this war will have all been for nothing. The Queen's determination to protect our water, to keep the peace in the region as your forefathers had done, all this must not be forgotten. These stones represent her reign, and her father's-father's reign. Keep them together as one, away from the enemy so that we may stay intact through them."

He lowered his head in respect, unsure if he had gone too far.

She nodded, and smiled. The princess had not taken offence.

"I am sorry for your loss, my Princess," he continued in a hushed voice. "It is a sad day. It is the end of an era, or even more. But perhaps, if I may say, I believe the gods took the Queen today…" he paused and looked out across the plain towards the General's encampment, "so that she would not have to witness what is to come tomorrow."

Afsineh thought about it, and nodded. She knew it was the end.

"Yes. It is over. But I will find a way to honor her, and our ancestors." She looked down at the stones. She knew what she had to do.

"I will bury these Royal birthstones with my mother, and they will remain with her for eternity. I will have a magnificent death mask carved for her. It will be carved from the gift from the gods itself. What better way to honor the mighty warrior Queen of Ashook than to have her mask carved from the sacred stone of Ashook?"

"This will be fitting," the young man said, his eyes smiling at the thought of it. "I trust the high priests will permit it."

She turned to look at him. "I will see to it. It will be permitted. Our remaining days on this earth are few; Even the priest's days are coming to an end, and they will not be able to protect the sacred stone from their graves."

"As it came from the centre of earth when the gods created the world," he said, "so it will return to the earth.

What better way to honor the Queen of Ashook than to be buried with the sacred stone?"

He smiled at the young Princess with approval.

"Yes! And the Queen will have her ancestor's birth-stones of every generation with her forever. I will have the mask inlayed so beautifully that the gods themselves will gasp. It will protect her, and our history. She will never be forgotten."

She looked at the guard through her tears. He smiled giving her encouragement.

"It would be wise to have the work started tonight, my Lady," he said, looking out to the west. A dark, menacing line could be seen in the dim light, encroaching across the plain.

"Reinforcements," he said quietly. He stared out at them. "There must be a thousand or more."

He stood upright, and took back his position as guard. "We will protect you, fight for you to the death, my Lady."

She whispered her thanks to the guard, but knew his efforts would be futile. The enemy was increasing in size by the hour. It was the end. Afsineh looked down over her city. Perhaps, she thought, for the last time. The city's fate, and all its inhabitants, was frightening. But now she had a purpose; something she had to fulfill before the final attack. She would immortalize her mother, the noble and just Queen of Ashook would forever remain deep below her beloved city, and protected by the mask.

She stood up and looked out into the darkness towards the General's encampment.

"You may succeed in removing us from this world General," she said defiantly into the night, "But our history will never be removed from this place. The sacred stone will remain here, protecting the Queen, and all our souls for eternity."

Chapter One

Present Day

Two men squatted behind the largest of the rocks that narrowed the pass down to a one-way track. They had been patiently waiting there for the distant hum of the car for over two hours and one of the men, who's uniform was particularly tight, was sweating miserably in the heat and having trouble staying low on his haunches. He stood up again despite his orders to stay hidden, stretching out his blood-starved legs and lighting a cigarette. He was bored and impatient, but before he could complain yet again, he was told by his accomplice to get back behind the rock. He cursed under his breath, and took a last stretch to get the circulation going again. He cracked his neck from side to side, and then reluctantly went back to squat in his uncomfortable post.

*   *   *   *   *

Natasha awoke feeling revoltingly sweaty. Her long hair was sticking to the back of her neck and the car seat, and she wished she had changed out of her hot jeans at the airport, as her mother had suggested. Through her half-opened eyes and the haze of the hot, afternoon sun reflecting off the hood of the old Land Rover, she could see that they were much closer to the ridge than when she had nodded off. That was a relief, she thought, they were almost there.

She looked across the sand dunes at the gigantic lump of rock shimmering in the heat. She could now see the vertical split in it that her mother had mentioned in her emails. Through the narrow split, or pass, on the other side, was the archaeological site of the ancient settlement where her mother had been working for the last two months.

As she watched her mother concentrate on keeping the car on the sand-blown track, it crossed Natasha's mind that she must be quite an important member of the team, being paid to stay out here in the middle of nowhere. She had never really thought about it before, she had always just been 'Mum'. But now she looked at her in a different light. Natasha's father had mentioned that the director of the dig had even helped her mother pay for their plane tickets, which was further confirmation that her mother was a valued member on the team. But still, Natasha felt torn; she couldn't help feeling resentful that her mother had been abroad for so long, taking a job so far away. So this new feeling of pride and respect was a little conflicting.

Her mother was an epigrapher. She drew and recorded in great detail everything that they unearthed at the dig *in-situ*. Why they couldn't just take photographs, Natasha didn't really understand. But, she thought, at least the job gave her and her brother the opportunity of coming out to an exotic country for the holidays. She had counted the days until she would be with her. Since the divorce, the novelty of staying with her father in his large, newly refurbished house on the other side of London, was wearing thin.

"His stupid girlfriend, Eva," Natasha had complained to her best friend, "doesn't look much older than us! She always seems to be at the house, pushing her way in, with her pathetic little voice and tight little tops. All the giggling and flirting makes me sick!" Natasha had also confided to her friend that she was spending more and more time up in her room just to avoid Eva. She wished her mother would come back to London so she could go home to some kind of normalcy. She had longed too for the end of term, when she could fly out and spend time with her. Even the thought of camping and living in a stuffy tent with temperatures topping one hundred degrees, had begun to seem inviting.

And now she was here at last.

The silence from the back seat told Natasha that Alex had fallen asleep. The early morning flight from Heathrow had knocked them both back a bit, so Natasha took the opportunity of having her mother to herself.

"Mum, how much longer do you think you'll be out here?"

"Oh, hello sleepy head, you've woken up," her mother said. She took Natasha's hand and squeezed it. "I've missed you, you know."

"Me too," Natasha said. "Will you have to be out here much longer? It's been ages, Mum."

"Not too much longer; a couple of months at the most I should think. Have you been OK staying at your father's? You seem happy in your emails." She looked at Natasha for confirmation.

"Yeah, it's fine." She shrugged. There was no point in telling her mother about Eva, she thought, but then out of the blue her mother asked her if her father had a girlfriend. Natasha replied that he had, but she didn't elaborate or give any more information about Eva than she had to. She changed the subject by asking about the excavation. To Natasha's relief, her mother seemed just as happy to change the subject too.

"Well, as you know, we're working on the site of a very large palace," she said. "From what we can tell, it was absolutely massive. It must have been an impressive sight in its day, with something like two hundred rooms within its walls."

"That's huge! Can you really tell what it was like just from the ruins?"

"Oh yes, there were courtyards, lavish bathrooms, kitchens, servant's apartments, gardens, and armories and a throne room. It had everything. It was almost a city in itself. Most of it is still unexcavated of course, and a lot of it has crumbled away, having been constructed mainly of clay bricks. But the quality of some of the things we have found so far is just incredible."

"What do you mean?" Alex interjected from the back seat. "Like treasure?" He had woken up and leant forward so he didn't miss a word.

His mother grinned.

"Treasure can be different things to different people, and it doesn't always have to be silver or gold or pieces-of-eight, Alex."

Alex sat back in his seat a little disappointed.

"But," she added, "I suppose in a way, you could say we've found treasure, even your kind of treasure."

"Really?" Natasha eyed her mother closely to see if she was joking.

"Yes, we did. It's been an incredible week."

She looked seriously at Natasha. "We've unearthed the tomb of a five thousand year-old Mesopotamian Queen," she said, and added quietly, as if sharing a secret. "We think it's the lost tomb of Queen Sorrea, a Queen who was thought of more as a legend, than a real Queen."

"Really?"

"Yes. Not only have we found her tomb, but her complete skeleton. It's all there, thanks to the dry air, and she has been totally undisturbed since the day she was entombed. That's pretty amazing, you know, that tomb robbers hadn't found it in all that time."

"Wow!" Alex said.

"And..." Natasha prompted her, "go on..."

"Well, if it is Queen Sorrea, and we are pretty sure it is, this will be a very, very important find," she said. "A lot of people from all over the world will be very excited."

"Wow, will we get to see her skeleton?" Alex asked.

"Of Course! Not only will you be able to see the Queen's skeleton, but also those of her guards, a young female who was probably a maid, and her horse, all of whom were buried in the tomb with her."

"That is so cool!" Alex couldn't believe his ears.

"No it's not," Natasha muttered pensively, she wasn't sure if she liked the sound of that at all. She decided not to think about it, and went in a different direction.

"But what did you mean about finding Alex's kind of treasure?" she asked. "Was the Queen buried with all her jewelry and things?"

"Yes she certainly was, but even more lovely than her jewelry, was her amazing death mask."

"*Death* mask?" Alex pulled a face. It didn't sound that wonderful to him.

"This mask is like nothing I've ever seen, Alex. It's incredible. It's carved from large, single piece of the most beautiful obsidian." She looked at him in the rear view mirror. "Do you know what obsidian is?"

"Nope."

"Obsidian is a rare, jet black, volcanic glass, and it is *extremely* precious."

"Oh, I've heard of that, I think," Natasha said. "Isn't it really hard? Didn't the Aztecs use it for daggers and stuff?"

"Yes, they did. It was often used for blades and weapons. Anyway, this mask we found is encrusted with the finest jewels and gemstones. It is exquisite; absolutely priceless! And it's inlaid so delicately and with such care, it is really quite stunning. I think it will become as famous as Tutankhamen's mask when the word is out."

"Wow! So is it still in one piece?" Natasha asked.

"Yes, miraculously, it is; not even a crack or a chip on it. It was covering her skull, and was found in exactly the same position that it was left in when the tomb was sealed all those thousands of years ago. In fact," she added, "it is so fragile, and so precious, that last night we wrapped and boxed it up very carefully. Since I was coming to meet you two at the airport today, we decided that I take it first thing this morning to the bank in Medinabad for safe keeping. It was just too risky to keep it on site with the other artifacts in the 'finds' room."

"Big responsibility, Mum!" Alex joked.

"Actually, it was, Alex. You can imagine how nervous I was; a priceless treasure strapped onto the car seat next to me here. That was a very slow drive, I can tell you."

"But what if you had tripped and dropped it?" Alex asked, "or driven over a hidden pothole or a stone; it could have smashed into a thousand pieces!"

"Well, she didn't did she," retorted his sister.

"Well, she could have been kidnapped then, and held for ransom."

"No one knows about it yet, stupid," Natasha said. "And anyway Alex, I don't think anybody gets kidnapped and held for ransom these days, that's only in films."

"Come on you two, there's no need for an argument. Anyway," their mother continued, "the mask will stay in the bank's vaults out of harm's way until the experts can examine and date it properly. As Alex suggested, we wouldn't want it getting into the wrong hands. It is priceless, and it really will become a national treasure once the press release is out and we announce its discovery in a couple of days."

"Wow, that's so cool, Mum, will you be rich and famous?" Alex asked.

She smiled and shook her head.

"Sorry Alex, it doesn't work like that. We're not treasure hunters. We're here for the love of it, not the rewards. I'll show you around the whole site tomorrow and you'll be able to see the tomb where we found the mask, and the palace - or what we've uncovered of it so far, anyway." She paused then added almost as an after thought, "oh, and I forgot to mention, Marcello's two children are here. They arrived a couple of days ago. You'll have someone your own age to hang out wi..."

"*MARCELLO*?" Natasha yelled. "Not *MARCELLO*? You never told us *he* was going to be here!"

Natasha folded her arms tightly and stared out of the side window, frowning. Julia immediately pulled over to the side of the road and stopped the car. She couldn't believe Natasha's sudden change in attitude. She looked at her daughter in astonishment.

"Natasha," she said, as calmly as she could, "I thought you knew Marcello was the director of this dig, surely you knew that he would be here, and even if you didn't, I'm sorry, but there is no reason to react like this!"

She looked at her daughter, who continued to stare out of the window tight lipped, her arms still folded across her chest.

Julia sighed, waited a minute, then calmly approached her daughter again, almost pleading. "Darling, come on, you don't have to make a scene, what on earth's the matter? Marcello is *such* nice man, and he is very fond of you both."

She waited for some kind of response from her daughter, but got none.

"Come on darling, don't make a drama over nothing. Please?"

Julia leant towards Natasha and tried to give her a hug. But Natasha wasn't having it. She wriggled on her seat as far away from her mother as she could, arms still crossed tightly, and continued to stare out of her side window.

"I thought we would have you to *ourselves*," she eventually mumbled under her breath. "I thought *he* was in Pisa digging up those stupid sunken ships he told us about."

Julia sighed again, remembering when the children had met Marcello when he was in London a few months ago. He had come over for supper before Julia had decided to take the job in Medinabad. She thought the evening had gone pretty well. Natasha never said anything which led Julia to think otherwise, so she was a little surprised, to say the least, by her daughter's reaction now.

Julia turned around and looked at Alex, hoping for some sort of explanation. He looked at her and shrugged his shoulders. He was just as baffled.

"I don't mind him," he offered happily as he checked for bandits and camels through his binoculars. "When Marcello came over for supper that time, he told me all about Herculaneum, and the problem they have of stopping it crumbling away. It's a big problem, you know Mum, being exposed to the elements and everything. Marcello said that the best thing would be to cover it all up again."

"Good," Julia said, only half listening, and turned back to Natasha. "And I will expect impeccable behavior and civility from you both when we arrive."

And with that, Julia jumped out of the car.

"Well, come on you two," she called as she opened the back door, "since we've stopped, we may as well have a break. And let's tie your hair back, Natasha; it's grown a lot since I last saw you. It's almost all the way down your back! I'll plait it for you if you like, it'll help you cool down. And you can both get out of those hot jeans."

After a drink and a change of clothes, Natasha and Alex felt a lot more comfortable. Natasha, although a little subdued, let her mother tie her hair back in a French plait, which she could never do so well on her own.

When Julia had finished, she gave Natasha a kiss on her forehead.

"Feel better?"

Natasha shrugged, looking at the ground.

"Come on, let's put it behind us," Julia said. "We're nearly there now."

"Sorry," she mumbled.

"Apologies accepted. Come on, hop in."

CHAPTER TWO

Natasha and Alex were surprised to see how high the cliffs rose above them. The ridge looked at least two hundred feet high, maybe more. Seeing it from a distance across the desert had been deceiving. Now that they were driving along its base, the jagged overhangs and outcrops looked dramatic as the sun cast shadows over the rock formations.

"Are we heading to where the flashing light was?" Alex asked. "I saw something earlier through my binoculars on top of the ridge."

"A light? Up there? I don't think you could have, there's no electricity out here, except a couple of over worked generators in the main tents in the camp. It's all very basic, Alex, I'm afraid, even the water has to be brought in by truck. We've no 'mod cons' at all. I expect it was just a reflection on your lens."

The bumpy track at the base of the cliff weaved between and around fallen stones and rocks, and then it turned to the left into the natural gap that split the cliff into two.

"Wow, we'll have fun exploring here, Natasha!" Alex said, examining the narrow pass. Above them, the sky had disappeared to a thin strip of blue, in places barely separating the tops of the cliffs from each other and keeping most of the hot sun out; the air was much cooler. Alex stuck his head out of the window and looked up. A falcon circled the top of the cliffs, then swooped down so low that Alex felt the rush of air over his head before it soared up high to the top of the cliffs again. Its high-pitched screech sounded eerie as it echoed off the rock face. He watched the falcon land on a ledge high up on the left, before it disappeared from view.

"Mum! Did you see that?"

"I did! I was hoping he'd come and greet us," she said. "He's usually around somewhere."

"It's probably being territorial trying to frighten us away, not greet us, Mum," Natasha said. "We're probably disturbing him, Alex."

Alex ignored his sister, and called out, "hello."

Back came the reply, "hello…hello… hello…"

The towering cliffs had almost closed in on them on both sides, and Alex's voice bounced off the walls over and over, softer and softer, until it had gone.

They neared the point where the pass was at its narrowest. Suddenly, two men, carrying guns, sprang out from behind a boulder and blocked the pass with their outstretched arms, taking advantage of two strategically placed boulders that narrowed the pass even more. They were shouting in Arabic and waving at Julia to stop the car. Julia obliged, and her hands froze tightly to the steering wheel. She kept the engine running.

The two men ran to the car, shouting and banging loudly on the side with their guns drawn, indicating that everyone should get out. The children were terrified and didn't move. The men indicated by shouting and miming at Julia that she was to turn the engine off. She reluctantly obeyed and quickly glanced ahead to the end of the pass in the hope of seeing anyone from the camp. But there was no one. At this time of day everyone would still be at the excavation site for another hour or two.

"Come on, we'd better do what they say. They want us out," she said as steadily as she could. "It'll be fine, don't worry, I won't let them hurt you."

She cautiously climbed out, her mind racing as to what she should do next. But she was immediately grabbed by the arm and pulled away from the car by the taller of the two men. He pointed with his gun to where he wanted her to stand. She refused to move away from her children, and pulled her arm from his grip. He became angry and waved the gun in her face, then again over to where he wanted her to stand a few feet away. Julia realized they were not joking. She quickly moved to where he was pointing. He shouted into her face. That was obviously a warning, she thought, but she refused to be intimidated.

"Don't you dare touch my children!" she shouted. "Who *are* you? And what on earth do you think you're *doing*?" she demanded.

She was ignored. They either didn't speak English, or they chose not to. She then tried in French and broken Italian, but to no effect.

The shorter of the two men pulled the children out of the car and indicated with a shove that they should stand by their mother, away from the car. The children were terrified and did as they were told.

"I *said*," Julia tried again, a little louder, putting her arms around her children, "what do you think you're *doing*? You just can't go around holding people up at gunpoint, looting at will!" Her voice echoed around the cliffs above them, but it had little effect on the men. She was completely ignored again. The echo made her realize how stupid that had sounded, since holding them up at gunpoint, and looting at will was exactly what they were doing.

So Julia and her children stood there, helplessly, watching these aggressive men open all the car doors and proceed to empty everything out of their bags and throw the disregarded contents on to the ground. They acted fast, and didn't seem interested in anything they came across, including Alex's camera and Natasha's ipod. Everything was cast aside around them.

"Don't worry, I don't think it's us they want," Julia whispered after a while. "I don't think what they're after is in the car, either."

The children looked at her and she gave them a wink.

Both men continued to empty the Land Rover of Julia's field equipment, trays, bottles of water, maps, ranging poles; they disregarded everything. The taller one was obviously giving the orders, as he was shouting at the heavier one, who was sweating and looking very worried and red in the face. Having tipped out the contents of the children's bags and emptied the car of anything loose, the two men then climbed into the car and lifted up the seats. They even took the spare wheel off the back door and examined it, then kicked it. They could find nothing, it seemed, that they wanted.

They were becoming more frustrated. The taller one clipped the other one around the head with the back of his hand. There was still a lot of shouting and waving of arms by both of them, and if it hadn't been so frightening, Alex thought, it would have been funny. He even had to concentrate on not giggling out loud. The tall one was now stamping his feet in temper, kicking at the dusty ground, and waving his gun around as if it was a toy, getting himself wound up and ready to explode. The fatter of the two tried his best to calm the other down.

When he had composed himself, wiped his brow and dusted himself off, the taller of the two men indicated to Julia, with a flick of his gun, to put everything back into the car.

Julia slowly walked over and carefully started to pick up the children's bags and clothes. She made the point of brushing everything off, carefully folding them, and re-packing them properly, looking at the men defiantly in the eye as she did so. She then walked around the car and slowly and meticulously proceeded pack her equipment back into the back, as if to make it known that they had been greatly wronged.

Natasha realized that her mother was showing them she was not intimidated. She took her time, and for the second time that day, Natasha felt proud of her mother.

The men grew impatient, and bent down to help Julia, muttering to each other bitterly. She even indicated that they put the spare wheel back onto the back door, and they did, to Natasha's amazement. They were in a hurry to get going, and Julia knew it. Another car from the camp, just around the corner could appear at anytime and catch these men red handed. She knew they needed to be quick so she continued to load up the car as slowly as she dared.

More words were exchanged, the men talked under their breath for a while. The taller man looked over at the children and beckoned to them to come over quickly and help finish loading, but Natasha and Alex weren't sure if it was safe to move, seeing that guns were still being waved at them. Realizing their concern, the fatter man put his gun in its holster in an over emphasized gesture, making sure the children understood they were not going to be shot. He then waved them over again, smiling, and talking in an overly friendly tone, which Natasha understood to mean, "I'm not going to hurt you, it's all a big mistake..."

His disgusting smile revolted Natasha, and she noticed he had a gold tooth on his bottom row, which she thought ridiculous; was he trying to look like a pirate or something? She couldn't bear looking at him. His accomplice also put away his weapon, gave an apologetic smile and went over and patted Alex on the head. He jerked his head away.

"Get off, you creep," he said under his breath.

The man laughed, almost over compensating for the children's expressions of distain. He tried to mime that it was all a big joke. He indicated that they go and help their mother pack up the car, and it was safe to do so. The children checked with her first before they moved, and she nodded that it was OK.

As Natasha walked past the shorter man, he whispered something in her ear, and stroked her plait as she went past him. Natasha turned round sharply and shouted, "don't *touch* me, you disgusting creep!"

Julia immediately stood up to see what had happened, and both men shook their hands as if to say, "sorry, sorry." The tall man quickly spoke, and the short man gave a fake laugh and threw his arms in the air to show it was all OK, or a sort of joke, a big, big mistake.

"Are you OK Natasha?" her mother asked.

"Yes, he's just a creep," she spat out, staring the man in the eyes defiantly.

Julia noticed he had a small flashlight protruding from his pocket. Alex had been right then, she thought. He had seen a signal after all.

With all their belongings back in the car, Julia and her children were told to get back in and go. Julia gave one last look at the men before turning the ignition key. She started the car, and sped off, leaving the men coughing in a cloud of dust.

Chapter Three

The three shaken travelers finally pulled into the camp. They were tired and glad to have arrived in one piece. Julia told her children to try to forget what had just happened. Though she was extremely shaken herself, she tried not to show it and made light of the episode. She emphasized that the men had obviously made a terrible mistake. It was clear they hadn't been interested in them or their possessions at all, and that's why they looked so foolish putting everything back in the car. She reassured her children that she would report the incident immediately and the men would be arrested in no time. She promised that nothing like that would ever happen again, and they could relax and enjoy their holiday.

"The area is really quite safe," she reassured them. "What happened today was a fluke, an experience that will never be repeated," she said. "In fact, I wouldn't be surprised if you found he rest of your stay a bit uneventful, even boring, after what happened today."

"That's Ok Mum, we'll take boring," Natasha said dryly.

"Yeah, but Tash, what a great story to tell our friends and at school next term! They'll never believe it!"

It was early evening, and the people working on the dig were starting to come back into the camp from the excavation site. As Julia walked her children through the little canvas village, they were introduced to a few of them returning to their tents. They looked tired, dusty and hot, but seemed happy to meet the children. Natasha commented on how young some of them looked, and asked her mother how many volunteers or students there were working at the site.

"There must be about twenty-five or thirty, from twelve different countries, I think. Most of them are probably in their late teens to early twenties. A few volunteers are a lot older though. They come out here and treat it as a working holiday. But the majority of the people here are university students, who volunteer their time in exchange for an amazing experience."

Natasha thought how interesting it would be to do something like this for her gap year before university when the time came.

"Mum, how does everyone communicate, with so many different nationalities?" she asked.

"Good question, but easy answer; mostly English!"

"But ov course," Alex said in his best French accent. "Zere ees no ozer language but Eengleesh."

"Yeah, lucky for you!" his sister said. She hit him with her bag.

They walked down an avenue of about twenty or so tents, until they reached the one that their mother called 'home'. Outside the entrance, under the shade of the attached canopy, stood a small foldaway table and an overturned box for a chair. On the ground, was an oriental rug that Julia told the children she had paid far too much for in the market in Medinabad, when she had first arrived.

"Can we go inside?" Alex asked, already untying the tent flap.

"Be my guest."

Apart from a camp bed, a couple of lamps, and a rug on the floor, there were papers, books and some camera equipment piled on one side of the tent. In the corner nearest the door, there was a metal grid leaning up against a pole, and a couple of trowels.

"Sorry about the state of it, I have to keep some of my equipment in here too; I do a lot of work in here in the evenings," she explained.

The children stood there for a moment.

"But Mum, where are we going to sleep?" Alex asked.

Julia pointed to the tent next door. "Come on, I'll show you. It's not exactly the Savoy," she said, untying the door flap. "But it's the best we can do."

"It's great, Mum," Alex said, already inside, and checking out one of the camp beds.

"Yeah, it's big," Natasha said. "It's great, Mum." She looked at her mother and noticed that she was looking a little uneasy, her mind was elsewhere.

"Would you two mind if I go and…"

"Mum, we're fine," Natasha interrupted. "Go and report those men. We'll be fine, honestly. We'll stay here and unpack."

"Sure? I won't be long."

"Just *go*!"

She quickly left to find Marcello, and the children checked out what was to be their home for the next couple of weeks. Their tent was one of those that could be divided down the middle by a canvas partition if needed, with a camp bed on either side of it. There were two little windows with mosquito mesh above each bed, and an oil lamp on two overturned boxes beside them. It was actually quite cozy.

Natasha sat happily on her chosen bed on the right, grinning at her brother while he fiddled with the mosquito nets. She put her clothes away in the box by her bed, and set her clock forward to local time.

"Come on, Alex, let's go and have a look around. I'm dying to find the bathroom; I'm about to burst. Coming?"

At the end of their row of tents, there was a very substantial, solid looking tent with a pitched roof and wooden floor. Alex suggested that it was probably an ex-army tent. It had wires and cables disappearing into it along the ground, and it had a padlock on the door.

"I bet that's where they keep all the stuff they find," Alex said.

"Who cares, come on, let's find the bathroom."

A few yards further on stood an even larger tent and from the noise coming from within, it sounded packed with people. It was obviously the camp's canteen. A sign outside showed the day's dinner menu, which Alex stopped to read but, but Natasha quickly pushed on.

"Come on Alex, aren't you coming? I bet the bathrooms are behind here somewhere."

Behind the canteen tent were two canvas blocks. Natasha ran into the one with a sign with a picture of a lady in a skirt and immediately came out again, horrified.

"*No way*!" she cried. "*No way* am I going in there. The walls are just thin fabric, and there's not even a roof! *Anyone* could look down from the ridge up there and see people peeing! They've *got* to be joking!" She was desperate, almost in tears, hopping on the spot.

Her brother laughed.

"Shut *up.* It's not funny Alex! Stop laughing. Do you think there's another one around here?"

"Nope," he smirked.

She ran back into the ladies room undoing her shorts, saying how she wouldn't have come out here had she known about the bathrooms.

When she came out again, she admitted that they weren't so bad after all. They were clean at least, and there were showers too, with taps hooked up to small overhead tanks.

"OK, I've seen worse," she admitted as they walked back towards their tent. "Remember when we went skiing with Dad last year? This was nothing compared to that dark wooden hut on the mountain with the hole in the floor. That was just unbearable!"

Alex groaned and pretended to stick his fingers down his throat at the thought of it.

"That was bad. Yup," he said. "That definitely takes first prize."

"I know, imagine how it was for me trying to cope with a one-piece ski suit, trying not to slip on that icy wooden floor; And stop laughing, Alex!" she thumped him on the shoulder. "You should be grateful you're a boy."

They walked back towards their tent, with the warm evening sun on their backs, happy to be in a completely different world from the one they had left that morning.

The hold-up in the pass wasn't even mentioned.

CHAPTER FOUR

Sitting across from Natasha and Alex's tent, was a young man writing at his table and enjoying a misty looking drink from a jam-jar. He had looked up when he heard Natasha and Alex approaching.

"Hello," he called to them, "you two sound happy. I could hear you talking and laughing from over here," he said. He spoke with a slight accent, and had very tanned forearms and Natasha also noticed he was at the prickly stage of growing a beard.

"Oh, we were just discussing the Alps," she said, hesitating and flushing, knowing it was only a half-truth, and hoping he hadn't heard what they really had been discussing. "I hope we didn't disturb you, sorry..." she felt a little embarrassed.

"Not at all, you've come just at the right time. Come, sit with me," he said grinning at them. "You must be Julia's two. I've heard much about you. Welcome to our little village!"

He indicated with a swoop of his hand for them to sit on the overturned boxes next to his chair. As he helped them pull the boxes closer to the table, Natasha noticed he wore a very worn string bracelet with a couple of brown beads on it around his wrist. She wondered if a girlfriend had given it to him.

"Thanks," Alex said. They sat down with him at his table.

He looked about twenty, maybe twenty-one, Natasha thought, but it was hard to tell. He had curly dark blond hair that was obviously growing longer than he was used to, as he kept brushing it out of his eyes.

"My name is Yanni," he said. "Would you like to try my own freshly squeezed lime juice? It's still a little sour, but I like it that way."

He poured the children their drinks into two jam-jars.

"I sweetened it already, but here is more sugar if you need it."

He placed a small bag of lumpy, grey sugar onto the table. He wiped a spoon that was on the table with his t-shirt and put it next to the sugar.

The children sipped the juice.

"Thank you," Alex said. "I like it like this. It doesn't need any more sugar." He looked at his sister for back up.

Natasha had lost her tongue.

Yanni leaned back in his chair, stretched out his long legs, and crossed them so they stuck out the other side of the table. Natasha noticed that his white socks had turned pale orange from the sand, and they almost matched the color of his suede ankle boots. His legs were tanned too and the blond curly hairs on his shins curled over the top of his socks.

She looked away and flushed.

He tipped his chair back and rocked it slightly, relaxed, holding his drink with both hands on his flat stomach.

"You didn't tell me your names," he said eventually, looking at Natasha.

She didn't say anything, and took a gulp of lime juice.

"Oh sorry," Alex said, looking at his sister, wondering why on earth she had gone so quiet. "I'm Alex, and this is my mute sister, Natasha."

"*Alex*," she protested. "I was *drinking*!"

"Ah, you have beautiful names, we have these names in my country also. You know, my real name is Maric Janowski, but here they call me Yanni for short."

"Where is your country?" Alex asked.

"Where it has always been! Ha!" he giggled.

"I *mean*, where do you come from?"

"Aha! I am from Poland, and I will be studding Business and Economics at Krakow University next year. I am taking a full year out before I start, for work experience," he chuckled to himself, and added in a sheepish, almost guilty tone, "the work should really be related to my courses, but you see, I also have a passion for ancient history. When would I get the chance to do something like this again? And with a man such as Marcello! Business studies can wait, no?"

He took a sip of his juice and Natasha noticed he had slender, long fingers, like a pianist might have.

"It is a privilege to be here," he continued, "but it is also hard work, especially in that pounding heat all day." He massaged the back of his neck with his hand and looked up at the blue evening sky, "but it is fascinating too, I wouldn't miss it for the world."

He smiled at Natasha, and asked her if she had thought about what she wanted to do when she finished school.

She took another gulp of juice, and a deep breath.

"I'm not sure, but I like history too, I mean, like my mother," she added quickly.

She glanced up at his face, and down at her juice again. He was still smiling at her. She saw that he had brown eyes, and that his sun burnt nose was peeling a little. Still looking down at her drink, she told him that she wouldn't mind taking a year out before university too, and then work on a dig like this one.

"It sounds really interesting," she said, "digging up the past."

"Oh my *goodness*," Yanni said excitedly, as if he had just remembered something extremely important. He sat up, and leant forward over the table to tell the children, "Interesting, is an understatement! Just this week," he said, pulling his chair in closer to them, "this week has been amazing! Fan-*tas*-tic!"

He was shaking his head in disbelief, and the curls over his forehead shook with him.

"Did Julia tell you what we found in the tomb? Un-be-*lievable*."

"Yes, she did," Natasha said, happy to share something with him. "Do you think it really is Queen... Queen..." she struggled trying to remember the Queen's name.

"Sorrea! Queen Sorrea!" Yanni said. "Yes it must be, it *must* be her! It can be no one else!" He was smiling at Natasha with almost childish enthusiasm.

"Finding her means so much, because she was always thought by scholars and historians as only a legend, you know, like your King Arthur. But now we have found her. Not just her palace, you understand, but actually *her*! It is just incredible. You know she was not only a warrior, a peacekeeper, but she had a very sophisticated city here. They traded with distant cities, and with other countries too, you know. Many trade routes passed right through here, from the East, and China, bringing the finest things the world had to offer."

"What happened to the Queen then?" Alex asked. "Where did it all go?" He found it hard to imagine, with nothing but sand as far as the eye could see.

"It seems that unfortunately for them, the climate changed rather rapidly. All the rivers dried up, and there was a massacre here."

"A massacre?" Natasha was horrified.

"There is evidence of flames and scorching on some of the bricks, which would indicate the people here lost their city in a violent attack. Probably an attack from some neighboring city. Who knows? But what is interesting is that the Queen must have died before the final attack, as she was entombed with order and method, and with possessions, which indicates that there was no battle raging at the time of the burial. They seemed to have had plenty of time to bury her rather nicely." He took a gulp of his juice again.

"Wow, that's fascinating," Natasha said.

"Tomorrow, Natasha you must come and see her..."

He was interrupted by Julia approaching his tent.

"Ah, there you are."

The children looked up to see their mother with her arms laden with drinks, panini and fruit. Natasha felt a little disappointed that she had arrived just as things were getting interesting.

"I wondered if you two had gone for a wander, I see you've found Yanni," Julia said.

"Hello," he said. "Yes, we are having a good chat."

Yes, and you're spoiling it, Mum, Natasha thought.

Julia told Yanni that Marcello was holding a meeting for the whole camp that night at seven o'clock in the main tent. It was important, and everyone was expected to attend.

Yanni looked surprised, and asked if anything was wrong. Julia shrugged and smiled at him, but didn't answer his question, and Natasha sensed that if she and Alex hadn't been there, her mother would have told him more. She knew what it was about.

"No problem, I'll be there," Yanni said. He understood by her silence that something was up.

They thanked him for the lime juice, and walked over to their tent.

"The meeting is to do with what happened to us today, isn't it, Mum," Natasha said. She sounded a little worried, the whole ordeal of the men in the pass coming back to her.

"Oh darling, don't you worry about a thing. Marcello just has to take steps to make sure that it doesn't happen again, that's all. He's going to tell everyone that they must report anyone they see not associated with the dig. From now on, everyone is going to have to check themselves in and out of the camp, that's all. He has informed the authorities about those two men, so they can deal with it and leave us to do our job here in peace. We won't be bothered again, don't you worry. But what I need you two to do before you go to bed, is to write down everything you can remember, separately, without conferring with each other or discussing what you both remember, so that the police can read both accounts and get as much description of the men as they can."

"Cool!" Alex said.

"You don't mind?" Julia looked at Natasha. "The Chief of police gave specific instructions for us to do it, I have just written my account for him. And when that's done, it will be the end of it."

"No, I don't mind, I'll do it, and then like you say, we can just forget about it once and for all," Natasha said.

"Exactly." Julia smiled reassuringly at her children. "Here," she said, "I thought you two might want a picnic in your tent tonight, you must both be very tired after your long day. How about an early night tonight, then you'll both be as right as rain in the morning."

They were tired. They wrote the descriptions out as well as they could remember and joked about the idiots who had held them up and had not even bothered to steal anything. They had a bite to eat and within the hour, they were both asleep.

Julia returned to pick up their papers and she kissed her children on their foreheads, and blew out the lamp.

"How lucky I am," she said to herself, as she looked at them in the semi-darkness. She had missed them dreadfully. She stood there for a minute listening to their breathing, so grateful to have them with her. They had both had a frightening experience today, she thought. They all had, for that matter; very frightening. They had coped with the situation very well, too. She was so proud of them. They were growing up fast.

Julia sat down on the end of Alex's bed, and put her head in her hands.

She sat there for a few minutes, going over and over the incident in her head, questioning herself for putting her children's lives at risk.

She realized though, after a few minutes that it was pointless to dwell on it. It wasn't constructive, and she couldn't change what had happened. What she could do, was think positively and do her best to make sure the men were caught quickly.

She picked up the two pieces of paper, kissed her children again and then reluctantly left them for the night.

Outside the tent, she made sure the zip was completely closed all the way to the bottom, and then she bent down and tied the two pieces of chord at the base in a bow. She laughed at herself. "Oh really, get a grip," she whispered. "As if that's going to make an iota of a difference." But she still made sure the little bow was tight, anyway.

She went to spread the word about the meeting.

CHAPTER FIVE

"BUONGIORNO! BUONGIORNO BAMBINI!"

Natasha opened her eyes with a jolt wondering where on earth she was. Ah yes; she remembered: the airport, her mother, the camp. She turned over on the creaky camp bed, and closed her eyes tight. Then she remembered those two horrible men, and Yanni.

"*Buongiorno*! Wakey, wakey, rise and shine, you two..." came the booming voice again from outside the tent. Alex had jumped out of bed and was already opening the flap.

"Hello, hello," said the thick Italian accent. "Are you two awake yet?"

"Well, we are *now*," Natasha murmured sarcastically. She sighed, and reluctantly rolled out of bed.

"Oh boy, here we go," she said to herself, and went outside.

Marcello was standing in front of their tent with his arms wide open, grinning from ear to ear waiting to greet them. He wore a worn floppy leather hat that Natasha thought looked as old as him, and a crisp white linen shirt that matched his teeth.

"Natasha! Alex!" he bellowed, "I am so happy you are here. Welcome, welcome!"

He went forward, and put a hairy arm around each of them, and kissed them both on their cheeks. He then spun them around to face Julia, and held them against him in a friendly grip under their chins. Julia laughed at him.

"Your children are almost as *beautiful* as you are, Julia," he said to her, and he kissed them both again.

Julia giggled and came forward to give him a slap on his shoulder.

"Oh stop it, Marcello! You're too much!" she said, turning red.

Natasha was nearly choking with revulsion; not only was he openly flirting with her mother, but Marcello's disgustingly hairy forearms were tickling her chin. She stiffly broke free from his bear-hug and the aroma of his aftershave as politely as she could, and stood by her mother, rather awkwardly, aware that she was outside in her pajamas.

"Why don't you two quickly go and get washed and dressed," Julia suggested. "Meet us in the canteen as soon you're ready. Marcello's children are already there having breakfast. They're very keen to meet you."

"OK," Natasha sighed, then forced a smile to cover it.

"I see you all in a few minutes... don't be too long," Marcello laughed.

"By the way," Julia added quietly to her children when he had gone, "you don't have to worry yourselves any more about yesterday's incident at the pass. It has all been taken care of. The Chief of Police was here last night until the early hours. It's all under control now and in the hands of the authorities, so don't even think of it any more. Promise? Today is a fresh start."

"OK Mum," they replied.

"Oh, and, by the way, before I forget," she added, "Marcello told his son about the little incident, but he said he would rather it wasn't talked about in front of his daughter, you know, she is younger and, well, a bit..." Julia struggled for a word, "a bit *precious,* shall we say."

Natasha and Alex looked at each other and rolled their eyes.

"O-K."

"Really, Natasha," Alex said, after Julia left them to get dressed, "that girl's got to be just awful! If Mum has to tell us to watch what we say in front of her, can you imagine what she's like?"

"I know, she sounds pathetic, and I refuse to spend any time with her, Alex. She's more your age, so I'm afraid she's your problem."

"What? You've got to be kidding! She's a girl! Sorry, Natasha, she's all yours! I bet she even wears frilly knickers and lacy petticoats. Sorry, she's nothing to do with me."

"That is *so* not fair! Just because she's a girl doesn't mean I have to be stuck with her!"

"Just because she's closer to my age doesn't mean she's lumped with me either. Sorry, you loose. She's a girl and pathetic, so that's that. She's all yours!"

And so the banter went back and forth until they reached the canteen tent.

With the smell of bacon and eggs wafting towards them, both children were reminded how hungry they were, and when they opened the door, the room was so packed full of people it took them by surprise and they forgot about the argument. There were rows of tables stretching right to the back wall of the tent, and every chair seemed to be taken. They stood in the doorway for a minute, not sure where their mother was in the sea of people in front of them.

"Over there!" Alex said pointing to the back of the tent. "See? Marcello's waving to us, over there."

"OK, I see them." Natasha saw her mother waving them over.

Marcello was standing up, grinning, waiting for them, and when they reached the table, he announced proudly, almost operatically, with his shoulders back and arm outstretched towards his children, "Natasha, Alex, may I present to you, my children, Gabriella and Lorenzo."

A tall, handsome, young man of about fifteen or sixteen, tanned, with tidy black, wavy hair, wearing a white shirt with the sleeves neatly turned back halfway up his forearms, just like his father's, had immediately stood up from his chair. He shook Alex and Natasha's hand with a small bow and a nod to each of them, which Alex thought was very cool. Natasha noticed he wore designer jeans with a crocodile belt. She thought how disgusting that was. No one wears crocodile *anything* these days.

Lorenzo said in clear, precise English, with an accent not quite as strong as his father's, "I am delighted to meet you. My sister and I have been keenly awaiting your arrival."

Natasha looked at him in disbelief, but he gave a very genuine half grin when he shook her hand that made her believe that he really was pleased to meet them despite the formal introduction. She thought too that he had very kind, twinkly eyes; He looked quite friendly, despite his carefully put-together look. She then reminded herself not to be easily taken in. She didn't like his disgusting father and she certainly wasn't going be fooled into liking Lorenzo either.

Natasha and Alex were offered the chairs saved for them each side of Marcello, but as Natasha sat down, Marcello held the back of her chair in order to help her slide it back to the table. She immediately turned and snapped at him, "I can do it myself, thank you!"

Julia flushed at her daughter's rudeness, and glanced apologetically across the table at Marcello. He gave her a wink, as if to tell her not to worry, it'll be all right, give it time.

Julia sighed, and got up to get her children's breakfast. As she passed behind Marcello, he gently caught her hand and squeezed it to give her further reassurance.

Natasha was preoccupied looking at Lorenzo's pathetic sister. She was about thirteen, and although she too had stood up to shake hands when she had been introduced, she seemed totally disinterested in Alex and Natasha, and didn't smile or make much eye contact at all. She had a frilly blue blouse on with flowers and tiny birds all over it, just as they had dreaded, and her dark curly locks were tied neatly to the sides of her head with matching ribbons. Way too old for the Gretel look, she thought. Gabriella looked at her 'Papa' and asked him in a whiny voice if there was anything different to eat because she didn't like the eggs he had brought her.

Natasha and Alex glanced at each other and tried not to giggle.

"O, *darling*, of course, I will go and see what I can find." Marcello stroked her cheek then rose from his chair to join Julia in the serving area.

Natasha and Alex looked at each other again and did their best not to burst out in giggles and the four children were left alone together in awkward silence.

Lorenzo was the first to speak.

"How is your tent, Alex? Were you able to sleep on the narrow camp bed?"

"Yes, like a log! It's very cool, I like it, don't you?"

Lorenzo shrugged. "It is OK, but it took a couple of days, or should I say nights, to get used to it," he said and smiled, "but it's very easy to make in the mornings."

While Alex was still taking in the fact that Lorenzo actually made his bed, Gabriella announced that she didn't like her bed at all. "The noises outside the tent in the night make me nervous," she moaned, looking unhappily at her brother.

"But Gabriella, I told you there was nothing out there. How many times do you need me to check for you? How can I convince you? There is nothing outside the tent, *believe* me." Lorenzo was using his hands to emphasize his frustration with her, and Natasha could see he was fed up with all her moaning and groaning as well. She sighed. The thought of being stuck with her for the Easter holidays made Natasha feel desperate. This girl was dreadful! How long were they here for? She decided to ignore Gabriella completely and talk to Lorenzo instead.

"Your English is very good," she told him. "How long have you been learning it?"

"Thank you," he smiled, appreciating the compliment. "I work hard at it. I would say I have been studying English for about five years, but last year we changed schools and we now go to the International School in Milano, so English is the first language; all the classes are in English. Even math."

"Wow, that's impressive," Alex said. "I wish I could speak French as well as you speak English."

"I can help you," Lorenzo said. "We are learning French also, I am becoming quite proficient, and we learn German of course, too."

Alex looked at him in awe, and wished he could go to the International school in Milan too. How cool it must be to be multi-lingual. Alex made a promise to himself to pay attention in French class when he went back after the holidays. It would be kind of cool, he thought, to be able to just break out in another language. He wondered why he hadn't thought of it before; all those months of joking around in French class with his friends, instead of obtaining a secret weapon to pull out at times like these! Damn! He thought!

"I am very glad you are here," Lorenzo was saying to Natasha. "Today is our third day, and my father is very busy, and my sister and I were becoming a little bored, to say the least. I do not really understand why my father wanted us to come here at all. The camp is of course deserted most of the day, while everyone is over at the excavation site. And after a while, even that becomes a little dull, watching people brush the sand off crumbling walls and broken pottery with little paintbrushes..."

He pretended to dust off his coffee cup with his knife, with a seriously intense expression on his face, imitating the archaeologists. They all giggled at him.

"But did you see the mask before it went to Medina-bad?" Natasha asked, eager to hear what it was like.

"Yes, I did, very briefly," he said, almost dismissively. "There was a lot of fuss and commotion when it was unearthed." He shrugged his shoulders. He had nothing more to add.

"Well, you don't seem too impressed," Natasha said under her breath.

"My father has been on the phone continuously," Gabriella added. "All day, every day, to people all over the world since they opened up the tomb. It seems to be a very significant find."

Her accent was very heavy, and she spoke a little stiltedly, but her grammar was impeccable. Natasha hadn't imagined the pathetic girl would speak English so well. It made her a little ashamed not knowing any Italian.

Alex was equally impressed with Gabriella's command of the English language, and did his best to equal it.

"Did you see the skeletons of the Queen and her entourage? I understand they were entombed with her."

Natasha had to hold her breath so as not to burst out laughing at her brother.

"Oh *please*," groaned Gabriella. "Do we have to discuss such things over breakfast? It makes me ill."

They all looked at her, and before Natasha or Alex could think of anything to say, Marcello and Julia had returned with trays of melon, ham, and rolls.

Julia told her children that after breakfast, she would take them over to the site and familiarize them with the area, and show them the different sections that they were working on at the moment. She looked at Lorenzo and Gabriella. "Do you two want to come along too? I expect you've seen it all already, but you're welcome to come and show the site with me."

"Mum, they really won't want to…" Natasha was cut short by Lorenzo.

"Yes, thank you Mrs. Blandford, may we?" he answered happily.

"Of course, Lorenzo, but on one condition."

"Mrs. Blandford?"

"That you stop calling me Mrs. Blandford. Please? My name is Julia, I would like you both to call me by my first name."

Lorenzo glanced at his father for approval, got the nod, and then thanked her. Gabriella stuck out her bottom lip and frowned.

"*Cara*, Gabriella, what's wrong, why are you not happy?" Marcello asked her in a very concerned tone. "Is it the food? The chef *is* Italian you know. He is from Piacenza," he added, hoping that would help his daughter's appetite.

"Papa," she moaned, totally unimpressed by the chef's roots, "it is not so much the food. It is the ...everything. I do not like sleeping in the tent. I hear noises at night, and when I wake Lorenzo to see what is out there, the noise stops. Nobody believes me, Papa; nobody listens to me. Nobody takes any notice."

She played with the ham and melon on her plate, and stuck her bottom lip out as far as it would go.

Pathetic, Alex thought. What an act. How could Lorenzo share a tent with such a spoilt brat?

"Darling, of course we believe you," her father tried to reassure his daughter. "I am sure it is only desert foxes looking for scraps of food. They are harmless. There is no need to loose sleep over it, darling. We all hear what you are saying…"

The alarm sounded on is watch. He glanced at it, and quickly finished off his coffee.

"Well, I have a conference call in a minute. Have a good day all of you," he said, rising from his chair and grabbing his phone off the table. "And see you in a little while," he said, beaming at Julia. He picked up his hat and his papers, then added as an afterthought, "oh, and Please, I would prefer if you four did not go too far from the site. You never know what could happen, especially after your little incident yesterday." He was looking at Natasha and Alex. "Always keep the camp or the excavation site in view so that you cannot get lost. Distances can be very deceiving in the desert."

Natasha and the boys reassured him that they would. Gabriella fiddled with her food and didn't answer. She had no intention of going anywhere. Where was there to go anyway?

Marcello made his way through the almost empty canteen to the door. He called out to them from the end of the room, patting the top of his wavy grey hair, "and please, wear your hats! Ciao!"

His cell phone rang; he put his own hat on, and was gone.

CHAPTER SIX

Further around the base of the ridge, about a quarter of a mile away from the camp, the ground started to rise into gentle, undulating hills. To their untrained eyes, these hills looked to Natasha and Alex as if they were scattered with rocks and rubble. But the rubble was in fact the remains of the magnificent palace, which had overlooked a small city of about five or six thousand. Julia took the children over to the first of the mounds to try to help them visualize the scene as it had once looked.

"This whole area," she explained, "was once the Kingdom of Ashook, where this legendary warrior Queen lived, five thousand years ago. Just imagine it, there were the rows of stable blocks down there, teeming with busy grooms and..."

"Wait a minute, you mean real stable blocks, like we have today?" Alex interrupted.

"Yes, legend says that this Queen had a cavalry of mounted archers unmatched by any King in history."

"That's so weird," Natasha said quietly. "Five thousand..." It was eerie to her, seeing only sand dunes where a city had once thrived. "There's absolutely nothing left of them. All those people, all those horses, all that time ago. It's all gone..."

"Well actually, that's not entirely true," her mother said. "There is quite a bit left of them, really. We just have to look carefully. We've already found the stable blocks, which is important, as this backs up the legend of the mounted archers. And over here," Julia pointed to her right, "is where the palace kitchens used to be, where we found remnants of the ovens. Imagine busy cooks in the kitchens preparing sumptuous dishes for the guests. The Queen would have entertained Kings, Princes and dignitaries from far away lands in these beautiful rooms over here."

"But Mum, wait a minute," Alex interrupted again, "you said all this was over five thousand years ago. That's three thousand years before Christ! That's… that's…."

Julia looked at him. "Well yes, Alex, that's right." She didn't understand his confusion.

"But I mean, were people really living in luxury and being civilized that long ago? I mean that's a really long time ago; Three thousand years BC, it's like…"

"Alex," Julia said, "just because it seems like a long time ago to us, it doesn't mean people were living in caves. Five thousand years ago is like yesterday, compared to the length of time people have been around. And this particular region, Southern Mesopotamia, as you should know from your history lessons, is known as the 'cradle of civilization'. Thousands of years before Queen Sorrea lived here, agriculture and farming had its roots here. It's where we humans became 'civilized' and built the first communities. This is where it all started! So we have a lot to thank Queen Sorrea's ancestors for. She is pretty recent history!

"But Mum, wait," Natasha said. "Now I'm confused. I thought you just said this Queen, Queen Sorrea, was only a legend, which would mean she probably wasn't real at all."

"Well, she was a legend, but that doesn't mean she didn't exist. Things get forgotten over centuries, and sometimes they are lost forever. Sometimes a legend is all we have to go on to give us a lead, and more often than not, it can turn out to be pretty accurate; all it takes is a clue, and a special person to find the clue."

"This city, Ashook," she explained, "wasn't exactly found by chance, you know. Only the locals and a few archaeologists had ever heard about the ancient city, let alone its Queen. But far away, on a dusty shelf in a tiny museum in Sri Lanka, lay some ancient scripts, just waiting to be deciphered by the right person; someone who had heard the legend, and who would bring the legend back to life."

"In Sri Lanka?" Now Natasha was totally lost. "But that's off the coast of Southern India. What's that got to do with this place?"

"Well, here's the amazing thing; these ancient writings had been in this museum for over a hundred years; dusty, unnoticed and insignificant, just waiting for the legendry Queen's name that was mentioned in the scripts to be recognized. And one day, that someone did come along, and did just that. He deciphered the writing, which eventually lead us here, proving that Queen Sorrea was in fact an historical person."

"Like a detective story!" Gabriella said, showing interest for the first time.

"Exactly! He followed the clues. All legends have some truth to them. All it takes is a bit of luck and determination to get to the bottom of it."

"So this was my father?" Gabriella asked. "The person who saw these manuscripts and put the clues together?"

"You mean the *special* person," Natasha muttered under her breath.

"Yes, it was, Gabriella. Queen Sorrea has a lot to thank him for!"

"So what were these ancient writings about, anyway?" Natasha asked. She resented the fact that Marcello was such a hero in her mother's eyes, but at the same time she wanted to know more.

"Well, for the most part," Julia said, "they seem to be reports written by a team of Indian surgeons, who spent three years traveling and teaching their surgical techniques to cities all along the old trade routes. But they also mentioned a certain Queen, Queen Sorrea of Ashook, who they had stayed with during that tour.

"What, even in those days?" Alex asked. "They taught medical stuff way back then?"

"Alex, you're being a dork again," Natasha said, giving him a thump.

"It seems from these scripts," Julia continued, "that these Indian surgeons had stopped here, which makes sense if you think about it. This used to be one of the larger cities on the southern trade route."

"So if it was so large, why on earth, or how, did it vanish?" Alex asked.

"It was probably abandoned. There was probably a dramatic climate change; perhaps a drought that dried up the rivers."

"Yanni told us that, remember?" Natasha said.

"Yes, but it's still weird," Alex said.

"Well the shape of the Middle Eastern coastline was actually a little different in those days," Julia explained. "The coastline used to be much closer to us here. Some archaeological sites in the desert to the south of us were actually on the coast five thousand years ago. They've even found ships buried in the desert. Last year a farmer came across an ancient boat beneath his date orchard! All the smaller rivers have long since gone, too."

"So you think those surgeons had actually come here?" Natasha asked. She looked out across the plain. There was absolutely nothing but sand and rock.

"You mean…" Alex joked, making a choking sound, clutching his neck, "before they all died… of… thirst…"

"Oh, grow up!" Natasha gave him another thump.

"Well not exactly Alex," Julia said. "We think what happened here was a major battle, probably against a neighboring Kingdom, which caused the final demise of the city and its people. It's terribly sad, really. There are arrowheads strewn all over the lower slopes of the city and the plains over there."

"That's so cool!" Alex said.

"No it's not!" Natasha snapped. "No battle is cool. It's horrific!"

It was still very hard for the children to imagine, looking at the sand, stones, and rubble strewn across four acres, that so many people had lived here so long ago. Julia said that some clay tablets found near the crumbled temple documented the production of wool, beef and grain, but she could see she was boring them. Gabriella for one, was looking hot and fed-up, and certainly not in the mood to listen.

"I think I will rest here while you go up the next hill," she announced. "I will be fine sitting here."

She found a rock with a little shade to sit on and checked it for scorpions before sitting down. She said she was content to busy herself drawing in the sand while the others carried onto the next mound.

Lorenzo, was just pleased to have company, and kept up with Julia. He looked at her curiously for a moment, and asked her what had drawn her to archaeology. He found it hard to understand why anyone like her, or his father for that matter, would choose to work weeks on end in the dust and pounding heat.

Julia thought about it.

"Well, Lorenzo, I suppose it's exposing something or someone lost in time, and bringing it or them back. For me a dig is all the more interesting when we find a personal belonging of someone who is no longer here. It's a way of remembering them. Rediscovering a real place that had been dismissed as legend, as Ashook was, is a way of showing that those lives that were forgotten, were meaningful, worthwhile and will never be forgotten again."

"I understand why you're doing it, Mum," Natasha said. "It's like trying to bring the people back. It's not just a mosaic floor, or a painted bit of plaster on a wall, or a dried up skeleton. It's about real people, who lived and breathed under the same moon and stars as we do."

Julia looked at her.

"Yes, you're right. Finding the missing pieces, doing the puzzles and letting it be known that they were here, is what it's all about. Well, for me it is, anyway."

In several of the trenches before them, there were people at work, carefully scratching the layers away with trowels and brushes and putting the sand they had removed into numbered buckets for sifting at the collection site. Natasha smiled at Lorenzo, remembering his imitation of the archaeologists over breakfast.

"You can see the different layers of colors on the sides of the walls down there," Julia was pointing to of one of the neatly dug trenches. "Each layer is a time-frame, and what we find is photographed, put into zip-lock bags and numbered, so the contents can be recorded and documented. When a really interesting layer comes to light I come and draw it too."

"How do they know how far down to dig? Do they just keep going until they find something?" Alex asked.

"Oh, goodness, no!" Julia was shocked at the suggestion. "As each layer is carefully removed, a supervisor checks the recordings before the next layer can even begin to be touched. They report to Marcello, and then he gives permission to carry on. This cuts out any guessing as to how deep to go and prevents mistakes being made."

"It never used to be like that, did it Mum?"

"No it was almost criminal. Artifacts used to be prized out of the earth and no one knew where they had come from or from what depth, so they couldn't even age them. Now we do it properly, thank goodness. Exactly where something is found is sometimes as important as the piece itself. Remember," she added, "it's not for fun; History books are written, and often re-written on the findings of archaeological excavations. It has to be very accurate."

"But I never thought it would be so slow," Natasha admitted. It must take ages."

"Well yes, it does," Julia said. "That's why you can't just go and dig on your own, Alex, it all has to be done properly."

Alex asked if they ever got impatient, having to take so long on each layer. He couldn't believe anyone would do the job so precisely without dying of boredom or heat stroke. He wondered if they cheated a bit when no one was watching just to get at the artifacts a bit faster. He knew he would.

"Let's ask those two working in the trenches over there," Julia offered. One of the ladies was taking measurements with her back to them, and the other was younger, about twenty, sitting on the edge of the trench, taking down the information that the other one dictated to her. As Julia approached them, the younger lady on the wall smiled at the visitors. She seemed happy for the interruption, and put her pencil and clipboard down and leaned over and got a drink from her bag. She was around twenty, and quite pretty with a short blonde bob, and Natasha noticed her nails had a French manicure. She didn't look as sand blown and weathered as most of the people on the dig; she looked clean and fresh, and Natasha wondered how she managed to keep looking so neat and out here in the desert.

"Hi, it's Amanda, isn't it?" Julia asked her.

"Yes, hi," she said with a smile, wiping her forehead with her sleeve. She nodded at Julia then took a gulp from her bottle.

"Do you mind if we interrupt you two for a minute?"

She said that she didn't, and that she welcomed the break. She had an American accent.

"This is my daughter Natasha, and Alex, my son. You've probably seen Lorenzo, he and his sister have been here a couple of days already."

"Yes, hi, I'm glad you guys are here. Will you be put to work like the rest of us?" she joked. "We could do with a few extra hands!" Amanda looked over to the other woman she was working with in the trench, expecting her to say something or respond to the group, but she hadn't even bothered to turn around or look up or even acknowledge Julia's presence at all, which made the atmosphere a little awkward. Natasha thought she was rude, especially since her mother was her superior, and there was no need for such an attitude.

Ignoring the rude woman, Julia was happy to address Amanda again.

"The children were asking me how you manage to be so patient," she said. "They were wondering if you ever wish you could dig through the layers faster. Can you fill them in on what it's like, having to be so meticulous?"

Amanda was about to answer, but the woman in the trench turned and looked up at the young faces.

"Patient?" she snapped. "Patient?"

She was about forty-five years old, maybe more, Natasha thought. She had long black hair tied in a messy knot that hung heavily over one shoulder. Her dark eyebrows were thick and almost met in the middle.

"It is not difficult to be patient," she snapped. "Patience is a virtue." She frowned and shook her head as she spoke, as if she was wasting her time answering such a stupid question. She turned and lit a cigarette with her back to them, then carried on with her job.

They got the distinct impression they were disturbing her. Amanda, still sitting on the edge of the trench, raised her eyes skyward without her work colleague seeing, implying she wasn't having the greatest time in her company, either.

Julia smiled and thanked Amanda for her time, and reminded her to take a break from the heat when she needed it. "It's a very hot day," she said. "Don't overdo it out here,

Marcello would want anyone getting heatstroke. Take a break when ever you need one."

Amanda thanked her, adding that she would stick at it a little while longer, and Natasha understood that her mother was probably hinting to Amanda to get out of there and away from the unpleasant woman as soon as she could.

"What's the problem with Miss Unibrow?" Alex asked when they were out of earshot.

"Well," Julia said, "I expect the heat gets to some people more than others. I wouldn't worry about it. And please, don't make personal jokes about people's appearances. It's not funny or clever."

Lorenzo and Natasha smiled at each other.

"Come on you lot," Julia called back over her shoulder at the dawdling group lagging behind, "get those feet moving! I thought you wanted to see the Queen's skeleton! Let's pick up Gabriella and go over to the tomb."

They walked back to Gabriella, who was sitting on a stone, sand at her feet, and Julia suggested they had a drink before they moved on. Aware that she was bored, Julia tried to think of something that would interest her.

"You know, Gabriella," she said, handing her a fresh bottle of water from her backpack, "I have a little Roman clay oil lamp sitting on the mantelpiece in the sitting room at home in London. Do you know why it is so special to me?"

"No," Gabriella answered honestly. She really didn't; Roman lamps filled every museum shelf and storage room in Italy.

"Well, it is not so much because of it age, or where it had been found, but because if you turn it upside down, at the base of the little handle, you can just see part of a thumb-print, unintentionally left in the wet clay by the potter who made the lamp all those centuries ago. Sometimes," Julia told her, "I touch the faint thumb-print, and I think of him making it all those hundreds of years ago. If he only knew that someone would be lovingly caring for it two thousand years later."

"I have something I treasure also," Gabriella said. "Something that belonged to someone who also died." She got up and walked a few paces away. Natasha thought how rude she was to just walk away mid conversation, but she hadn't seen the tears in Gabriella's eyes. Julia hesitated and wondered if she should go after her and check she was all right, but decided against it.

Natasha, seeing that the spoiled child had her mother's attention, sided up to Julia.

"It's strange how objects stay on while the owners have to go, isn't it, Mum," she said quietly. "I often think of it when I sit in your grandfather's big old chair at home; the leather on the seat is all worn away from his using it for so many years; it looks like he has just left the room for a moment, even though he has been gone for so many years. Is that like the kind of feeling you get with the Roman lamp?"

Julia smiled at her daughter. "Yes it is, and it's that sort of thing that makes me love archaeology," she said, and glanced over to Gabriella to check she was all right. "It's the closest I'll ever get to the people who lived in the world before me. It's my reminder that we just borrow the world for a few years and then pass it on. Finding out who has passed it on to me, is what makes me tick, I suppose."

Natasha looked at her mother. She had no idea that that was how her mother felt too. It was weird. She wanted to tell her mother how alike they were, but she couldn't. It would sound way too soppy.

"Mum," Natasha said, moving closer to her so she could confide out of earshot of the boys, "I think I have decided to do archaeology."

Julia smiled at her daughter. "I had a feeling you might," she said quietly. "I think you will make a good archaeologist." She kissed her forehead, and Natasha got one of those secret smiles, and it felt good.

"Come on Gabriella, we're moving on," Alex called. "I want to see this skeleton before I turn into one myself! You're holding us up and it's nearly lunch time!"

Gabriella came running back into the fold. "Do you think this is anything?" Gabriella asked, holding out her hand. She had a piece of thin, weathered metal in her palm. It was about three inches long, and split down the centre. Julia took it and examined it carefully.

"What's this, Gabriella?" she asked. "Where did you find it?"

"It was sticking out of the sand at my feet over there," she offered.

"Gabriella, this is amazing! Show me, where exactly?"

Gabriella led them over to the spot where she had sat waiting for them earlier.

"Just there," she pointed. "It was half on the surface, and half buried, and I pricked my finger on it when I was drawing in the sand. What is it?"

Julia examined the small area nearby, and saw another one, which Gabriella hadn't noticed. It was half buried to the left of the stone she had been sitting against. Like the first piece, it was thin and delicate, but with a scooped flat circle about the size of a small coin at one end of it; it looked like a very delicate, small, shallow spoon.

"My goodness, Gabriella, the first one looks like a pair of pincers, or tweezers, and this one looks like some kind of spoon, don't you think? Perhaps for measuring powdered incense, or medicine. This is amazing, I can't believe it! We'll find your father and he can get an area excavation started over here. My goodness, these could be medical instruments… Gabriella, this is amazing!"

"Cool! You think they belonged to those Indian doctors?" Alex asked. "Can we do some digging and see if we can find some more?"

"I'm sorry Alex, you know it has to be done methodically."

He looked disappointed.

"But you're right; they could have belonged to those visiting doctors," Julia added, "though the Queen probably had her own team too. Remember the Indian doctors would have come to teach their methods to physicians, not laymen, which would mean there were physicians here already. Now do you see how exciting it is out here? There is just so much to learn and discover."

With Gabriella's help, Julia placed the artifacts back in the sand where she had found them, and they all helped gather some small stones and marked the area so it would be easily located again for Marcello. They then started their way over to the Queen's tomb.

Natasha took a long hard look at Gabriella. She was now not only walking, but almost skipping alongside her mother and chatting happily with Alex. How dare she find those ancient artifacts! Natasha thought, especially when she has no interest in archaeology whatsoever! Natasha couldn't believe her audacity.

"Come on, Natasha," Gabriella called back to her. "Now you are falling behind!"

"Oh great! This is going to be the holiday from hell," Natasha grumbled under her breath.

She sighed, and wished she were back at home with her father.

CHAPTER SEVEN

In a sparsely furnished room, three men were sitting cross-legged on a worn Persian carpet. They had taken over a small, run-down farmhouse on the outskirts of a dusty hamlet, about an hour and a half from Medinabad, not far from a track that lead to the ridge. Along with their shoes, their guns were lined up in a neat row near the door and the men slurped piping hot, sweet, black tea from small tumbler glasses.

The unobtrusive, flat-roofed farmhouse was ideally placed for the cunning operation at hand. Facing the ridge in the distance, it was the perfect base for the gang. The typical, very poor, peasant farm was one of many to be seen dotted about on the edges of the desert outside hamlets and villages. Scrawny chickens, a donkey and a few goats shared a small shaded area under a cluster of date trees at the back.

The farmhouse had been taken over by the organization soon after their infiltrator at the dig had told them that the excavation behind the ridge had uncovered the priceless mask. A close watch had been put on the excavation as soon as permission had been given to dig there, and when the news of the mask's discovery had been leaked, the gang moved into the nearest farmhouse. No one would suspect the building as a base for such a risky operation.

The old farmer and his wife, whose home it was, had been obliged to wait on the men hand and foot ever since they had arrived. If they had refused, they were warned that they would not even live to regret it. The men had helped themselves to everything the poor couple had, including taking several blankets and their only mattress away from the property. This confused and upset the old couple and they prayed they would be returned when the men's task was done, whatever that may be. The husband dared not ask them if or when he would get his blankets back, despite the pushing and nagging from his wife to find out.

From the back yard and the expanse of desert beyond it, the men were offered a clear and unobstructed view of the ridge that rose out of the desert in the distance. Any transportation to and from the cliffs could be seen quite clearly, even from this distance, and communication with a flashlight from the roof of the house to the top of the ridge was easy, or so it should have been.

It was early evening and the temperature was dropping for the night. But despite this cooling of the air, two of the men, Hasim and Abdul, were particularly hot and uncomfortable sitting crossed-legged on the rug. This was not because of the steaming tea they tentatively sipped, or because of their newly 'acquired' rather tight military uniforms, but because they were waiting for the arrival of the boss.

They had met him only once before, when they had been hand picked for the operation, and did not expect, or indeed particularly want to see their boss again. Their instincts had told them at their first meeting, that it would not be a pleasant experience if they did, and they were right. Now they were contemplating having to explain to him what went so wrong with the disastrous hold-up in the pass the previous day. Their stomachs churned at the thought of it.

He was angry, and they knew it was not going to be a pleasant meeting.

The information Hasim and Abdul had received from Maha, their informer at the dig, which had led to the hold-up in the pass, had turned out to be inaccurate. Either that or they had misunderstood the information she had given them.

Whatever the problem had been, it was of little consequence to their boss. The damage was done and Hasim knew he was about to take the bulk of the blame for the blunder. Hasim also felt a little peeved, to say the least, that Maha wasn't there with them waiting to explain herself. It was too difficult and risky for her to leave the camp, even to explain what had happened. She now had to stay there at the camp and draw as little attention to herself as possible, especially since she had apparently been noticed and had direct contact with the English woman who they had held up in the pass. This was not in the plan, and was dangerous to the whole operation.

A car was heard pulling up out outside the farmhouse, and a then a car door was slammed closed, and Hasim and Abdul looked at each other and waited. Hasim wiped his brow.

"Keep the engine running. This will not take long," the voice outside instructed the driver.

Their boss walked in, cigar in hand, followed by a burley, armed bodyguard.

Seeing there were no chairs in the room, he waited for someone to jump up and fetch him something to sit on. He certainly wasn't going to sit on the floor in his suit. The third man of the three, who's job had been to secure the farmhouse and keep the owners of the house from escaping, quickly produced a stool from behind the screened door. His boss took out a silk handkerchief and wiped it before sitting down. He then sat down and faced his men.

He was in his early sixties, with slick black hair combed back in straight lines and stuck in place with shiny gel. He had a very thin trimmed moustache, which made his lips look plump and swollen, but otherwise his face was clean-shaven and pale. He was immaculately dressed in a pinstriped suit, a crisp, pale blue tailor-made shirt with gold cufflinks and a silk tie with a matching gold tiepin close to the knot.

The bodyguard stood by the door with his hands behind his back and stared into space. Hasim noticed the revolver bulge under his jacket. It made him want to wipe his brow again.

"Salaam Alykum, salaam." The boss greeted them politely.

"Salaam Alykum," they replied.

The pleasantries were over; the boss got straight to the point.

"Hasim," he said, "…it is 'Hasim', is it not?" he asked, addressing the sweating man.

"Yes, Excellency."

"Then, Hasim, would you be so kind as to explain to me why you believed the priceless mask to be in this particular truck at this particular time?" He spoke quite slowly and calmly, causing Hasim's stomach to churn. "Why you put the whole operation at risk, not to mention severely damaging my credibility and reputation? That is, besides possibly scaring my South American client away for good, and ruining this multi-million dollar deal completely? Hmmm?"

He half smiled at Hasim, but the smile was not one made in kindness. It was a challenge, and his eyes narrowed as he stared at the sweating man. He opened his plump, well-manicured hand towards Hasim in a gesture that was the queue for him to start talking. The diamond on his finger caught the light in the bare overhead bulb.

The silence in the room thumped in Hasim's ears. Hasim bowed respectfully at his boss, buying time.

He cleared his throat and swallowed hard.

"It was an unfortunate misunderstanding, sir." His words came out too quickly, and his voice sounded higher than usual. He cleared his throat again. "Our informer at the site, Maha, is unable to communicate using the mobile phone due to the reception here, nor the radio for risk of being overheard. We use flashlights, you see, sir. There must have been some kind of a miscommunication in deciphering her messages sent from the top of the ridge. We, Abdul and I, apologize for the terrible blunder. We will get the mask for your client, you can assure him, sir."

He felt he had done well. He had cleverly informed his boss who it was who had messed up the assignment with him, by naming Maha and Abdul, hopefully reducing the blame on himself considerably.

His boss nodded slowly.

"Hasim… Hasim… Hasim, he said slowly and thoughtfully. He took a long drew of his cigar. "Do you know what happens to those who fail me, Hasim?" he asked softly, "who lie to me, or even try to blame others for their own mistakes?"

"Excellency, I... I…"

"You do not know? Oh, well, let me tell you, Hasim. There is a very gentle remedy for people like you. It was, I am told, perfected by a certain tribe of Native Americans, I believe, who became a little tired of the white invaders lying to them, cheating them, and taking their land by force, slaughtering their women and children, you see. Nasty little business..." He took a long drag on his cigar, and exhaled slowly in Hasim's direction.

"They took these men, Hasim, the liars, and the cheats, and tied them down, on their backs, face up to the sun, you see. So simple, no? And there they were left tied up in the desert, for nature to deal with them. Perfect, is it not?"

"I shall have the mask for you soon, I swear, Gracious Lord."

"Oh yes you will, Hasim. You will indeed. And you have five days, and five days only. After that, you, your family and everyone else who messed up this deal will be staring up at the sun as the last thing they see in this world. Do you understand, Hasim? And you?" he asked looking at the other two. Abdul and the other man were not off the hook either. "I shall be waiting," The Boss added. He examined the lit end of his cigar, then tapped the ash onto the carpet and rubbed it in with his shoe. He looked over at the other man sitting very quietly. Neither him, nor his family were exempt from this 'American' solution.

False pleasantries were exchanged as the boss stood up to leave. He brushed his suit off and left the room with his bodyguard. The car door slammed shut and the car drove away.

The three men sat in silence.

"How will we get the mask?" Abdul asked, looking absolutely shaken. "How are we to *get* it?" There was panic in his tone.

"I don't know. It's not exactly easy. We don't even know where it is," Hasim hissed.

"We will need to watch very closely. We shall set up camp on the ridge," Abdul said.

"But what if the mask has left the camp for good... what if..." the third man started, but Hasim cut him off. He wasn't listening. He had a plan.

"I have just realized, it is of little consequence where the mask is. It does not matter at all. There is another way. It will come to us." Hasim's voice was calm and confident. He lit a cigarette and inhaled deeply. He sat back and leant against the wall, using his bent knee as an elbow rest while he smoked his cigarette. He felt relaxed. His plan was foolproof. It would work.

Abdul looked at him, waiting.

"Well?"

"The children," Hasim said, exhaling and examining his cigarette, mimicking his boss.

"We *take* those children. Wherever the mask is, it is of little consequence, it will appear soon enough into our laps, when we take the children."

Chapter Eight

"Joooo-li-aaaa…" Marcello's call echoed across the sands. He was standing outside his black Bedouin tent, the site headquarters, perched on the highest mound commanding a panoramic view of the whole excavation site. Holding his cell phone to his ear with one hand he beckoned Julia over with the other.

"I'd better go," she excused herself to the four children. "And I need to tell your father about your interesting find, Gabriella. But if you continue to walk that way," she pointed further along to the left, "you'll find Yanni and his team. I'm sure he would love to show you the Queen's tomb. I'll let Marcello know you're going over there now. See you later, have fun!"

Natasha felt hurt that it had only taken one call from Marcello for her mother to drop them, and go running over to him. OK, she thought, it was probably work-related, and she understood that she had to tell him about what Gabriella had found, but still, she didn't have to go straight away; those bits of metal had been there five thousand years. They could surely wait another hour.

Natasha now felt grumpy, and didn't feel like talking to Lorenzo, who was obviously bored with the whole archaeology thing. He was asking Alex where they lived in London and if they had been to any good concerts in the park. Natasha's only joy was the thought of seeing Yanni. She walked on quickly ahead of the three of them to try to get to Yanni before they did.

Yanni and his team of four were working in a large, shallow 'area excavation', which was about the size of a tennis court, but only a couple of feet deep at the most.

"Hello, hello!" Yanni called out and jumped up to greet them, grinning. He seemed happy to see them.

"Have you come to see what we are doing? Look here!" he pointed to the ground with his trowel. Natasha looked for a sign that he was happier to see her than the other three; a secret smile or glance perhaps, but she really couldn't tell; he just seemed thrilled about the excavation he was working on.

"It's a mosaic floor… Ha! Fantastic!" he laughed to himself in disbelief looking down at it, and wiped his brow. "Fantastic! These little squares that make up the floor are all painted clay pegs, Natasha, and onyx, glass and enamel. Look Fantastic! And not a Roman in sight for another three thousand years! Who would have thought they had mosaic floors then?"

Natasha smiled at him. She had honestly never seen anyone so enthusiastic about anything before. And did he just address her specifically? She forgot about being angry with her mother and Gabriella, and asked Yanni to tell her more about his ancient mosaic floor.

"This was the main entrance to the palace. It would have been a wide galleried hallway with a series of columns leading to the principle rooms to the side."

He pointed to the perimeter of the excavation, and explained that his team had first exposed a small section there, just to check it was the hallway. Now they were concentrating on the vast room that led from it. Yanni explained that Marcello had first recognized that this was the floor of the entrance hall, and not the great reception room, by the slightly larger pieces of tessarae, and the thicker layer of cement that held them in place, compared to those a few feet away.

"He is so smart, no? I would have missed the clue completely," he laughed.

Natasha tried to understand why the size of the little pieces of stone told so much about which room they were in. She felt too shy to ask what he meant, but nodded knowingly.

"Because the entrance to the palace had a lot more foot traffic than the room over there," he continued, "the floor is a little more tough, and the pieces a little larger; A little more, how do you say in English, hardwearing? It makes sense, no? Those pieces of tessarae over there in the side rooms are a little smaller, you see? More delicate. Less traffic and more grace."

He picked up a piece from the reception room floor and a piece from what would have been the entrance hall, and showed Natasha the difference between the two sizes. Yanni told Natasha that this large room they were excavating had probably been where the Queen would have entertained her guests. It would have been lavishly decorated to impress them. He showed Natasha that there was an intricate design emerging as they uncovered the floor, and Yanni was obviously very excited to be working on it.

He walked over and showed Natasha where the great fallen pillars of the entrance hall would have stood. He squatted down and pointed to the darkened colorations in the ground on each side of the wide gap.

"These two dark areas in the ground indicate that there was once wood here," he said. "What do you think this would have been?"

She was suddenly put on the spot, and had to quickly rewind in her head what he had just been talking about. She had been watching him so closely, that what he had been saying to her was almost a blur. She flushed. "Darker wood in the ground? That means something made of wood… oh, door posts?" She went bright red in anticipation of her being wrong.

"Yes, yes, exactly, Natasha, the massive door posts. See the diameter? Big and heavy; can you imagine them?"

She let out a sigh of relief, hoping he wouldn't ask her anything else.

He stood with both arms out stretched as far as they would go and took several steps from one side to the other to demonstrate the size the massive palace doors would have been.

"But there aren't any trees here," Natasha said. "Are you sure there were wooden door posts here?"

"Ha! I asked the same question to Marcello exactly! Ha! The posts would have been transported from hundreds of miles away to the north of here, probably from Syria. Marcello explained to me that there had never been trees like these here in this part of the world."

Natasha smiled at him; he looked so good in his faded jeans that she was still having trouble concentrating on what he was saying. She stood there watching him as he spoke with such amazing enthusiasm and energy. She felt so stupid being only fifteen; She wished she was sixteen or seventeen, at least.

He asked Natasha if she wanted to see the inlaid floor more closely that he had been working on for so many weeks.

"OK," she said nonchalantly. If he only knew, she thought. She tried to sound cool and collected, but her heart was pounding and she wished the day would never end. She hoped she was disguising her feelings well enough.

She hovered on the side of the excavated mosaic floor, wondering if she was supposed to step down off the little wall onto it or not.

"Come, give me your hand; jump down, Natasha."

Natasha took his hand. She absorbed every second of the contact. She jumped off the wall as gracefully as she could and onto the floor where he and his team were working.

"Here, I can show you something, he said."

He squatted down and wet the floor with a little water he poured from his flask. He spread the puddle around with the palm of his hand.

"Look at the colors," he said lovingly, stroking the tiles clean. "Beautiful! Reds, black, white, blue. See the shape emerging?" He was pointing along the outline of a curved creature. "Look. It is a horse. Ha! See the neck, the shoulder, the reins; I think that is a foot of the rider down there. And look over here, a surprise…"

He took three giant leaps sideways. "The feet and part of the legs of fifteen foot soldiers behind the mounted rider. I have counted them, thirty feet with sandals! The floor is fantastic Natasha!"

She tried to focus on the floor, but was finding it hard. She loved his enthusiasm. She loved everything about him.

He took four more large steps to the edge of the excavated area, and pointed to where the design continued under the earth. Natasha followed him, and enjoyed his excitement. She had to admit it, uncovering this palace was fascinating. She wished she was allowed to be on Yanni's team and help excavate the floor.

Yanni looked up to see if the others wanted to have a closer look too, but realized that Alex, Lorenzo and Gabriella had walked off and left them; Probably some time ago.

"Oh, I must have bored them," he said, looking a little deflated.

"Oh, don't worry about them or what they think, *they're* the boring ones. You can't force someone to be interested."

He looked at her thoughtfully, and smiled at her.

"Where is your mother?" he asked after a moment. "Wasn't she showing you all around?"

Natasha pulled a face and shrugged her shoulders. "Well, she was, but *His Majesty*, Prince *Marvelous* over there…" she looked over to the direction of Marcello's tent on the hill, "…called her over, and she just dropped us like a sack of potatoes."

She looked down, and thought perhaps that had been a bit harsh, even immature. But she had said it now, so what's done is done.

Yanni looked at her and thought for a minute. He gently put his water bottle down next to his trowel on the low wall. He continued to look down at them, thinking.

He eventually broke the silence.

"Do you want to go for a walk? I can show you around. Come, Natasha; let's walk a little."

Natasha thought she would faint. Her heart pounded.

"OK," she managed to say.

CHAPTER NINE

"When I was fifteen, Natasha, my father had an accident on our farm. Our tractor that he was driving overturned. It was very old and it used to belong to my grandfather before him. We were not rich, and the tractor had been repaired many, many times. But one day, in heavy rain, the front axle broke in half, you know, the bar that holds the wheels, it broke completely."

Yanni showed with his hands how it had snapped.

"The tractor slipped in the mud, and went down the hill, down, down, over and over, and my father with it."

Natasha looked at him, surprised.

Yanni paused. He sat on the edge of a large stone.

"My father, he died a couple of weeks later of his injuries."

"I'm so sorry," Natasha said. She was shocked. She wondered why Yanni was sharing this terrible story with her.

"Thank you," he said. "That was over three years ago. But what I want to tell you, is this Natasha. I have four brothers; three older, and one younger than myself. My mother had a very difficult time, trying to control and keep us younger ones out of trouble on her own, and running the farm also, after my father died. You understand, it was not easy."

He looked up at Natasha, and she nodded.

"The older brothers took care of my mother, of course they felt they had to take the place of my father. They protected her. But they were not good at it."

He paused. "You see, a couple of miles away, in another village, there lived a man who had been a friend of my father for many years. In fact they had been at school together when they were very young. Well, he started calling once a week, you know, on foot, to check that everything was well."

Yanni looked at Natasha, to see if she was following. She nodded, wondering what on earth was coming next.

With his elbows resting on his knees, and his head down, Yanni slowly ran his fingers through his hair. Natasha knew he was going over something very difficult. But why was he? What on earth had brought this on?

He held his head in his hands and he sat there, staring at the ground between his boots. The silence made Natasha want to run. Had he forgotten she was there? What should she say? She felt terribly uncomfortable. She looked around to see if anyone was nearby so she could make an excuse to go.

"Well after a month or so," he continued, "the visits increased, and this friend of my father, he would usually say he needed some eggs. We had some chickens, you see."

Yanni paused again for a while; Natasha could see it was so painful for him to remember.

"You don't have to tell me, Yanni, it's OK," she said, hoping he would stop.

"…He then started to come on Sundays, in his best suit, and then Wednesdays, and again on Fridays. My brothers and I were not stupid. We knew he was interested in the farm, or more so my mother. Maybe both."

Silence.

"It was a long walk for him, Natasha, from his cottage, his village, you understand, maybe five or six miles round trip. He often came in the rain, to buy our eggs."

Silence.

"So one day, after discussing it amongst ourselves, you know, the brothers, we waited in the trees down the lane for him to come one Sunday. When he approached our property, my two eldest brothers confronted the man, how do you say, a threat?"

"Yes," Natasha said. "They threatened him?"

"Yes, we threatened him, and we told him we knew what he was after, and that he was not welcome here anymore and he was not to come back. We told him if he came back he would be sorry."

Yanni stared at the ground. Natasha hated the silence more than the story. She didn't know what to say.

He picked up a pebble. He rolled it in his hands, still staring at the ground. It seemed like ages before he spoke again.

At last he continued.

"So life went on for my mother. The man stopped calling, a couple of years passed, and we brothers grew older. We never told my mother that we had stopped him coming. She must have wondered until she went crazy why the visits stopped. We had no phone of course, it was very rural. We didn't think about this, or what we had done, in our ignorance, or selfishness or even arrogance. I don't know, we thought we were doing the right thing. The truth is, we *didn't* think."

Yanni looked up at Natasha, and smiled at her. His eyes were moist. He looked like he needed a hug, but she couldn't.

"We were thinking of ourselves, Natasha. You see, we were wrong to do that; Very, very wrong. And one by one, all of the brothers left the farm; we didn't want to be farmers. We wanted a better life. So, my mother, unable to manage the farm on her own, had to sell it. Now she lives alone in a small apartment on the seventh floor on the edge of Krakow."

"Oh. I'm so sorry. And your father's friend? What happened to him?"

He shrugged. "I don't know, as I said, he didn't come back."

Yanni threw the pebble into the distance.

"But we learned that he had his own chickens," he added quietly. "He didn't need more eggs."

"Oh." Natasha didn't know what to say. She felt sorry for his mother, and the old man. She didn't like to see Yanni so miserable. The whole thing was horrible.

"So, Natasha," he said, clearing his throat and standing up again, "don't interfere with nature, it is not in our hands. If your mother likes Marcello, and he likes her, be happy. Better that, than one day having a lonely old mother left sulking on her own with no one to talk to. You and Alex will be gone in a few years, no? She will be alone, no? Or are you planning to live with her and take care of her forever?"

Natasha shook her head. Now she understood why he was telling her the story.

Yanni brushed off the seat of his jeans, and he added, "do not give your mother a difficult time, life is too short, Natasha. Look at these ruins; we all turn to dust in the end. Let her enjoy life while she has it. Believe me, it will work itself out one way or another. I know it is hard for you; it is hard for her also. I think she will need your understanding and love, more than your anger and jealousy, no?"

Natasha looked down remembering her behavior in the car. She felt ashamed.

"And believe me," he added quietly, "she could do a lot worse than Marcello."

Natasha was still looking down and Yanni came close to her and gently lifted her chin up with his finger. He was so close she could feel his breath on her face. Her heart nearly burst. He paused, then smiled at her, taking a small step back.

"It's OK, don't worry Natasha. Things will work out."

He teased her and pulled her plait. He walked on ahead.

Chapter Ten

"Hey, Yanni!" Alex called from beside the tomb when he saw him approaching. "Are we allowed to lift up this cover and have a look underneath?"

"No! Do not touch anything!" Yanni called back. He ran over to them. "Please, you must wait for Marcello. He will be coming in a minute."

Alex was standing with Lorenzo and Gabriella next to what looked like a very unassuming stone platform with three layers of steps around it. The platform sat in the middle of a flat, recently excavated area of about fifteen foot square. The whole area was swept clean of loose stones and sand, and looked like it was still very much an ongoing project, with buckets, brushes, red and white striped ranging poles, all in a neat pile to the edge of it.

The carved stone block platform in the centre was about six feet square, three feet high, very smooth, plain and without any engravings or decoration. Natasha noticed that its corners were still sharp and well defined, and she presumed this was because it had been buried and protected by the sand for five thousand years. She had seen pictures of obelisks and columns in Egypt, that were chipped and damaged at the top where they had been exposed to the elements, but beneath the level where the archaeologists had removed the sand, the stone was as new and unblemished as the day they had been carved.

Long, oblong, tightly fitting slabs formed the roof of the platform, and one of these pieces on the end had been removed, and was now lying on the ground beside the steps. It was this opening that Marcello had temporarily covered with a large piece of tarpaulin to protect what lay beneath, and was what Alex was so eager to lift up.

"Please, just a quick peep, Yanni?" he begged.

"Look, he is coming, Alex," Yanni said. "We must be patient, careful, and also respectful to the dead. This is the Queen's resting place, remember. "Stand back a little, please, and as I said, we wait for Marcello to come." His voice was serious, almost commanding, and Natasha liked the way he took control.

Marcello came over and joined the children.

"Ah, my little archaeologist!" he said to Gabriella. "You know, the instruments you found are very interesting. I was just over there to have a look at what you found. We will have to do an excavation at that section to see what else we can find! You are so clever, my little Princess…"

Gabriella beamed as he kissed her forehead, and Natasha walked away before she said something she shouldn't.

"Ah, here he comes!" Marcello said, ready to greet another man who had followed him down the hill to join them. He looked a little older than Marcello and was introduced to Natasha and Alex as Signor Muretti. He was apparently a close friend of Marcello's, and his chief supervisor. Marcello explained that they had worked together for years in many parts of the world. Marcello also mentioned that he was also acting as press coordinator during the announcement.

"What announcement?" Alex asked.

"*The* announcement!" Marcello laughed. "The Queen's day of rebirth! The day she becomes fact and not fable! The day an Egyptian boy King, Tutankhamen, who has held the limelight for almost a hundred years, will finally be overshadowed by a beautiful Mesopotamian Warrior Queen! The day the exquisite Mask's existence will be announced to the world…" He laughed and looked up to the heavens at the thought of it.

Mr. Muretti added for Alex and Natasha's sake, that the press conference was being held there at the site in a couple of days. He wanted them to understand that it was a very important day for history books, as well as Marcello and his team.

"Yes, but until then, we must push on," Marcello said, coming back to earth and thinking of what had to be done before then. He walked towards the Queen's tomb, and Signor Muretti asked Natasha and Alex if they had seen a skeleton before. When they both said they hadn't, he laughed and told them the first time was always the best.

"Especially if it is a Queen! Not everyone is as privileged as you are to see an ancient Queen in her tomb." He said it lightly, but he meant it.

Yanni made sure the children were a few feet away from the tomb before he and Marcello carefully lifted the cover off the exposed corner. They put it down next to a ladder that was lying on the ground nearby, and Gabriella and Lorenzo stood a few yards away. Neither of them wanted to look down there again; they had seen it the day it was opened up, and once was enough. They walked over to the shade of a low wall a few feet away, and sat down and waited.

"Ready?" Marcello asked, looking Natasha and Alex in the eye with all sincerity. They nodded that they were, and then he added in a serious tone, "and please, when you see her," he paused, "…please look with respect. Although it is a skeleton, she is still a Queen. She was a real person, not an object. This has been her resting place for five thousand years. We are all extremely privileged to be able to see her."

Alex and Natasha nodded. They understood what Marcello was saying. It was to be a memorable moment in their lives. Natasha was a little apprehensive, if not a little nervous. It was an experience she wasn't going to forget, and she knew it even before she looked down into the tomb.

He nodded back to them as if to confirm the seriousness of what they were about to see. Then Natasha and Alex, Yanni, Signor Muretti and Marcello knelt down against the side of the tomb. They very slowly leant over and peered down into the dark chamber.

To Natasha's surprise, its floor was about six feet below them, and it seemed to be a much larger area down there than the size of the stone tomb on the surface. The chamber even seemed to go back underneath them.

"I can't see anything," Alex whispered. "It's too dark."

Marcello switched on his flashlight.

And there she was. A real, ancient Queen, lying only a few feet below them. A white skeleton, lying there in a shallow pit, staring up at her inquisitive audience with her hollow eyes and her grinning, open jaw looking as if she wanted to say something.

Natasha shuddered. She felt a musty draught rise into her face. Ancient, thick air, she thought. Dead people's air. She lifted her head up and took a deep breath of clean air before mustering the courage to look down into the chamber again.

After the initial shock, looking at the skeleton again, Natasha found that she wasn't really afraid of the dead Queen's bones, in fact she was able to look beyond the bones, and felt sorry for the Queen as a person. She stared down and wished she could apologize to her for being so invasive. She felt that by staring at her like this took away the Queen's dignity. Her clothes had rotted away, and the way she was lying on her back, with her arms crossed over her chest, almost seemed to Natasha as if she was being modest, as if she was trying to hide her nakedness. It just didn't seem right to be staring at her.

There were a quite a few handfuls of beads scattered around and in between her bones, and Marcello told the children that these had once been woven into her cloak.

"The cloak must have been very heavy," Alex said. "I bet she didn't wear that every day."

Although Natasha still felt uncomfortable being so intrusive, she found it fascinating looking at the bones. Her eyes followed the light of Marcello's flashlight, and she saw more bones clustered together to the right of the Queen.

Marcello was explaining how she had been buried with her most loyal and closest servants, which Natasha really didn't like the sound of. She couldn't stop thinking that these were real people down there, who had once had names; these people hadn't seen the light of day in thousands of years. If they could talk, she wondered, would they be happy to be uncovered like this? It bothered her, and she began to wonder whether they should be looking at their bones at all.

Then her thoughts then went in a different direction, and she thought about the actual logistics of them being buried down there. She wondered how the servants had died. Had they drunk poison? If they had, was it willingly? Or would they have been forced to die, like their final duty as loyal servants?

Whatever the truth was, Natasha now felt the urge to cover them all up. A part of her felt it definitely wasn't right to disturb them. She wished she could talk to them somehow, sort of telepathically, and apologize.

"To the left, under there," Marcello was saying as he reached down into the chamber, shining his flashlight underneath the ground directly beneath them, "...the chamber goes a lot further back."

They strained their necks to look down into the tomb, but couldn't see much from their position at ground level.

"Can I go down there and have a better look?" Alex asked.

"I'm sorry Alex, it is not possible. We have to treat it as carefully as we would a forensic scene. But I can explain to you a little better what is down there. Under here, below us, is a side chamber, and there is the skeleton of the Queen's horse, and another human skeleton, who we presume is the groom. Next to him is the Queen's chariot, in rather bad condition, I must add. It looks as though it was badly damaged before it was put in here.

"You mean like battle damage?" Alex asked hopefully.

"It is probable, yes, more than likely. But it was not really built to be robust. It is very lightweight, built more for speed. There is ample evidence that a battle took place on the plain outside the city boundaries. Shortly after the battle the city seems to have been abandoned, however. "

"Why?" Natasha asked.

"We think from lack of water. The whole region was probably drying up. It can happen in hot climates every few hundred years or so. A city can almost completely vanish over time! There used to be two rivers near here. Now it is only possible to tell this from the air. My suspicion is, that the city was under attack for its water supplies; there was a very sophisticated irrigation system here in this city. Large stone water tanks held an enormous reserve just over there," he pointed to the right, "on the outskirts of the city. I should think this was probably the cause of the Queen's downfall; Her city died trying to protect her most valuable asset. There are some arrows and spearheads all around the tanks. It makes you realize that no silk, slaves, spices, salt or even gold was worth more than water."

"Wow," Alex said. "I never really thought of water as more precious than gold!"

"Well of course it is, Alex! But, unfortunately it seems it was a fruitless battle, the region was already turning to desert; the wind and sand took over very quickly, and it was all gone."

"It's so cool that you can find out what happened here, just from digging," Natasha said, forgetting she didn't really want to converse with Marcello.

"Yes it is interesting what the earth can reveal to us. You just need to you know where to look, and what to look for."

"How much more is there down there in the tomb?" she asked.

"The tomb goes back that way, and there are a lot of things yet to be examined."

They were silent for a few minutes as they looked into the tomb, lost in their own thoughts.

"Where is all her jewelry?" Alex asked, peering further down into the darkness. "I can't see anything sparkling down there. Isn't there anything like treasure? Have you taken it all out, Marcello?"

"Oh yes, we have to remove it, in case it is robbed. Your mother spent hours here drawing, photographing, and measuring everything before it could be touched of course. It is safely locked up with all the other artifacts that are being catalogued over in the main tent. It is a time-consuming process, but it has to be done properly. I will show you what we have over there if you are interested, Alex."

Alex shook his head. "No, don't worry, but thanks. Jewelry isn't really my thing." Marcello smiled at him, then looked back at Natasha. She was still peering down into the tomb thinking about the Queen and all the other people down there, almost stranded in time.

Marcello continued, "we are of course able to leave the pots, all the crumbling artifacts and the skeletons *in situ*, you understand, they are not of interest to robbers, not like the jewelry is, or the mask of course. Come, Natasha," he said standing up again. "Shall we let the Queen sleep?"

The children stood back while Yanni, Signor Muretti and Marcello lifted the protective cover back over the tomb opening and tied it down safely.

"There are still many weeks of work to be done down there, but now we don't have to rush, we must take our time and do it thoroughly. Any treasure seekers will not bothered with bones or artifacts. In a few hours the equipment will arrive to examine the bones, and perhaps tell us a lot more about the Queen and those buried with her."

"Really?" Natasha asked. "What will you be able to find out?"

"Hopefully what illnesses or diseases they had, if any; their ages, what they had eaten, and perhaps even how they had died."

"What else did the Queen have with her down there apart from her chariot and horse?" Alex asked.

"Well the mask of course was the most stunning artifact. That goes without saying. It is magnificent."

"Can we see it?" Natasha asked. "I really would like to see it."

"You will see it Natasha, eventually. It will be in all the papers. But I am sorry you will not see it here with the Queen. Not this year anyway. My aim is to be able to one day leave it here forever. But there is a lot of work to do first, no? Signor Muretti?"

Signor Muretti's eyes looked skywards and he shook his head at the thought of what was still to be done, and Marcello slapped him on the back laughing.

"But what else is still down there with her?" Alex asked.

"She has a harp, in fact that is only *just* there, it is made of wood and inlaid with ivory, and it is in very bad condition. It is at the other end of the chamber and not visible from here. One of her servants is lying beside it, cradling it, with a hand across it." He demonstrated with his arms. "Like this, as if still playing it. Very beautiful, no? And there are remnants of long black hair on, and beside the skull."

Natasha gasped. "How terrible. How *awful*. She was probably a young girl," Natasha said. "Maybe a girl who loved music and had been talented enough to have had the honor of playing for the Queen, so much so that she had been buried with her. It's awful."

"You could be right," Marcello sadly agreed.

Then Natasha's mind raced thinking of the logistics of how she had come to be down there. Surely this meant that she, along with the Queen's servants, guards and grooms, *must* have all died or been killed before they were put in the tomb. You couldn't get all those people and the horse, to lie down in the right positions and then tell them to just die in an orderly fashion. This awful thought changed Natasha's perception of the 'good', kind Queen. Their bodies must have been arranged and staged like that after they had died. Perhaps Queen Sorrea and her court weren't so nice after all. Natasha felt a little deflated. It was too horrible to think about.

"Sad, Natasha?" Marcello asked, distracting her from her thoughts. He saw that Natasha was frowning, and he smiled warmly.

"Does it upset you, Natasha?" he asked softly, leading her a few feet away out of earshot of the others, "I think about them also. Especially when I lie awake at night. It is very sad, no?"

She shrugged, a little embarrassed, and didn't know how to reply. She felt a bit emotional, but didn't want to say anything to Marcello, especially in front of the others. She wouldn't be able to put how she felt into words, anyway.

He put his hand gently on her shoulder, and squeezed a couple of times, making her look at him. He smiled at her tenderly again, and she felt he knew what she was feeling. She felt a little uncomfortable being so transparent, and so close to him. He lead her a few feet further away from Yanni and Signor Muretti who were explaining to Alex how the string grids worked.

"I tell you something," he said quietly, almost confiding in her. "At Herculaneum, Natasha, it was bad. You know what is Herculaneum, no?"

She nodded that she did. She knew it was the town less visited by tourists on the lower hills of Vesuvius, which had also been completely submerged and covered by lava and pumice just like Pompeii had been. She hadn't been there, but she knew it was better preserved than Pompeii.

"I tell you, it was very bad there for me at Herculaneum," Marcello whispered, frowning. "Very bad, Natasha. Much, much worse than Pompeii. You know, Natasha, around three hundred skeletons of men, women and many children were found, huddled together in groups, still exactly in the positions in which they had died when the volcano was smothering them. Many were even sitting up, some leaning against the wall..." he paused, and exhaled loudly, remembering them. It was still difficult for him.

"These people are not photographed or seen as the famous odd person found at Pompeii are seen and photographed by tourists and television shows. No, these three hundred people are less famous. These people had taken shelter under the strong, vaulted chambers by the shore, you see," he corrected himself, "I mean it *had been* the shore, before Vesuvio had finished emptying its devastating belly. This row of vaulted rooms was probably where the fishing boats and nets would have been stored off the beach for the night. The arches were open, facing the sea. But they became instant tombs for these poor people who took refuge in them. These people are haunting."

Natasha looked at him.

"There are about thirty to forty people to a section, or a room," he continued. "I suppose they all thought they were safe from the volcano, protected, huddling under these stone arches, being open to the sea, you see, with the volcano behind them. But of course they were not safe at all. These people suffered a terrible death. It haunted me for many years, Natasha, for many, many years. Because these people became so real to me, so human, all trying to save their own lives, and all huddled together. Their skulls and teeth also told us a lot about how they died, too. I cannot tell you, it was very bad, very bad indeed."

Marcello stared beyond Natasha as the memories of that excavation came back to him.

Natasha tried to imagine what Marcello had seen as he uncovered these people. She didn't even want to know about their skulls and teeth. It must have affected him quite badly, whatever it was.

"You see," he continued, "had I been there, at the time of the eruption, I too would have hidden in the same place. I would have taken your mother there. I would have taken Lorenzo and Gabriella there too, and you two..." He shook his head, and thought. "Yes, uncovering these families was a very strange experience. Very strange; I will never forget it. You uncover one skeleton here, one skeleton there, it's OK, it's archaeology. But when many die together, it tells a very sad story, a very human story... like here."

They looked at each other in silence. They were both thinking of the people a few feet below them in the tomb buried with the Queen.

Alex's voice distracted them. He came over to them.

"Anything else down there? Any weapons and stuff, Marcello?"

"O yes, *many* things, Alex," Marcello replied, and winked at Natasha. The moment was over. He turned to Alex and gave him his full attention.

"Well, let's see. There are remnants of weapons with the guards. We haven't examined them in great detail yet, but it looks interesting, Alex. These long bows are of an extraordinary length, I've never seen anything like them before. If you come to my office later, I can show you the photographs. There is also a small wooden chest down there that once contained food, which still has to be examined."

"But the *mask*! What about the mask?" Natasha asked.

"At last. At last! I thought you would never ask! The mask!" he repeated, pretending to cry. "The mask!" He put his hands together as if in prayer. "It is magnificent! Of *all* my years in Herculaneum, or in Egypt, or in the Sudan and on Adriano's wall on the Scottish borders, *this* is the one; this is what it is all about. The mask is the most wonderful, the most beautiful…."

He put his hand across his heart and patted his chest softly, and looked up to God.

"O *Dio*, *grazie*!"

Marcello looked at Natasha, and he bent down to her eye level and said very slowly and precisely, as if he was conjuring up a spell with his words.

"It is like magic; the face is of the purest obsidian, carved to flawless perfection. Blackest black you can ever imagine, but it shines like a bright star on a clear night. It draws you in like a magnet. It is strong and powerful, yet it is soft and feminine. It makes you want to touch it, to feel it, to stroke it, but most of all, to protect it. It is encrusted with jewels, precious stones and pearls that would make a thousand Kings gasp. It is absolutely breathtaking, Natasha."

Natasha said nothing, but grinned at him, appreciating his theatrical description. She was distracted by Yanni's chuckling at him beside her. He understood Marcello's passion, and envied him being able to do what he loved for a living.

"So when do we get to see it?" Alex asked, untouched by the poetic performance.

"It will come back here one day, for good," Marcello said quickly in his normal voice, "when the museum is built. Perhaps you will see it then."

Natasha watched Marcello with interest as he walked over to his two bored children, who were still sitting patiently by the wall. Poor Marcello, she thought, all this meant nothing to them. She felt a bit sorry for him, and despite herself, she was definitely beginning to soften towards him. He was quite sweet, really, she mused, for an old man of fifty-something.

The party broke up, and Yanni said he'd better get back to his mosaic floor, and Marcello told him he'd be over later to see how things were going. Natasha waited for an invitation to join Yanni. But to her disappointment, it didn't come. Instead, all Yanni did as he walked past her was pull at her plait for the second time that day. Interestingly though, she noticed, it was Marcello who glanced back at her before he left to go back up the hill with Signor Muretti. He looked sideways at her, and gave her a smile. It was an understanding smile; a friendship smile, a smile to acknowledge that they had shared something together, and she was glad for it.

Watching him, as he walked back up the hill towards his tent deep in conversation with Signor Muretti, Natasha remembered the joke, that if you tied an Italian's arms down at his side, he wouldn't be able to speak. Now Natasha could clearly see how that had come about. She hated to admit it, and she tried to resist it, but the old man was growing on her.

CHAPTER ELEVEN

"Now what?" Alex asked.

Natasha shrugged her shoulders. She didn't like the fact that the four of them were together in the same predicament. She didn't want to be part of a group. But like it or not, the fact was, they were left standing like lemons in the middle of an archaeological excavation, with nothing to do and nowhere to go. She felt stuck. She wanted to go off on her own without the others. She really wanted to go to Yanni.

"Know any good jokes?" Alex asked.

"Oh shut up, Alex!" she barked.

"Sor-*ry*," he said. "Who let the *cat* out?"

"Next time we are all together," Lorenzo quickly said, "it should be in our home in Milano, and you both must come and stay with us. It is a lot less dusty, and it would be more interesting than being here in this heat the middle of nowhere. And believe me your room would be a lot different than the tent and camp bed that is on offer here."

"And there are no dead people to look at," added Gabriella happily.

Natasha looked at her. It wasn't even worth responding to.

"Thanks," she managed to say to Lorenzo. She wondered how on earth she was going to survive the rest of the day with his sister. The irony was, here they were inviting us to stay with them in Italy. Extraordinary! Lorenzo, Natasha admitted to herself, seemed OK, he was friendly enough, but this girl was something else.

They left the dig behind them, and walked back in the thin strip of shade along the base of the cliffs to the camp. Natasha walked ahead quickly, in an effort to keep her distance from Gabriella.

Lorenzo caught up with her, and asked if he could join her. She said she didn't mind. He slowed her pace a little, and took her by surprise by asking if he had upset her.

"Oh no, not at all!" she said, but wanted to add that it was his sister who was driving her mad, not him. She felt a bit guilty that she had been so transparent, so she thought she should at least try to talk to him a little, to show it wasn't him she was upset with.

"So where do you live? I mean, I know you said Milan, but are you in the heart of the city, or on the outskirts?"

"Well, actually neither. Milano is the nearest large city and international airport. And it is easier to just say Milan. We are in fact nearer Piacenza, but if I had said that, you wouldn't have known where we were at all."

"I might have," Natasha retorted, not liking the fact that he presumed she didn't know. She didn't, but that was beside the point, she thought.

Lorenzo explained how he and Gabriella lived in his father's family home south of Milan in the hills of the Trebbia Valley with their grandmother. She had, for the last few years, practically brought them up single-handedly since their father was always busy and traveled so much. During the week in term time, they lived with their Aunt in an apartment in Milan, as their school *was* in the city, but they went home to the Valley on Friday afternoons. Natasha noticed that Lorenzo didn't mention their mother, and she felt she shouldn't ask.

Lorenzo explained that one day, the family home would pass down to him, as it has been passed down to the eldest son for centuries. Natasha slowed her pace right down and listened with interest. She didn't even notice that Gabriella had caught up with them and was walking beside her.

"'Montesonnellino', our family home, has been in the family since the fifteenth century, when it was built by an ancestor as a wedding gift to his young daughter," Lorenzo explained.

"It was a way of keeping your daughter close by," added Gabriella. "She was almost seventeen when she married. She had grown up on the estate on the hill across the valley. This way, with their daughter still in view, her family could feel close and visit often and still be in her life."

It sounded lovely to Natasha. Even the name of the home was enchanting. She loved the way the Italians have always been so family orientated. Gabriella talked about her grandmother, and that how in her eighties, she was still a formidable figure, one to be reckoned with.

"Even my father does what he is told," Lorenzo said, laughing. "But she really has a heart of gold. She would welcome you both with open arms, and you could stay for as long as you wanted, and never be in the way."

"Yes," agreed Gabriella. "Please come and stay, it is very lovely. We have fountains in the gardens, with statues and many interesting things to look at," she said. "Natasha, you would like the fountains, they are very pretty. I would love you to come home with us."

This took Natasha a bit by surprise. Was Gabriella totally oblivious to how much Alex and she were trying to avoid her? Natasha had to admit though, that Gabriella was better when there were no adults around, especially her father. She was less pathetic.

She thought about the unexpected offer. Natasha had visited her mother's friend's house outside Florence, which sounded similar, with beautiful formal gardens and grounds, and every room in the house almost heavy in history. She looked at Alex, and he shrugged a 'why not?' sort of shrug back.

"Thanks," she managed to get out. "We'd like to visit one day, and meet your grandmother, I suppose."

She just thought how weird this was, as they hardly knew each other. Perhaps Gabriella and Lorenzo were a bit lonely stuck out in the country. It would certainly drive her mad, she thought.

"You two are welcome to come to England and visit my grandmother," Alex offered. "But I think you'd be bored silly. *We* are. She lives in the country, and there's nothing to do at her house except take the dogs for walks across fields or sneak off to the little village post office down the lane to buy sweets. She even hides the television under a table, with a big round cloth covering it just to make it awkward to get out and watch."

"I don't mind," Gabriella said honestly. "Grandmothers are interesting. I love to sit with mine and hear stories about her childhood. I am sure your grandmother must have some interesting stories too, Alex, no?"

Alex shrugged his shoulders. "Dunno, never asked. She tells a good ghost story though."

"She was evacuated as a child to the North of England during the war, because of the Germans dropping bombs in the South, which is where she lived," Natasha said, not wanting to sound as disconnected to her grandmother as Alex was. "I think she had a terrible childhood because of the war. She didn't see her mother for years and ran away from horrible families who abused her and treated her like a servant."

"That is so terrible!" Gabriella said, looking genuinely worried. Natasha wasn't sure if Gabriella meant 'terrible' because her grandmother had been treated like a servant or because of the bombs.

"Was she? Really?" Alex asked Natasha. "Evacuated?" He had no idea.

"That is very sad," Gabriella said. "How she must have suffered." She paused, then added, "I sometimes escape too, you know. We have horses, and I have a very special horse that I love more than anything in the world. When I miss my mother," Gabriella lowered her voice, so as to be out of Lorenzo's earshot, "I sneak out at night and go and sleep in the stables with Artamis. He is the only one who understands me," she said. "He is my best friend in the whole world."

Natasha understood by this, that her mother must have died. She felt very sorry for her. That probably explained her attention-seeking behavior when her father was around. Natasha felt a bit guilty at dismissing her so quickly as being pathetic. She *was* annoying, but there was a reason for it.

They walked on in silence, and Natasha could tell that Gabriella was close to tears.

She put her arm around her, and they followed the boys back to the camp.

Chapter Twelve

Alex made a point of walking back to the camp with Lorenzo to suggest to him on the quiet, that it would make a lot of sense if the boys moved in together in one tent, and then the two girls could share their own tent. But as good as it sounded to Lorenzo, he had to decline, saying that he felt his sister would feel happier if he slept in the tent with her.

"She is scared enough at night with me there, hearing noises and imaginary things outside the tent, so without me I am afraid, Alex, she would be inconsolable."

"You're right, Lorenzo," Alex sighed. "I suppose Natasha needs me to protect her too; we guys should do our duty. Hey, look," he whispered, nudging Lorenzo, "there's that awful woman again, Miss 'Unibrow'."

She scurried past them as they neared Lorenzo's tent. She was in an obvious hurry and walked quickly in the direction of the excavation site. She reluctantly nodded to Alex and Lorenzo when they said hello to her, but was more concerned with shoving something into her jeans pocket. Her odd behavior didn't go unnoticed by the girls either, and they presumed she must have forgotten something from her tent and had come back to get it.

"Well what ever it was must have been shiny," Alex said. "It seemed to catch the light for a split second. It must have been a lighter or something; remember she was smoking in the trench?"

"Oh forget about her," Gabriella said. "She is of little interest. Let's have a soda in our tent. We should have some cold cans in the cooler."

They sat on the two beds in Gabriella and Lorenzo's tent with their drinks, and talked about how on earth they were going to pass the time for the next couple of weeks.

"What was my father thinking when he told Gabriella and me that he wanted us to come out here this Easter? It is crazy!" Lorenzo announced. "We have never had to come to any other of his excavations before, in fact, he has even discouraged us. Remember Gabriella, when he was at Herculaneum two years ago? He was even living in a villa on the coast, with a pool and a tennis court, but he said it would be too boring for us to join him as he wouldn't be able to spend much time with us, remember? He thought *that* would be boring! What was he thinking bringing us here?"

Natasha flushed. She remembered her mother going to Herculaneum about two years ago. It was her first job abroad since her had parents had split up. She kept quiet.

"Yes, I do remember Lorenzo, and look at us here," Gabriella was saying, "living in tents! And no private bathrooms! I can't even use my hair dryer, it is ridiculous."

The children laughed. But Gabriella didn't. It wasn't a joke. For once though, Natasha thought she was right.

"Well, thank goodness you two are here," Lorenzo said to his two new friends. "At least we can talk and complain together!"

"I'll drink to that!" Alex said, and he raised his can of soda. "Cheers!"

Natasha smiled at her brother. She was glad he was here. Although she would never admit it openly, the eighteen months between them seemed to be narrowing, and she didn't see him as such a dork of a younger brother any more. She looked at Gabriella and Lorenzo, and then a thought crossed her mind about what Lorenzo had just said about their father wanting them out here in the desert with him;

was it a coincidence that the four of them were brought out here? Was it orchestrated by their parents, for reasons other than having each other's company? She quickly dismissed the thought. But then she thought about it again. She remembered her chat with Yanni. And then there was something else she remembered; when Marcello was confiding in her about Herculaneum and finding those bodies, he had said he would have hidden her mother under those arches to keep her safe. And then he went on to add his own children and Alex and herself! What was all that about?

She feared something was definitely behind it and wondered if she should say anything to Lorenzo about her suspicions, but decided not to. She could be wrong; so she decided to keep her observations to herself.

"Knock, knock!" a voice said from outside the tent, jolting her back. "May I enter?"

Lorenzo lifted the flap and let the visitor in.

"*Ciao a tutti*!"

"Hello Claudio," Lorenzo said. "Thank you for the ice and cold drinks. This," he turned to Natasha and Alex, "is Claudio, the chef from Piacenza. He takes very good care of us, and our appetites!"

He shook hands with Natasha and Alex.

"Any special requests from the kitchen for the new English taste buds? I know you like your breakfasts!" he said in perfect English. He was clad in a chef's white jacket, blue and white loose gingham trousers, and clean white clogs on his feet. He was quite young, probably in his early twenties, and with a big Roman nose, and an army buzz-cut which could have made him look a little threatening had he not smiled so much.

"Cereal," Alex said. "And I don't mean boring old Corn Flakes. I really can't stand healthy chopped fruit and oats and all that other stuff either, I need proper sugar-coated cereal."

Claudio looked blankly at him. He was thinking more on the lines of omelets or French toast.

"Alex, don't be so rude!" Natasha said, giving her brother a dig in the ribs.

"We're fine, thank you, Claudio, we really eat anything," she said apologetically.

"Do we get iced drinks in our tent too?" Alex asked. "Absolutely!" he said. "There is water, and I can add a selection of fruit juice and sodas. The only rule is you must dispose of the empty cans in the proper place behind the canteen. No trash is allowed, especially anything that will attract flies or desert rodents."

"No problem," Alex said. He would do anything for a bit of room service.

Natasha asked Claudio, out of interest, how he got the job out here, or more to the point, *why* he took the job out here. She liked the way he was proud of what he did and seemed to go out of his way to please people, and with a smile on his face, too.

"Well, Marcello had given me an offer I couldn't refuse, an almost crazy offer, to cook beautiful, healthy meals for the camp every night. Marcello told me that the way to a happy camp is through the stomach. He is paying my expenses himself, you know, since he would never get funding for such an extravagance! ' If I must sleep in a tent like a nomad,' he said, 'at least I can eat like a Prince!' "

"So you really don't mind being stuck in that tent, cooking?" Lorenzo asked.

"No!" he said with a grin. "I think of my friends at home doing the same old thing in the same old place and I am here doing something totally different! I can breathe here; you have all been to the top of the ridge, haven't you?" he asked, pointing to the ridge behind him. "The sunset is something!"

They said they hadn't.

"Well, it is definitely worth the climb. Most people here do it when they first arrive, but now it is old news. Now, no one bothers to go up there, or takes much notice of the moon, the sunsets or the stars, after their first week."

Alex's eyes lit up. He was thrilled at the thought of climbing the cliff. Why hadn't he thought of it before? What a waste of an afternoon he had had, wandering around the camp when he could have been exploring up there at the top of the ridge. He went outside the tent and looked up at it. It didn't look too hard; quite 'do-able' really, he thought. He examined the cliff face and he saw that there was a snake-like track that wound its way to the top.

Back in the tent, Alex announced that he was going to climb the ridge, and asked if anyone else was up for it. Natasha immediately told him that he should check with Marcello and their mother before they went scrambling up the cliff face. "Especially after what happened yester…" she stopped in her tracks and looked at Gabriella to see if she had noticed.

"It's all right, Natasha, I know what happened," Gabriella said, sighing. She sounded frustrated. "Lorenzo told me everything."

"Ah yes, the bandits," Claudio said. "*Idioti*! We were told about them. People do such stupid things. Even, it seems within this camp itself."

"Within the camp? What do you mean?" Lorenzo asked.

"Stealing food when it is quite unnecessary."

"Stealing food?" Natasha asked. "What do you mean?"

"I had some food taken from the kitchen yesterday. I don't understand it; all they have to do is ask for it! Why steal it? I give them whatever they want to take to the site for their lunches, and I make sure the meals at breakfast and in the evenings are plentiful! So why take from the kitchen without telling me? It just isn't necessary. There is more than enough, Marcello makes sure of that!"

"Maybe it is those animals outside my tent," Gabriella suggested. They looked at her not knowing if it was a joke or not. She let out a smile.

"We're getting sidetracked," Alex said, wanting to get back to what was important. "Any chance then, of a few sandwiches to take up to the top with us, Claudio?"

"OK, we'll do a deal," he laughed. "You forget about the breakfast cereal, and I'll make something for you to take with you. I don't think they have cereal out here, anyway. Give me a few minutes to prepare the sandwiches, and then you can pick them up."

"Cool. Thanks," Alex said. "This is going to be fun!"

Gabriella and Natasha headed back towards the canteen with Claudio to find Julia and Marcello to check it was OK to do the climb. They eventually found them in his office, his Bedouin tent, on the hills overlooking the site.

Initially Marcello was adamant they shouldn't do it, but after a lot of pleading by Gabriella, Marcello eventually relented, but not before they were given a lecture about safety, responsibility, and staying together.

"Gabriella, are you sure you want to go, darling?" her father asked one more time. Natasha rolled her eyes. Here we go, she thought.

"It's very steep," he continued, "especially in a couple of places, remember, Julia?"

"Yes, yes," Julia answered. She almost added something, but decided not to. She looked a little flustered. Marcello looked at her, and smiled. There was an awkward silence.

"Your mother hasn't a head for heights," Marcello said, still looking at Julia, almost covering for her. They laughed quietly together. It was obviously a private joke.

"But she did very well," he continued. "It was worth the climb in the end, no, Julia?" he added, almost out of the children's earshot. "The sunset was magnificent, no?"

She looked at Marcello. "Yes, beautiful, Marcello."

Natasha couldn't wait to leave the room. She felt sick. Now that she knew what was happening between them, she didn't want to know. It was all so weird, and she really didn't want to face it. She couldn't get out of the tent quick enough. She quickly said 'bye' and left Gabriella in there. She needed fresh air. It was too stuffy in there. She went and picked up the picnic from Claudio and put it out of her mind.

Within the hour they had all met as planned at the base of the cliff behind Gabriella and Lorenzo's tent, which, according to Claudio, was the easiest point to start the climb.

CHAPTER THIRTEEN

The path was steep, dry and dusty, which made for a poor grip under foot. But Alex led the way, in his element, periodically checking the girls behind him, offering help and advice on how to tackle the tricky parts. Loose stones sometimes made it very unstable, and a small avalanche of pebbles and dust would roll down to the person directly behind the one in front. Sometimes both hands were needed to scramble up and over large rocks, often followed by a smooth section where they could continue quite easily on to the next level. It was strenuous in places, but exciting.

Gabriella was a little scared but she pushed herself on, not wanting to be the last one up. With Lorenzo's encouragement from behind, promising his sister he would catch her if she slipped, she did surprisingly well. Alex was surprised at her tenacity. Not bad, he thought, for a girl. He had almost expected her to give up, or even not to have come at all. But she was actually pretty good, he thought.

The path became narrow in places, and at one point, Natasha lost her footing and slid down backwards about six feet into Gabriella. She grazed her hand on the path while trying to stop herself sliding, and sat down and wiped her palm on her shorts, carefully picking the grit out of the scraped skin on her palm and wincing as she did it. She looked up and saw Lorenzo at her side.

"Are you alright?" his eyes told of his genuine concern. He dampened the bottom of his Polo shirt with water from his bottle, and took her hand and gently wiped the wound clean. It stung and Natasha winced, instinctively withdrawing her hand. Lorenzo apologized, gently took her hand again, and softly blew over the graze.

"My mother used to do this for us when we were hurt," he said. He blew again very gently. "Is it feeling any better?"

Natasha felt embarrassed with the attention, and wasn't sure if the mention of his mother was a lead for Natasha to ask about her. She told him it wasn't stinging so much, and thanked him for his help, and got up to carry on. She noticed that a large patch of his spotless white polo shirt was now smeared with a mixture of dirt, water and her blood. She apologized, but he didn't seem at all concerned.

"Here, give me your good hand, I will lead you the rest of the way," he said. He called to Alex to slow down and keep apace with Gabriella.

Before Natasha could protest, he had taken her hand and was leading her along the path. Natasha had never held a boy's hand before, except for a handshake, or a helping hand like Yanni had offered her earlier. Lorenzo's hand was strong and in control. She felt safe with him. A bit like an older brother might be, she thought. Her grazed hand was very sore and throbbing, but it didn't matter. She was smiling inside.

Lorenzo lead her gently up the path and over and around the rocks that sometimes blocked their way. He warned her of another loose section ahead of them, and then of a particularly tricky part, and kept hold of her hand through the worst of it. He was in control, and was being an absolute gentleman. She discovered that she liked the feeling of being taken care of.

Occasionally, Lorenzo called to Gabriella to check that she was OK.

"Gabriella, *sta bene*?"

"*Si, Lorenzo, sto bene. Alex e qui con mei.*"

Alex was doing a good job of watching over Gabriella, and ten minutes later, the four young teens had reached the summit. They were tired, dusty and hot, but they had done it. They found themselves standing on what seemed to them, the top of the world.

CHAPTER FOURTEEN

"This must be how God feels!" Gabriella called to Alex, standing a few feet away; her arms were outstretched wide, catching the breeze.

"I know. It must be. And this is His part of the world too!" he said, stretching out his arms and catching the breeze too. "It's great being on top of the world looking down!"

The view was incredible: A three hundred-and-sixty degree panorama. They looked out into the distance and could see the whole delta spread out before them in every direction until it merged with the sky on the horizon: miles and miles of sand dunes, as far as the eye could see. It was fantastic. The four children stood there in awe of the view and majesty of the whole experience.

"I can see why the Queen had her city here, this is the perfect spot," Natasha said. "Come on, let's go and check out the other side."

They made their way to the north side of the ridge, across a rocky escarpment, and then another area so smooth and clean, with shallow hollows and gentle slopes, exposing the many beautiful colors and shades of the rock in wavy horizontal lines, which Alex said would be great to skateboard on. And further on, beyond a few more loose rocks and boulders, they came to an abrupt stop. They stood a few feet away from the edge of the cliff, and looked out into the endless expanse of desert.

"Look, you can make out the road in the distance," Lorenzo pointed out.

"And look over that way, are they camels? See, that straight line down there?" Natasha was pointing to tiny dots far in the distance to the left. "They're moving, see? They look like camels to me! And look down there, those look like donkeys!"

"Donkeys? I doubt that!" Alex said. "But isn't it is amazing how anyone could live out there. You can just see the dried-out riverbeds that Mum was telling us about in the car, Natasha, see? Over there."

They all looked to where he was pointing. It was a faint snake-like mark in the valley floor.

"Rivers? There are no rivers around here. It must be something else," Gabriella said. "Just a line in the sand."

"No, there used to be rivers, believe me," Alex told her very convincingly. "I can give you the history about the area sometime if you like. I know a lot about it." He sounded very matter of fact.

Gabriella looked at him. She was impressed.

"Can you teach me about the history, Alex, I would like to know more."

"OK, any time," he said, secretly hoping he would have the chance to ask his mother a bit more on the subject before Gabriella mentioned it again.

The sun was beginning to set, and they the decided to make their way across the top of the plateau to the other side of the ridge to see the sunset; the shadows were becoming longer and the air was now cooling. The children hiked back to the south side, and they sat by the edge of the cliff and watched the gigantic orange ball sink into the horizon beyond the desert. Natasha found a nice flat, smooth boulder, just the right height for a seat. As she sat on it, she wondered who might have sat on it before her thousands of years ago. The boulder was in such a perfect position overlooking the ancient ruined city with the sunset beyond it, that someone must have sat here, she thought, to take in the view and the sunset all those centuries ago when the city was alive and thriving. She smoothed and patted the thin layer of fine, dry sand under her feet, and then she noticed a darker patch of sand close to the rock beside the boulder. She wondered if there had been something wooden in there at one time; wasn't that a sign to an archaeologist? Isn't that what Yanni had told her, that a dark spot in the earth was where wood had once been? Perhaps it had been the torchlight of a lookout guard. She felt the smooth surface of her stone chair with her fingertips, wishing she could know who had sat there before her.

"Funny how people are here for such a short time, doing their best to survive for as long as they can, and then things like rocks and stones live on."

Alex turned round and looked at his sister.

"Yup, very strange. And here's your sandwich Natasha. And by the way, in case you hadn't noticed, rocks don't actually 'live'. Did Claudio give us any mustard or mayo? Mine's a bit dry…"

The low sun shimmered and glowed, and then it was gone.

They enjoyed the panini that Claudio had prepared for them, and they sat for a little while longer before they started to feel the chill in the air, and they made their careful decent down to the camp.

Chapter Fifteen

Late that night, while the camp slept, Alex lay on his bed, wide-awake. Natasha was breathing heavily on the other side of the partition, almost at the point of snoring. She was mentally and physically exhausted after her full day of emotional highs and lows, plus the climb to the top of the ridge and down again in the dark had all but knocked her out for the night. She had fallen asleep instantly, much to her brother's envy.

Alex just couldn't get to sleep. He kept tossing and turning, feeling too hot, then cold. He threw his pillow down to the bottom end of his bed. He thumped it with his fist, then turned around, slammed his head down on to it, and lay facing the opposite end of the tent. He put his hands behind his head and looked out of his little side window with the mosquito netting.

From this position, he faced the ridge. Not that he could really see anything; it was much too dark. But he could see the stars in the black sky above the plateau. They were very bright. Wow, he thought, they were bright! Much brighter than the stars at home, he noted. And twinkling! They were twinkling so much, they almost looked fake.

He sat up to get a better look. One of the stars in particular was so low and bright; it could have been hovering on top of the ridge. He watched it for a few moments. How close the night sky is here, he thought.

"Wait a minute," he said out loud. "That *can't* be a star!"

He sat up. He pressed his eyes so close to the mosquito netting for a better look, that his eyelashes bent back.

"There's no way that's a star… or is it?" He decided he needed to check this out.

He went to the door-flap and started to un-zip it as slowly and as quietly as he could. "Why is it that at night," he muttered to himself, "when you try so hard to be quiet, the sound is multiplied by a million?"

He gave up trying to un-zip it quietly, and opened it with a fast upward yank just to get it quickly over with. He glanced over at his sister's side of the tent. The noise hadn't woken her; she hadn't stirred. She was still breathing heavily.

He crept outside, and walked round to the back of the tent, where he had an uninterrupted view of the dark cliff-face behind the back row of tents. He could make just make out its silhouette; the moonlight and stars had given him some light, but it was a weird light that reminded him of something nasty, but he wasn't sure what. He couldn't quite pinpoint it exactly. He felt that something might jump out at him; Werewolves sprang to mind.

"Get a grip," he whispered to himself. "Concentrate; the star."

He looked up, and there it was again. That same, big twinkling star. Except, he realized as he watched it, this star seemed to twinkle at regular intervals. It almost seemed like it knew the Morse Code, or something.

Very quietly, he walked along the back of the tents, so he could get the flashing star lined up directly above him. Looking upwards and walking straight ahead in the dark isn't a good combination, especially behind a line of tents. He waked into a guide rope and tripped over, giving out a yelp.

"Ouch, ouch, ouch! That hurt!" he said, rubbing his shin.

Suddenly, he was blinded by a bright light shining directly into his face. He put his hand up to shade his eyes. He still couldn't see anything, it was so bright.

"Alex," whispered the voice behind the flashlight, "for Heaven's sake, what are you *doing*?"

Alex thankfully recognized the voice.

"Oh, Lorenzo, it's you!" he whispered. "OK, OK, put the flashlight down, you're blinding me! I'll tell you!"

"Sorry." Lorenzo lowered his flashlight so that Alex could see.

"But *Alex*, what on earth are you doing out here? It's almost two in the morning!" He had been woken by Gabriella again, who had heard noises, as usual, and had sent him out to investigate.

"Shh, I know, I know. Lorenzo, listen, I need to show you something weird. Turn your flashlight off, quickly!" Alex whispered.

Lorenzo did what Alex asked.

"Look up there. There's a light."

Lorenzo looked up to the plateau where Alex was pointing. "Yes, you're right, Alex, many lights. They are called stars."

Alex raised his hand as if to tell Lorenzo to wait and watch. They waited, and they watched. They waited a little longer. And watched.

Nothing.

"What, Alex? *What* did you see?" Lorenzo sounded frustrated. "You are as bad as my sister! What am I supposed to be looking for?"

"There was a light. At first I thought it was a really bright shining star or something, but it wasn't, it was a light, and it was flashing some kind of a code."

"What do you think it was? Someone signaling? For what? And why at two in the morning? Alex, you read too many adventure stories. People have mobile phones now if they need to communicate, in case you hadn't noticed. They don't use flashlights."

Alex sat down on a rock. He felt confused. He looked up the cliff face, hoping the flashing would start again so that Lorenzo would believe him. Whatever or whoever it was doing the flashing had stopped now. Perhaps seeing Lorenzo's flashlight had put them off.

"Just wait a couple more minutes…"

"Look Alex," Lorenzo sighed. "I am cold standing out here. And I need to sleep. Can we discuss it in the morning when we are fully dressed and thinking clearly?"

"OK, fine, fine." Now he felt a bit silly. Had he imagined it? And anyway if he hadn't, so what? What's the harm in a person with a flashlight? So what if someone was up there?

He reluctantly said goodnight to Lorenzo, and went back to his tent, checking the cliff top behind him as he went. But the flashing had definitely stopped.

Alex tried very hard, but he couldn't convince himself it was nothing to be bothered about. He lay on his bed again, looking out of his little window up at the stars, but nothing was twinkling anymore. Nothing was flashing. All was quiet on the western front.

He closed his eyes, and eventually fell asleep.

Chapter Sixteen

"What? You want me to climb up there again with you? Why?" Natasha looked at her brother in amazement.

She was trying for the third consecutive time to do a neat, even, French plait. She was determined to do it without her mother's help. The bandage on her hand didn't help either. The top part of the plait close to her head always gave her trouble, and she had to concentrate hard with her eyes closed as she did it. Now that she had been distracted by Alex and his plan, she had to undo what she had begun and start all over again.

"Alex, wasn't the climb enough for you last night?" she asked him. "I thought we would hang around at the dig and see if anything else from the palace is excavated today. Gabriella found something yesterday and I was hoping to find something too."

Then she added as nonchalantly as she could, "and Yanni was going to tell me more about his floor that he's working on. *You* may not be that interested in the dig, but *I* am."

She stopped talking for a minute while she concentrated on the plait.

"Is this bit even?" she asked him.

"Yeah, great." He didn't even look. He was annoyed that she didn't want to go up again.

She finished the plait. She felt it, it was fine. She flicked it behind her back. She could now concentrate on Alex.

She was torn. Going up to the top of the ridge again would be fun, and now with a purpose too. Alex had explained to her as soon as she had woken that morning about the flashing light, and she was interested. It did sound very odd and it was certainly worth checking out. But she had looked forward to spending the day with Yanni, and talking to him as he worked on the mosaic floor. She couldn't seem too keen though, or Alex might be suspicious and start teasing her. That would be disastrous.

She thought about it, then sighed.

"Well if you are going, I suppose I'll come too," she said reluctantly. "Let's get some breakfast and ask if Lorenzo and Gabriella want to join us. Come on, it's late. It's nearly ten o'clock. The whole camp will have been working at the dig for a couple of hours by now."

"Yeah, it'll be nice to have the canteen to ourselves. More for us to eat."

"Pig!"

"Pig yourself!"

Alex had been right; the four children had the canteen completely to themselves. That is, almost to themselves, as the grumpy lady known to them as Miss 'Unibrow' from the trench came in, poured herself a coffee then sat two tables away from theirs. She ignored the children, and started wrapping a bandage around her wrist as she obviously had a minor injury and wasn't going to work. Lorenzo had politely said, 'good morning' to her as she had sat down, but she pretended she hadn't heard, and ignored him, making it very obvious she didn't want to talk. Alex tapped the side of his head, indicating to Lorenzo that she was crazy, and they all tried not to laugh.

So over their ham, melon and fresh bread heaped with chocolate nutty spread, the four children ignored the woman, and discussed the flashing light at the top of the ridge, and what it could possibly have been.

"Well what ever it was, I think it needs further investigation. I'm going up there after breakfast with Natasha to check it out," Alex announced. "I reckon it's the men from the pass. They're spying on us."

"*Alex,* we can't discuss... *that*, remember?" Natasha hissed under her breath, "because of, *you know*!" She gave her brother the look that meant 'zip it'.

"I told you, I know *everything*," Gabriella announced happily.

"It is true, she's not as scared as she seems."

"Oh, good," Alex said, a little perplexed as to why anyone would want to act even more girly than they really were. "And I wouldn't call those two idiots 'gentlemen', you're far too polite Lorenzo."

"Yes, I've got another name for those two, but I wouldn't say it here." Natasha said under her breath.

"They are *bastardi*!" Gabriella announced, loud and clear.

They looked at her in shock, and then laughed. Natasha almost liked this girl!

"So, Gabriella, the animal noises that you hear outside your tent at night, you're not *really* afraid of those, are you?" Natasha asked her hopefully, now that she knew she really wasn't half the wimp she made herself out to be.

Lorenzo and Alex looked at each other trying not to laugh, remembering their meeting last night behind the tent.

"I *meant,*" Natasha clarified her question, "the *animals* you heard *before* last night. Stop it, you two! Be serious!" She kicked her brother under the table for laughing.

"Yes," Gabriella replied emphatically, totally ignoring the boys.

"Er... you mean, yes... what?" Natasha asked. "Yes you are afraid of them, or yes, you're not afraid?"

"Yes I am afraid," she said, "because they certainly are not animals. They are humans."

The three of them looked at her in amazement again.

"You mean *before* last night, before Alex and Lorenzo were out there, you heard humans? I mean people, outside your tent?"

"Yes, Natasha. Alex was there last night, someone else was there the other nights." She was serious. She looked at her brother directly in the eyes. "I am sure of it."

Silence.

"*Ma*, Gabriella. What do you mean, that someone is creeping around our tent every night? For what? It is too ridiculous." Lorenzo was trying not to become irritated with his sister.

Natasha looked at her.

"Lorenzo, what if Gabriella wasn't imagining things?" Just because she was spoilt, Natasha thought, didn't mean she was making things up.

The woman at the next table got up abruptly and left the canteen, leaving her empty coffee cup on the table. They watched her leave.

"I had forgotten she was there," Lorenzo said. "Do you think she was listening?"

"Dunno. What for? I shouldn't think we're very interesting to her. She's made that pretty obvious already."

"Listen Lorenzo," Natasha said, turning her mind back to Gabriella's noises in the night. "It might not be so ridiculous, you know, about Gabriella hearing someone outside your tent, I mean." She looked at Gabriella. "Gabriella, I was just sort of wondering, did you hear the noises, or, I mean the people, the first night you arrived?"

Gabriella thought for a moment.

"No, it was after our first night. I remember the first night; I could not sleep because the bed was so uncomfortable. I was awake for most of the night, and I heard nothing outside the tent."

"So?" Alex said to Natasha. "What are you getting at? This is *boring*, Natasha."

Natasha looked at him.

"Wait a minute, Alex. Bear with me for a second. Listen, Gabriella and Lorenzo arrived the day after the tomb was opened up for the first time, right?" She looked at them for confirmation. They nodded at her. "Right. And that's when you started to hear the creeping around near your tent. Right Gabriella? After the mask had been discovered." Lorenzo and Gabriella nodded again.

Gabriella shrieked. She looked terrified. She understood where Natasha was leading.

"Oh no, the Queen! She is coming to haunt us! You are right Natasha. It is the Queen and her dead guards. My father opened her tomb and let the spirits out!" She was terrified and grabbed her brother's arm. "I want to go home, we have to get away from here!"

Natasha tried to calm her down.

"No, no, Gabriella, listen! I don't think it is the Queen, or her ghost or anything like that. But it could be someone looking for something that belonged to the Queen. My mother told us she took the Queen's mask to Medinabad the morning the day we arrived. Probably only a handful of people here know that. Most people probably presume the mask is still in the camp, locked up in that 'finds' tent, with the jewelry and all the other things they're working on. I bet you they're looking for the mask. That's what those noises will be. I'm sure of it. But I'm not sure why you hear noises behind your tent, the mask is obviously not there, or anywhere your tent, but I bet all this is somehow linked to that priceless mask."

"That makes sense," Alex said. "I think you may have something. I *bet* it's the mask they're after. That's what those two plonkers were searching our car for!" he said. Then he paused and thought for a moment. "But why search a car on its way *back* into the camp, if they thought the mask was already *in* the camp? That doesn't make sense at all."

The children were stumped.

"I know," Alex said, answering his own question, "what if they somehow got word that the mask would be leaving the site, but didn't know exactly when?" He felt he was on to something.

"Yes," Natasha said. "Maybe they missed their chance when our mother was leaving the camp with it. After all, she said that she had left really early that morning. What if they presumed it would return with her later on in the day. They would have waited, and held up the car on its way back."

Lorenzo was shaking his head.

"No, no; But why? Why would they think that anyone would bring such a valuable object all the way back into the camp once it had been purposely taken away? They wouldn't presume that at all. It is ridiculous. It is just not logical... and wandering behind our tent at night? It just doesn't add up."

Lorenzo always has to be logical, Alex thought. But anyway, logical or not, unfortunately he had a point. Why *would* they think the mask would be brought back again? Why did they search the car on its way back *into* the camp? The whole thing just didn't make sense.

The four of them sat in silence. It felt like they had hit a dead end again.

Gabriella broke the silence. She had an idea.

"They did not know that it was going to be locked in a bank. How could they know? I am sure my father only discusses such things with Signor Muretti, and of course your mother. We didn't know, did we Lorenzo, where the mask was going? Maybe these men thought the mask was just going to be examined and valued or photographed. They probably thought my father wouldn't want it out of his sight for too long, as it is so precious."

They looked at Gabriella.

"Gabriella, you are right!" Natasha said.

Alex stared at her, wondering why he hadn't thought of that.

"Yes Gabriella, after all, everything else from the tomb is still here," Lorenzo added. "Even the Queen's jewelry. It is all still in boxes in that tent, waiting to be catalogued, it is no secret. So to these men, it would make perfect sense that the mask would come back to be locked up here with the rest of the contents of the tomb."

Lorenzo seemed happy with this explanation. He was definitely getting into it now. It was becoming quite interesting to him.

"Well I'm off," Alex announced, grabbing his back-pack. He stuck his finger in the chocolate spread jar, and scooped out a dollop.

"Alex, that's disgusting!" Natasha yelled at him. "All your disgusting germs!"

"Oh, yeah, you're right, sorry." He licked his finger clean and put the lid back on, then popped the jar into his backpack.

"For energy," he explained. "And so you don't get my disgusting germs! All this thinking makes me need a bit of extra energy. Well, I'm going for an explore, and I have a change of plan. I think today I will go back to the pass to check out the spot where we were held up instead of going up the ridge. Maybe we will find some clues or something. Remember Natasha," he said, "I saw a light flash on our way here in the car before those men held us up? I'm going to check it all out. It's all falling into place. Anyone want to join me, Lorenzo?"

The three sat there thinking about it; the thought of walking anywhere in the heat wasn't appealing to any of them.

"Oh come on you lot, we can't mope around in the canteen all day. It's more fun than looking at a decaying old floor at the excavation site! I'll leave in twenty minutes from my tent. Anybody is welcome to join me. See you!"

CHAPTER SEVENTEEN

"Maha, this is driving us crazy. In God's name, where are they? I cannot feel my legs anymore from squatting like this for eternity. Are they coming or not? The boss will have our heads if we do not..."

"Abdul, they are coming, they are coming." She tried to calm him down. "I heard them plan their day. I told you, I was sitting right next to them. The English boy said he was coming up here to check things out. They will be here, have patience." She sounded confident, but now she was actually having doubts herself. It was almost three hours since she had left the canteen, having heard their plans to come to the top of the ridge, and there was still no sign of the awful brats. She especially hated the older girl with the long blonde hair. She seemed too pretty for her own good, and Maha had a special surprise planned for her.

"What's the bandage for? Have you hurt your hand?" Abdul asked her.

"Don't be ridiculous," she snapped. "It is so that I can be absent from the trench. If I am questioned, I have an excuse."

The two men were squatting behind a boulder on the top of the ridge. They were tired, irritable and uncomfortable. The cramped wait in the heat was getting to them, especially having spent their second night on the hard floor of their cave with only one mattress and a few miserly blankets between them. Maha had practically run up the steep path to wake and inform them that it was to be this morning, and they were to be ready. She had even managed to take bread and cheese for their breakfast without the camp's chef noticing. That was now exactly three hours ago. She squatted behind an adjacent bolder in wait for the children.

"They will make it easy for us. So just be patient and be ready to pounce," she whispered. "Do you have the ropes from the farmhouse? You know what to do. This is our last chance. Don't mess it up this time or our lives will not be worth living!"

"The ropes are here, it is all under control, Maha."

"Good. Did you bring my gun from the cave?"

"Yes, it's here."

"Good, then the mask will soon be in our hands, and by tomorrow we will have a very happy boss and we will all be as rich as Princes. It will be out of the country in no time with the foreign collector, and we can get out of this stinking desert once and for all."

"God willing," Abdul muttered. "What is the knife for? We have guns. What need of the knife, Maha?"

"The blond girl. She needs to be taught a lesson," she answered.

He grinned at her. "Oh yeah?"

She got up from her hiding position. Her legs were cramping. "I will check if they are coming. Stay here."

She walked to the edge and carefully peeped over the plateau. She saw nothing. No one coming at all. She cursed and then walked over to the edge at the top of the pathway. She looked down to see if she could see them. She cursed again and swore under her breath. There was still no sign of any of the confounded children. She lit a cigarette and walked back to the other end of edge of the ridge, towards the pass. As she approached, she startled a large falcon, which had been sitting on a ledge jotting out of the cliff face a few feet below her. It flew off into the pass, screeching, and the noise bounced off the cliffs echoing over and over.

"Stupid animal," she hissed.

Then she thought she heard voices. She looked down over the side of the ridge, and she couldn't believe what she saw. Her anger seethed inside her. There they were, the two boys and the two stupid girls, going for a stroll down in the narrow pass below her.

"*Idiots*! Confounded *idiots*! I don't *believe* it! What are they doing down there?" She was furious.

She threw her cigarette down beside her in temper, and then ground it under her boot until it disintegrated.

* * * * *

It had taken over half an hour for the four young explorers to walk from the camp, along the base of the ridge, to where it turned to the right and into the cool narrow pass. They were glad of the shade; it was now midday and the sun was scorching. They rested on a boulder and had a drink.

The towering cliffs each side of them made the children feel tiny as they looked up to the slit of open sky high above them. The falcon that Alex had watched from the car before the men had jumped them, was circling high above, searching for unsuspecting prey below.

Alex watched it, fascinated. He thought how he would love to learn falconry and have a bird like that of his own.

"It's quite an art, you know, Lorenzo, training your bird to hunt for you. Of course, the Arabs were always the best at it; they've practiced and perfected the art of falconry for thousands of years."

"That's interesting Alex," Gabriella said. Natasha rolled her eyes and bit her tongue to keep quiet.

They watched the falcon circling above them, and Alex wished he could see it hunt and catch something. It soared higher and higher, then it swooped down, screeching, as if warning the four intruders not to trespass in its domain. The high-pitched screech echoed around them, making the children feel a little uncomfortable. It then flew back up to its ledge high on the side of the cliff, and disappeared, just as Alex had seen it do before.

"Natasha," Lorenzo said, bored with watching the bird and wanting her attention, "show me where you were exactly, when the men stopped your car."

Alex and Natasha walked on a little further and showed Lorenzo and Gabriella the narrow spot where the two men had jumped them. They discussed the incident and went over it in great detail. Alex imitated the two men and over-emphasized their mannerisms making Lorenzo and Gabriella laugh. But there was something else on Lorenzo's mind that hadn't come up before, and he was concerned.

"Where was their car parked?" he asked them.

Alex and Natasha looked blankly back at him.

"Well, what kind of car was it? Was it an army truck or a regular car?"

They looked at each other and shrugged.

"Well, you must have seen it parked *somewhere*," Lorenzo said.

They stood there thinking for a moment, trying to remember.

"I didn't see a car, did you, Alex?"

He said he hadn't. And there was nowhere to hide one either. The boulders were only large enough for a person to hide behind, but not a car. That was very weird, he thought. He didn't know why he hadn't thought of that before.

"So where do you think they hid their car?" Lorenzo asked, scouring the area carefully.

"Well, suppose they didn't have a car," Alex suggested.

"Why wouldn't they? They would have had to have had a car, this place is miles from anywhere," Natasha said.

"Maybe it would have been too dangerous for them, too easy for us to identify," Alex said. "Think about it, they would have to be pretty stupid to park a getaway car where it could be seen by the people they were holding up, and there's nowhere to hide one Look around, I reckon they didn't have a car."

Lorenzo laughed. "But they'd have to have some kind of transport; they were expecting to rob you!"

"Well, perhaps they moved around by camel," Alex suggested. "No one would think of questioning anyone traveling across the desert by camel, dressed as a nomad, would they? We passed at least two groups of people on camels that day coming from the airport. The last thing that came to my mind when I saw them was that they were involved in criminal activity. Let's face it; it would be a great means of a getaway. It would fool anyone. Look at the Three Kings, for example, they came from afar with treasures; were they mugged or held up by ancient police? No, of course not."

"Yes, but these men weren't dressed as Nomads, or Kings, they were in military uniform, you dork!" Natasha laughed.

"Ever heard of a disguise, Natasha? Look, there are plenty of little shaded nooks and crannies to hide a couple of camels around here." Alex pointed out several places along the base of the cliffs.

Lorenzo thought about it.

"No one could expect to escape with a priceless mask across the desert on a camel, it is too slow. Too much risk involved too; it's a precious piece of obsidian, which is glass, remember. Sorry, I just can not see it happening by camel."

"Well, what's the alternative? You think someone picked the men up, and gave them a ride out of here?" Alex asked.

"Or," Gabriella said quietly, taking a few steps towards her brother, "maybe, they're still here. If they didn't have a car, and they didn't have camels, it means..."

Lorenzo quickly dismissed the whole thing.

"Oh please, why are you all so fascinated by these stupid men. I am sorry I brought it up. Who cares where they are, or where they parked their car or camel!" he said. "Does it really matter? They are not here now, Gabriella, that is certain. The police have them now. Remember? It is a pointless conversation. You're all making much too much of nothing. Come on, I want to go back."

What Lorenzo said though, and what he felt, were two different things entirely. Now he didn't know what to think. He suddenly felt the weight of responsibility on his shoulders. This place, he realized, was still not safe. And having no getaway car, either meant the men had been picked up, or, as suggested, that the men were still around.

But that was ridiculous, he tried to convince himself. Of course they are not still here. That would be madness.

Or was it?

Lorenzo kept his concerns to himself, but he couldn't help wondering if the police hadn't caught the men. His father said it was all in the authority's hands. He hadn't said they had actually *captured* the men. And everyone, including himself, had been ignoring Gabriella when she tried to tell them about the noises outside their tent. It was all fitting into place and he didn't like it. He began to feel an unfamiliar sensation of internal panic. He tried not to show it, but he kept thinking of the path up the side of the ridge. The path! The path is directly *behind* our tent. Oh, how stupid he had been, he thought, how blind!

He looked up at the cliffs above him. They seemed oppressive. He felt like they were closing in on him. Were they being watched? He needed to get out into the open.

He calmly said to the others that he was dying for a drink, and needed to get back. He suggested they start walking back, and he tried to hurry the pace. As they talked and chatted trying to sift through the clues and possibilities, Lorenzo walked in silence. He felt sick inside. If the men were still hiding somewhere, he had risked his sister's, and

Alex and Natasha's safety in coming here. Not only that, the thought struck him that they had all left the camp without telling his father where they were going. *Anything* could happen between here and the relative safety of the camp. His throat felt tight with anxiety. He was sweating. His mouth was dry. He couldn't wait to get back now.

He could think of nothing else.

"Hurry up, will you?" he called back to them. "Let's get back and have a soda in our tent."

He went over and over the possibilities in his mind. Suppose the men were watching? They must be here, he thought, they wouldn't leave without such a priceless treasure if they thought it was still here. And had the four of them tempted fate by walking into the lion's den itself? Looking up and around the high cliffs, Lorenzo prayed that the lion was not watching them now, waiting to pounce.

Now he also had to face the fact that when he reached the camp, he would have to explain to his father why he had been so irresponsible in taking his sister somewhere without telling him. His father was not going to be pleased. He turned and yelled at the dawdling group to hurry.

CHAPTER EIGHTEEN

'Natasha and Alex, Please come to my office as soon you get back. Thank you, Marcello.'

Alex handed the note to his sister. It had been pinned to the entrance of their tent so they wouldn't miss it.

"Oh bummer, do you think we're in trouble?"

Natasha thought for a minute.

"Yeah, Looks like it. And I suppose we can't really blame him, can we. We shouldn't have gone to the pass without telling anyone where we were going. We were supposed to report in and out, remember? Anything could have happened to us, and no one would have known where we were. He did tell us specifically to stay within sight of the camp at all times, remember? I suppose it was a bit stupid of us, especially after what happened, you know, before."

Lorenzo and Gabriella were approaching their tent. Lorenzo had showered, changed, and looked fresh and clean. He too was holding a note in his hand. He didn't look too happy.

"I see you have one too," he said. "I'm sorry. It is my fault, I am the eldest, and I take full responsibility for our actions as a group. We were irresponsible to go wandering so far, and not tell my father where we were going. I should have considered this. Perhaps our parents were looking for us today and were worried in light your experience the other day. I am totally to blame, I should have known better. As I said, I will take full responsibility."

"Look," Natasha said. "We're all in it together, and we will all take the blame together. It wasn't your fault and we don't expect you to take the blame just because you are the oldest."

"I agree," Alex said.

"We should all apologize," Natasha continued. "And while we're there, we can tell him about the flashing light that Alex saw last night, and everything we've discussed today. We could say that we were so wrapped up in all of this, that we totally forgot to stay in sight of the camp, and also forgot to tell anyone where we were going."

Natasha looked at Lorenzo for a response and support. He nodded solemnly. He certainly was going to tell his father about his suspicions, he thought, and more. But there was no need to worry Natasha or the younger two about it. He decided to lead the conversation in a different direction.

"OK, but be warned, my father does not tolerate disobedience, and today we were a little disobedient, and thoughtless."

"Well, it's the truth, Lorenzo; we forgot!" Gabriella protested. "Our father is very fair when we tell the truth, and Natasha, don't let my brother make you afraid of my father, there is no need of it. He always listens and is very reasonable." She frowned at Lorenzo.

"Well, I wasn't afraid until you just said that," Natasha sighed. "Oh this just sucks. Do we have to go?"

"Come on, let's get it over with," Alex said. "At least we can say we all kept our hats on."

"But we didn't keep our hats on," Lorenzo said. He was confused.

"No, but I said, we could say we did!"

When the four children arrived at the main tent, they found Marcello already inside waiting for them. He had set four chairs in a row to face him, and when they entered the tent, Julia, who was standing next to him, beckoned the four children to sit down. The fan spinning noisily in the corner of the tent seemed to be making the hot air hotter, and Marcello wiped the perspiration from his temples. Neither Marcello nor Julia said a word. The atmosphere was heavy. The children knew they were in for a very severe reprimand.

When they were all seated, Marcello eventually broke the silence.

"Thank you all for coming."

Silence.

He seemed to shuffle on his feet and fidget with his signet ring. He cleared his throat.

"There is something I would like to say to you all. We, I mean Julia and I, brought all four of you out here to Medinabad for the Easter holidays, not only to see our respective children of course, but also to find out if you could get along with each other."

He looked directly at Lorenzo.

"It seems to us, that you have, so well in fact, that today you ignored my earlier instructions about keeping the excavation or camp within sight, and informing us of your leaving the camp."

He looked at Julia. She nodded.

Lorenzo took a deep breath and opened his mouth to start his rehearsed apology, but his father cut in before he could say a word.

"But we are not here to discuss that now." He paused, and cleared his throat again.

The children looked at each other wondering what was coming next.

Natasha saw that her mother was looking down. She looked like she was trying to hide a smile.

Natasha flushed. Oh no, could it be? Before she could think straight, Marcello had put an arm around her mother's waist, and announced proudly, "Julia and I have decided that we are to be married."

The four children sat there speechless. Julia and Marcello were looking at each of them in turn for some kind of reaction.

Marcello prompted his own children, by saying quickly under his breath in Italian that he was hoping that perhaps they could find it in their hearts to give their blessing… or something.

Gabriella sprang up and put her arms around her father. She then hugged Julia.

The other three were still taking it in.

Lorenzo was happy for his father, and was thinking he should have known in hindsight, since his father had been more relaxed and easy going recently. He was also a little relieved that he didn't have to account for his irresponsible behavior just yet. He got up and hugged his father, then kissed Julia on each cheek.

"Father, I am very happy for you," he said, and added smiling to Julia, "I had noticed when we first arrived here that my father was looking happier, younger, in fact. Now I understand why. It is a surprise, but a good one. I am happy for you both, truly."

Although Natasha had been prepared in a way, by Yanni, and having her own suspicions about her mother's relationship, having it confirmed and hearing it directly from the horse's mouth was still a shock to her system. She wasn't sure how to react. She felt a little numb. It was all so sudden. She watched Alex as he congratulated them, he seemed happy enough. Was he so fickle and oblivious? Didn't he understand the consequences of what had just been announced, how life was going to change? What would happen to *them*? Would they now have to move to Italy, and go to a different school, and what about Dad?

She looked up at her mother. Julia was looking at her with pleading eyes.

Natasha remembered what Yanni had said, about giving her mother all the love and support that she needed. It was hard for her to do right now, but her mother looked so vulnerable. Yanni was right, it wasn't right for her to judge her mothers' decisions.

Natasha got up and gave her mother a hug. They squeezed each other for some time. Natasha felt better. She felt reassured.

"It won't change anything, darling, I promise," Julia whispered in her ear. "I still love you just as much, and I know we'll all be happy."

Marcello suggested that they all go for a little walk. It had been a momentous announcement for him to make, he felt a little emotional and shaky and needed some fresh air.

The soon-to-be family of six walked towards the palace site, and sat on the highest hill that looked out across the vast desert before them.

They sat quietly and took in what had just happened. The children's earlier exploits of the day were now put aside for a while, if not forgotten. Even Lorenzo had put his fears about the men and the mask aside. Now wasn't the time to bring that up. He could pull his father aside any time tomorrow and tell him his concerns. Now there were more important things to contemplate.

"So where is everyone going to live?" Alex asked his mother. "What's the plan?"

Julia and Marcello admitted that they weren't sure what was going to happen. But the best thing, they said, would be to keep every thing as it was for now, as there was no rush to change anything straight away. Things would work themselves out in good time.

"So for now Alex, the only difference is that you will have three homes; your mother's, your father's, and mine." Marcello smiled at him. "Will that be OK?"

Alex thought for a moment, then nodded.

"Cool."

Gabriella was thinking about Natasha. She said quietly to her father in Italian that she always wished for an older sister, and now it had come true. She kissed his cheek, and leant against him. He put his arm around her.

"I think Mamma would be happy that you are not sad and alone any more. I think she would be very happy for you, Papa."

Marcello smiled at his daughter. It was still painful to talk of her mother. Part of the reason he had spent so much time working away in distant countries was to escape the awful memories of her passing. But now he would be spending more time at home with his children, and this was a good thing. He was turning a new page in his life. It would be better for everyone. He looked at his daughter. She was so brave, he thought; His little warrior.

"Yes, I think so too, Gabriella, she would be happy for us all."

That night, it was Natasha who had trouble getting to sleep.

Chapter Nineteen

"This evening, after work," Marcello announced over breakfast the following morning, "when we have showered and changed into our cleanest, most dust-free clothes, we are all going to downtown Medinabad for dinner to a little restaurant I know, to celebrate the joining of our two wonderful families in love and friendship." He put his arm around Julia and kissed her hand.

Despite his offer of a trip into town, the four children insisted as politely as they could, that he and Julia should go out and have a romantic evening without them. They told their parents that they would be just as happy staying at the camp for dinner.

"Perhaps Claudio could prepare something special for us to eat here at the camp to celebrate," Alex suggested.

"Yes," Natasha had added enthusiastically. "And this way, maybe Yanni and Amanda could join us too. We could have our own little party here."

This argument for staying was eventually accepted by both parents, and the children were relieved that they wouldn't have to watch their parents swooning over each other all evening over a candle-lit dinner. Natasha was also very pleased with herself for coming up out of the blue with the suggestion of asking Yanni to celebrate with them, and no one had seemed to realize why. She had added Amanda as a cover for any suspicion of her intentions.

Although the incident in the pass and the subject of the Queen's mask had, for the moment, been thrown into the background in light of the momentous announcement from Marcello, the children found that by the time they'd finished breakfast, and the engagement had been discussed, although a little gingerly, the obsidian mask and the men in the pass did begin to creep back into the conversation.

Lorenzo was still feeling a little stressed about it, as he still hadn't managed to find the right moment to let his father know his concerns about the noises Gabriella was hearing at night outside their tent, and that he thought the men who held Natasha and Alex up in the pass could still be prowling around. He knew his father had been very concerned about the hold-up after it had happened. Lorenzo had overheard him talking about the camp's security with Signor Muretti. However Marcello had put his complete faith in the competence of the Chief of Police and had obviously put it all out of his mind, especially, Lorenzo now realized, as he had things of a very different nature to think about.

Lorenzo decided to keep quiet for now, and let his father enjoy his day, but he would wait up for his father's return from Medinabad that night to tell him his concerns.

So the young adventurers spent the day on the sandy hills at the site, helping to prepare the area for the influx of guests who would be arriving the following day for Marcello's press conference. Alex and Lorenzo helped sort out and arrange the guest's seating. A truck had delivered more than one hundred stackable chairs, which all had to be put into straight rows opposite the little stage that Marcello had built so he could address the world's press and tell them about his Queen of Ashook and her mask.

Natasha and Gabriella spent most of the day in the shade of the sorting tent with Amanda and six other workers. They were shown how to gently wash the shards of pottery and how to put them in some kind of presentation order. They made labels for them, and when those were ready, they helped the supervisors by carefully brushing clean the best of the hundreds of clay tablets before they were sorted into groups and boxed. Natasha and Gabriella enjoyed being part of the team, it gave them the chance to become involved in the dig and meet some of the other international students who were studying archaeology at university. Gabriella mentioned that she had found some kind of instrument quite by chance, and Amanda congratulated her, which put Natasha's back up as all she had done at the time, was poke around in the sand drawing flowers and hearts with her finger. On several occasions Natasha looked at Gabriella, still shell shocked at he thought that she was going to be her stepsister. Several times she found that Gabriella was already looking across the table at her with a grin on her face. Natasha hadn't quite known how to handle it, and immediately looked away pretending she hadn't noticed. She decided to think of something else, something less problematic, and of course, Yanni sprang to mind.

Natasha initially thought she would ask Amanda if she wanted to join them for supper, but in truth she didn't really want to. It wasn't that she didn't like her; Amanda was actually very friendly, she thought, but she really wanted Yanni to join them on his own and she really didn't need another girl around him. She had only mentioned her name earlier to her mother and Marcello so as not to make it too obvious that Yanni was the reason for the whole plan. So she didn't mention anything about eating together to Amanda, and nothing was said about their parent's engagement. She thought the news would leak out anyway before long, if it hadn't already, on the quiet.

"So have you got a boyfriend?" Amanda asked out of the blue, looking at Natasha.

"Err not exactly," she admitted. "Have you?"

Amanda smiled to herself. "Not exactly. But there's someone I kind of like."

Natasha looked at her. She felt quite glad Amanda had opened up to her and shared her feelings. Firstly, it meant she wasn't interested in Yanni, which was great news to

Natasha, and secondly it meant Amanda had accepted her, despite there being a few years apart.

"Me too," Natasha said. They looked at each other and smiled.

For the most part, the excavation of the palace had come to a halt while the preparations for the conference were under way. The only excavating still taking place was the large mosaic floor, where Yanni and his group continued to work non-stop to reveal the beautiful design hidden beneath the sand. Marcello wanted it completely exposed for the media and guests to see; it was so dramatic and in such good condition, and a wonderful example of Mesopotamian art and craftsmanship. He wanted to stun his audience with it. Natasha had hoped to spend time over there with Yanni, but she had been kept so busy and hadn't had a chance. She had also hoped he would find the time to come and see her, especially since she was doing something so useful and worthwhile like cleaning and sorting the shards. But he hadn't come, and by lunchtime, after standing on her feet for hours and working so hard, she was feeling a little grumpy. She had plenty of time to think as she brushed and cleaned the small pieces given to her, and she decided she was definitely not going to go looking for him in her break, which had been her first instinct, especially as she had spent most of the time thinking about him.

She was half expecting to feel a tug on her plait from behind, and she had even played out in her mind how she would turn around and look surprised, or a little nonchalant at seeing him. But he had never come over. Not once. So she was annoyed and decided that playing it cool was her best plan of action. If he wanted to talk, he should come and find her.

By late afternoon, when Marcello was confident that the preparations were almost complete, he and Julia left for their romantic evening in Medinabad together. The children planned to meet up at the end of the day back at Natasha and

Alex's tent after they had showered and cleaned up. Natasha decided to forget the meal with Yanni and make herself scarce so that he would wonder where she was. Perhaps if she went up to the top of the ridge again, she thought, that would work; he might even go looking for her. She might even have some time alone with him up there!

So with her little scheme in mind, Natasha asked Alex if he wanted to go up to the ridge again, with the pretence of looking for evidence of the men from the pass. She knew this would get Alex up there like a shot. Sure enough, it worked and he was keen to go. She then put it to Lorenzo and Gabriella, that since they are all about to become related, there was so much to talk about, they could sit up on the ridge and watch the sun go down and chat, like before.

"Yes! That would be better than eating dinner in the hot canteen or our tent," Gabriella said happily.

"It would be nice, but no," Lorenzo said in his concerned voice. "We can not do this, Natasha, unfortunately my father and your mother have already left for Medinabad, we can not go anywhere without asking them first. I already have to tell him about us going to the pass without permission." Then he added as an afterthought, "but if we go up to the top of the ridge, that could knock out my having to tell him about the pass, since we all got back safely and without incident. I could perhaps call him on his mobile phone to ask him permission. I'm sure Signor Muretti wouldn't mind if we borrowed his phone. Mine does not have a signal out here."

"But what if they say 'no' Lorenzo?" Alex protested. "I think we could go up just for an hour or so, then come down again, and they'll never know we went! They won't be back for hours. We could tell them that we had gone up there later when they come back tonight." He tried his best to convince Lorenzo.

"And if we sit near the edge, we can keep the camp and the palace site in view! That is all Papa wants of us, no,

Lorenzo? To keep everything within sight?" Gabriella looked hopefully at her brother. She was more interested in the change of scenery than finding evidence of anyone looking for the mask. Her day of cleaning shards had been exhausting. She had never done so much work in her life before, and her hands were chaffed and dry. She also feared that if she stuck around the site any longer someone might find some more cleaning of shards for her to do. She had been putting layers of hand cream on since they had finished. She really wasn't planning on doing any more.

Alex however, was impressed with her reasoning about keeping the camp in sight from the top of the ridge.

"You're right. Keeping it in sight was all Marcello asked of us, really. Good thinking, Gabriella! I should have thought of that one."

Natasha had a better solution.

"We could even leave a note on his tent, like he did on ours. As you said, Alex, we'll be back down again and asleep in our beds way before they get back. But we can leave the note anyway, just as a precaution in case they come back early and find us gone."

Lorenzo hesitated, he thought for a moment, and agreed.

"OK, good enough," he sighed. "Let's do it. As long as we keep the camp in sight." He felt better. He could relax for the evening without feeing guilty. He was keen to go up to the top one more time, if anything, just to convince himself that there was no one up there lurking around who shouldn't be. He wanted to prove to himself that his worries about those men had all been totally unfounded. Going up and looking around was the only way to put all these worries to rest. He could then sleep well tonight, especially if he could convince Gabriella there was no one and nothing lurking around their tent.

He showered, changed his clothes, and found a fresh shirt for the occasion. It felt good to be doing something positive.

Natasha volunteered to write the note, and pin it to the zip of Marcello's tent, where he couldn't miss it. She carefully attached it with four pins, one on each corner of the paper for security. She attached it at eye level, with two of the pins inserted through the zip itself, so that there was no chance of Marcello missing it in the dark.

"Even if it was pitch black when they returned from Medinabad, he would still feel the paper, and would have to remove it in order to unzip his tent," she said to herself. As she attached the note, the weird Unibrow woman from the trench walked slowly past Natasha, and looked sideways at her through the corner of her eye, as if she was checking on her. Natasha nervously half smiled at her, but got nothing in return except a cold glare, and it made Natasha feel uneasy. It was blatantly obvious the woman was letting her know that she didn't like her. Natasha hurried back to her tent, feeling very uncomfortable, to tell Alex.

"Hello Natasha."

She looked up. It was Yanni.

CHAPTER TWENTY

"Natasha, I was expecting to see you this afternoon!" Yanni exclaimed. "You didn't come to see my floor! I looked for you; I uncovered much more of the rider on horseback. I wanted you to come and see it!"

He was on his way back to his tent, his shirt off, obviously having just showered as his hair was wet and combed back off his face. His towel was flung over his shoulder and he was carrying his wash-bag.

She didn't know where to look.

She took a deep breath and tried to be cool, calm and collected.

"Oh, I..." she was about to reply with her rehearsed speech, but Yanni butted in excitedly.

"It's a lady you know, I know it is for certain the Queen. The colors are truly, truly magnificent. But I was instructed not to uncover the face until Marcello is there with me. We will do it tomorrow, early. He wants to see her face before anyone else."

Natasha completely forgot about her cunning plan of being off-hand.

"Wow! That's great, Yanni. I'm so sorry I couldn't come and see the floor today, I wanted to come over this afternoon, but I was so busy, cleaning shards and making labels for tomorrow's presentation, you know."

There, she thought, she got it in. She was a part of the team, and far too busy to just watch someone else excavating a floor all day. Well, sort of, she admitted to herself; he'll never really know how much she missed him.

"Don't worry Natasha, it is not important. Tomorrow, we shall uncover the face, and that you *must* see. I think Marcello wants us to cover it up after we have seen it and then uncover it again officially in front of the cameras later on in the day. Ha! Marcello, he is very excited! You know, Signor Muretti has already left for the airport to pick up the experts on carbon dating. They are flying in from Scotland. They're hoping to have the X-ray equipment working in the tomb before the morning. They will be studying the Queen's bones. It is all coming together very well for him."

"Why?" Natasha asked. "I mean why do they want to X-ray and study her bones?"

"Well, so we will know her age, and her diseases, if any, by tomorrow morning. In time for his lecture."

"Oh, I see."

"You will watch tomorrow as the face in the floor is revealed to the world, Natasha? It is very important. We will be in all the newspapers. It is going to be a very, very exciting day."

"I know, of course, we'll all be there. I wouldn't miss it for the world."

She looked down and twiddled the end of her plait. She wanted to confide in Yanni about her mother's engagement, but she didn't quite know how to change the subject. He was so excited about the Queen's bones and the identity of the rider on his floor, she thought she had better not. She continued twisting the end of her plait round her finger, wondering what to say. He was smiling at her, she could tell.

There was an awkward pause.

"Come over to my table while I get a drink of lime juice," he said suggested. "You look like you could do with one too. And if you continue to do that with your finger you will wear it out!"

They walked over to his tent. He disappeared behind the door flap for a minute, and emerged wearing a clean t-shirt. He offered her a drink of his juice in the familiar jam-jar and looked at her and then over to the old overturned box. His eyes told her to sit.

She sat down next to him.

He waited.

"Well?"

"Well," she started slowly and cautiously, "well you know what you said about Marcello and my mother, you know, about it being OK if they liked each other, and everything…" she paused, and waited. He nodded.

"Well, yesterday," she paused again, subconsciously twiddling her plait, "they announced to the four of us, that they were going to get married."

She looked down in case her face gave anything away. She still wasn't sure if she was happy about it.

"Ha!" Yanni slapped the table, threw his head back and combed his fingers through his wet curls. He sat back in his chair grinning and nodding knowingly.

"*Fantastic*! I am very happy for them. Marcello is a good man, and your mother? I don't know her so well, but I think she is a very kind lady. And beautiful, of course. It is very good news. Very good."

Natasha didn't quite know how to take the comment about her mother's looks, so she ignored it, and continued with what she wanted to say.

"Well, I suppose I wanted to thank you really, because you sort of taught me to think about my mother's feelings, and well, about the whole thing a bit better. I'm not sure how I would have reacted to Marcello's announcement if we hadn't had that talk, you know, about your brothers and your mother. I think I reacted a little better for your advice. I hope I did anyway."

She continued to look down at the table, feeling his eyes looking at her.

She didn't dare look up in case he could read what she was really feeling now. Which was, of course, to give him a kiss on the cheek, or at least a little hug.

"It is OK Natasha, I know how you are feeling."

She quickly glanced up at him, surprised.

"And do you know," he said, "something else good came of talking with you about my mother. You know, I have written a long letter to her and I apologized for my behavior, and my brother's actions also. I explained to her everything, from my heart, that we had confronted her friend without telling her, and scared this poor man away. I also told her to maybe write to him, because you know, he is perhaps still alone also, and thinking about her."

He took a gulp of his juice. He examined the jar and was quiet for a while.

Natasha was a little surprised at what Yanni had done. She wondered how his mother would take the confession. It probably was all a bit too late now, the man could have found someone else, or worse still, he could have died by now! But she didn't want to tell Yanni that.

"Your mother might be upset, Yanni," she said after a while, "because of what you did."

"Yes, yes, upset. But it is better to tell the truth, even if it is five or six years late. And things may have a chance to be put right, no?" He turned and looked hopefully at her.

Natasha nodded. She was actually thinking how furious she would be if she found out that someone had interfered in her business like that. But still, it would be better to know about it, she thought.

"Do you think your mother will contact him? It would be so nice if she did. I suppose I'll never get to hear the outcome though." Natasha thought it was a bit like reading a book and then finding the last chapter missing, even if it was a sad ending.

"So, I will write to you and tell you what happened. You have a computer at home?"

"Yes, you mean, will you email me?" Her heart was pounding.

"Of course, and something else, Natasha. I have been thinking seriously about changing my major at university. *Business*," he said with distain, screwing up his nose, "you know, it is not for me, really. I have been thinking these last few days, seeing Marcello's enthusiasm for his job made me a little envious of him. Then I thought, well, *I* can do that too! Why not? There is nothing to stop me. Who knows, after Queen Sorrea's Palace, maybe University in London to study ancient history!" he slapped the table, leant right back in his chair and rubbed the back of his neck.

She was stunned.

"You know Natasha," he continued, "Marcello has already spoken to me about coming to work in Italy with him. Do you know, when he leaves here, he and Signor Muretti will be excavating ships that have been buried under the city of Pisa for centuries." He paused, "you know where Pisa is, yes?"

"Oh, yes!" she nodded enthusiastically.

"Well, these ships, they sank over a period of eight hundred years, each layer of mud contains ships from a different period in history. It's fan-*tas*-tic! Some of these ships are piled on top of each other, you see." He indicated with his hands how they lay overlapping each other. "It is just incredible, they are actually under the Pisa railway station!"

"Really?"

"Yes, really Natasha!" he laughed. "And the mud has preserved them and their contents. They are like time... time... er… how do you say…"

"Capsules?" she offered quietly. She was still in a daze.

"Yes, exactly! Like time-capsules!"

He poured himself some more juice and smiled at Natasha, realizing he had got a little carried away.

"What do you think, Natasha? Shall I come to London to study and work with Marcello during the holidays in Italy? It would be better than boring business studies, no?"

Natasha flushed. She couldn't believe her ears. She wasn't sure how she should respond without looking childishly ecstatic. She felt like fainting, jumping up and down. She felt like hugging him. He wants to come to London. He wants to come to London! The words kept ringing in her head. And he would work with *Marcello*!

Deep breath.

"That sounds like a good choice, Yanni. You are so passionate about archaeology," she managed to sound level headed. "Somehow, I can't ever see you as enthusiastic about business and working in an office. And it would be pretty cool if you came to London, I mean to study. It would be great, in fact."

She couldn't conceal it. She smiled the biggest smile of her life.

Man! How this trip is turning out. Would there be any more surprises around the corner? She doubted that anything could top what had happened today, ever.

"Good! Exactly what I was thinking, Natasha," he said. "I have already decided. I have told my mother this also in the letter. I am going to study in London. Ha!"

He slapped the table. It was a done deal.

CHAPTER TWENTY-ONE

The children met as planned behind Gabriella and Lorenzo's tent. Having inspected the cliff face in some detail, Alex had confirmed that this was definitely the easiest and smoothest point at which to start the climb to the top.

Natasha was still reeling with Yanni's news. She wished she had mentioned the weird Unibrow woman to him, or asked him what he knew about her, but she had totally forgotten about her as soon as Yanni had bumped into her. She realized that she had also forgotten to tell Alex and the others about the little encounter with the woman, but she thought she could discuss everything when they were at the top of the ridge and could think straight.

As she followed the crumbling path up the slope, slipping occasionally and remembering how dangerous it could be if she lost her footing, she now realized she hadn't mentioned where they were going to Yanni! Oh how stupid! How would he come up and join them for the evening if he didn't know where they were! The news of his coming to study in London had seemed to wipe everything from her mind.

She thought of everything that happened in the last few hours. She still couldn't believe that Yanni would be working with Marcello, her stepfather to-be, which would ensure that she was *bound* to see more of him. She smiled to herself as she followed the others up and over the rocks. She now couldn't help liking that the brother and sister nattering away in Italian ahead of her, would soon be her stepbrother and sister. It was unbelievable really; her life was changing for the better. This permanent connection to Marcello and his family was actually a good thing all round, she thought. She could get used to Gabriella too; she wasn't so bad really. All in all, it had been quite an eventful trip, and she hadn't even been here a week yet.

To her surprise, Natasha quickly found herself at the top of the ridge. She had hardly noticed the climb, being so preoccupied in her thoughts. It had taken less than twenty minutes and now the four children were taking in the panoramic view again, and loving it. They sat down for a rest and took out a drink from their backpacks.

"I wish we could set our tents up here, it would it be nice to sleep up here tonight, don't you think?" Gabriella sighed. "I just love it. It is the top of the world! Do you think Papa would let us sleep up here one night, Lorenzo?"

"Perhaps, we can ask tomorrow," he shrugged. Lorenzo had absolutely no intention of sleeping up there. In fact he couldn't think of anything worse. He liked the view, but not that much. At the back of his mind he still wasn't sure they would be alone, anyway.

He did notice that he was the only one now looking around for anything suspicious. Those men who had held Alex and Natasha up seemed to be far from Alex's mind, he could see that. Gabriella was enjoying the view, the breeze and the sense of freedom and Alex was preoccupied throwing stones over the cliff into the hazy abyss.

Lorenzo looked at Natasha and offered her some pistachio nuts.

"Oh, thanks," she said.

"You seem to be deep in thought, are you OK Natasha? You've been preoccupied with a smile on your face for quite a while."

"Oh, have I?" she flushed.

"Are you happy about the engagement?" he asked her quietly. "It will be strange, no? For everyone, I mean."

She nodded, "Yeah." She wasn't sure what to say.

"Let's move on," he said, and they walked on in silence.

Lorenzo had been thinking about his father's engagement to Julia. Weird, he mused, to suddenly have a sister his own age, and an extremely pretty one at that. He gave her a sideways glance. Her long blonde plait down her back was swinging from side to side with her stride, and it made him smile. It was cute, he thought. He could imagine his two closest friends back home being very envious of him and joking about his good luck! If Natasha and Alex ever came to live in Italy, his friends would be over every weekend. That, he imagined, would be really weird. He didn't like the thought of that at all. Now he felt protective towards her.

He decided to think of something else. He focused back on the men who had held Natasha and Alex up in the pass. He scoured the rocky plateau, but saw no one lurking in the shadows at all. Lorenzo decided, thankfully, that the four of them had probably been making a mountain out a molehill over the whole thing because they had been bored and had let their imaginations run wild. He relaxed a little. He chuckled to himself at the apt expression; molehills, mountains, the English language is so fun, he thought.

"You know Natasha," he said, catching up with her, "I was thinking that anyone who wanted the mask so badly, would be very welcome to it. It may be valuable, but it is really quite ugly, and *I* certainly wouldn't want it staring at me from a wall in my living room."

"Well at least you've seen it to have an opinion, Lorenzo."

He shrugged and smiled at her. "True…" he said, then added quietly, "…sister."

She flushed, and they headed further along the plateau towards the edge of the notorious pass, where they could look down with a bird's eye view of the whole pass below them. They stood a few yards back from the edge.

"You know what?" Alex said, "I bet you I could jump across it if I had a long enough run without all these rocks in the way!"

"Alex, you do that and we'll have to burry you with Queen Sorrea!" Natasha said, tightly grabbing the back of his t-shirt. "It's much further than it looks, Alex, don't be an idiot, and I'm not going down there scraping you off the ground!"

"I know, I know, I was only kidding, but you have to admit, it does look close. You can let go of me, Natasha!"

"Look down there," Gabriella said pointing below the edge. "It is that bird of prey."

They knelt down and peered down over the edge. About fifteen feet below them the falcon Alex had seen when they first drove into the pass was perched on a stone ledge that protruded a few feet from the cliff-face. It was scouring the scene below its ledge, ready to dive into the air when it saw the opportunity for a meal. It was startled when it heard the children above it, and suddenly took off screeching into the pass.

On its ledge, was a small pile of baked, bleached droppings. And as Alex pointed out, there were bits of 'things' in the droppings that weren't entirely identifiable.

"Look, you can even see a piece of brown fur and some small bones. That would be some kind of rodent, I bet," he said.

"That is disgusting, Alex. Don't even tell me, I do not want to know!" Gabriella said, moving away from the edge.

"Look, if you lean over a bit more, you can see that the little ledge goes back into the cliff. Cool place to live," Alex said. "I wonder how far back it goes?"

"Be careful, Alex, don't lean over too much," Gabriella pleaded, pulling him back by his arm.

"Lift him by his shorts," Natasha offered. "Give him a wedgie! That'll stop him!"

Alex immediately jumped to his feet and stepped away from the edge.

"We could just hang out here for a while," he quickly suggested. "We could watch the sun go down on this side of the ridge, it's better than going back to that spot overlooking the camp again."

At the back of their minds they all remembered Marcello's rule about keeping the campsite or palace in view, but not one of them wanted to remind each other that they were breaking it. Lorenzo told himself to stop feeling guilty; he was almost sixteen, and had the right to make a few decisions for himself. No one was being irresponsible, he reasoned; they were just enjoying the evening together. Surely his father wouldn't object to that!

They found an area of rock surface where the rock had been hollowed and smoothed away by years of wind blown sand, forming a shallow dip, which had collected about three or four inches of sand, creating a perfect, soft, comfortable cushion, just wide enough for all four of them to sit on.

"The great thing about being up here is that we have such a fantastic view of the pass below. We can see anyone approaching for miles," Gabriella said, turning onto her side and resting her head in her hand. "So when we see our father's car approaching, even in the dark with the headlights on, we will have plenty of time to get back down to the camp before they even know we were up here."

"Gabriella! I do believe you are joining the human race! I hope it's not us influencing you!" Natasha joked.

Gabriella giggled. "I don't know, but it is fun!"

"Fun until we are caught, Gabriella," Lorenzo added. "But until then…" he shrugged, not caring much about the consequences.

"This is pretty cool," Natasha said. "You know, not many kids get to do things like this."

"Well that's lucky, or it would be pretty crowded up here," Alex said.

The enormous red sun lowered in the sky and the children sat in silence for a while, enjoying the breeze, the vastness of their surroundings and the sense of freedom. They started to talk on the subject that was on all their minds, but a little difficult to tackle: the engagement of their mother and father.

Lorenzo approached the subject first by asking Natasha about her father, and what the arrangements were since her parent's divorce.

"Well, we live with him in Hampstead, which is an area in North London, when our mother is working away. Otherwise we live with her the other side of London by the river. The real bore," she said, "when we do stay with our father, is crossing London on the underground twice a day to get to and from school. Our school is in Putney, you see, not far from our mother's house. We have to trek across London on the tube when she's away, which is really horrible in the morning. Alex calls it the 'crush-hour'."

"Our Dad has a much larger house than our mother's," Alex added. "He bought a dump that needed everything doing to it. He scooped it out. It's very modern and the rooms are massive. Do you like snooker?" he asked Lorenzo. "He's got a whopping big basement with a home cinema and everything under the sun down there. It's great! You will *have* to come and stay."

"*Alex*!" Natasha hissed, "I don't know how that will go down with *Dad*, I mean, you know, Marcello's children staying, considering the circumstances? They are nothing to do with him."

"Why? Oh yeah, I didn't think of that."

"So your father has not remarried then?" Lorenzo asked Natasha quietly.

She shook her head. She told him a little about Eva, the latest one, and admitted that she didn't really like her. She told him how it embarrassed her when her friends came over and Eva was there, because she looked really young, and even if she wasn't, she tried hard to be.

"It just doesn't put my father in a very good light. I suppose he's going through some kind of male menopause, and it is very embarrassing," she said.

"They all look the same to me," Alex said. "They're all idiots. But I'm not bothered by his girlfriends like Natasha is."

Natasha fiddled with her plait for a minute, then continued, "I hope you don't mind me saying this, don't be offended, but I didn't really like your father either, I mean before I got to know him. I didn't mean not to like him, but I couldn't help it."

Lorenzo nodded. It was blunt, but he understood.

"It is normal," he said. "You resented him." He unfolded his legs from his sitting position to lie on his stomach.

"My father..." he hesitated, "...my father has been away from us for most of the time since our mother died five years ago," he explained. He smoothed the sand under his hand. "At first, I thought it was because he was not interested in Gabriella and I. I thought he loved only his work. It was particularly hurtful for me the first couple of Christmases and I was very upset with him for not being home. But my grandmother explained to me that my Father found the memories being at home too painful. He had apparently told my grandmother that he couldn't bear to be in the house, and that it was easier for him to be away. I had not thought of it like that, and although I was still angry by his absence, I understood him a little better."

"But he has been very happy on this excavation, *e vero*, Lorenzo?" Gabriella said, putting her hand on his shoulder. "He is laughing and joking and being noisy as I remember him before. He is different now. I see it in him. At first I did not see it, but now I know our father is happy again. It is wonderful, really." She smiled at Natasha and added, "It is your mother who has made him so!"

Natasha nodded at her, then looked down. She felt a little guilty. She could hardly look at Gabriella. Here was a girl, she thought, two years younger than herself, who was totally unselfish, and only worried about the happiness and well being of her father. Gabriella was genuinely happy that her father had found someone new to love. Natasha felt deeply ashamed. The jealousy and childish dislike she had felt for Gabriella's father, and even Gabriella and Lorenzo when she had first met them, now made her feel so stupid and immature. She now realized how childish she had been. So self centered and pathetic. To have to learn from the behavior of a girl younger than herself! Yanni must have been shocked. Natasha blushed at the thought of it. No wonder he had that talk about his mother and his awful brothers.

The four children lay on their stomachs, and discussed all the possibilities that lay ahead of them as a family. They realized it was going to be very different from now on. Different, they agreed, but interesting. There were probably going to be a lot of trips between London and Milan until their parents decided who was living where.

Alex told Gabriella and Lorenzo about life in London, about school, about the free concerts in the park, about tennis at Wimbledon, and all the cool things they had done recently. Natasha added that Gabriella would like the King's Road, and told her about all the places she shopped with her friends.

"I will look forward to it very much," Gabriella said. "But Natasha, you have not *lived* yet if you have not shopped in Milan!"

"You and Alex have so much freedom compared to Gabriella and I," Lorenzo said. "You are so lucky, you have no idea."

"Really?" Natasha looked at him.

"We have to be driven everywhere," he said. He sounded exasperated. "And the driver usually waits for us for as long as he has to, to bring us home again. Even visiting a school friend needs some forward planning. Living up in the hills, a long drive from anywhere has such limitations," he sighed. "And even when we are in Milan during the week, our Aunt does not like us roaming around with our friends unaccompanied. I must admit I like the idea of being let loose in London. I shall look forward to a little freedom when we..."

"Hey, look! Sorry, excuse me, Lorenzo," Alex interrupted, "but look what's buried in the sand here! Cigarette stubs! That's *revolting*!"

Alex had found three stubs next to his elbow.

"And I have some more here," Gabriella said. That is not very nice, leaving dirty cigarette ends in this beautiful spot. Who would have been here and sat long enough to leave all these behind?" She was annoyed, and muttered something in Italian. How awful, she thought, her idyllic place had been used and spoiled by someone before her.

They all sifted their fingers around in the sand a little deeper.

"Look, there are more; Quite a few more. In fact, they're *everywhere*!" Natasha said.

"I wonder who's been sitting here?" Alex said, "I don't blame them though, it is the most comfortable place to be on this rocky cliff top, and you do get a great view of the whole pass and the approach to it for miles. Look, you could see a car coming half an hour before it got here."

Lorenzo was quiet. He had turned pale. A shiver went down his spine; He felt sick.

He looked across at Natasha, to see if the same thought had struck her too. She looked over at him, and Lorenzo could see even in the dim light that she was terrified.

Suddenly, before anyone could say anything, huge hands grabbed Lorenzo's ankles and he was abruptly dragged back from the edge of the cliff.

CHAPTER TWENTY-TWO

Gabriella and Natasha screamed. They were dragged back on their stomachs, and their faces were pushed down into the sand to keep them quiet. They were held down with a knee in their backs while their hands were tied behind them. Alex kicked and wriggled trying to free himself from the grip around his legs, but he felt something cool and metallic against the side of his forehead, which he knew could only be the barrel of a gun. He froze, and reluctantly had no choice but to lie still and do what was demanded of him. He was red with anger, and took deep breaths to calm down and think straight.

The three men pulled the children to their knees, and after all their hands had been tied securely, they were shoved in the back, and ordered to walk. When they refused or hesitated, guns were pointed at their faces. Gabriella was whimpering with terror. One of the men threatened to hit her if she didn't stop. She did her best to be quiet.

Natasha was in shock. She was trembling and felt sick with fear. She heard Lorenzo telling Alex under his breath not to struggle now; it was too dangerous with the guns, and better to save his strength for later. She felt a little stronger hearing this and was glad of Lorenzo's strength of mind.

They were pushed towards a cluster of boulders.

"Look at the men, Alex, Natasha," Lorenzo said quietly "Do you recognize any of them?"

One man shouted at Lorenzo and threatened to hit him with the gun if he spoke again.

Alex looked at their faces closely in the semi darkness. It was hard to tell. What he did notice was a shiny tooth in the shorter one's mouth. He remembered the two men who had held them up. This was one of them all right, he thought. This was the shorter one of the two. He looked at the other man in front of him, and recognized him too.

"Yes," Alex said to Lorenzo, loud and defiantly. "It's them!"

Alex was kicked from behind by a third, smaller person, and he yelped.

"Don't *touch* my brother, you jerk!" Natasha screamed.

"Don't worry, I'll get him back." Alex reassured her.

The fat man turned and came and stood close to Natasha.

"You nice, velly nice hair," he stroked her plait. She stepped away in disgust.

"Don't touch her! Get away from her!" Alex shouted, ramming himself against the man with all his force. The man fell over and Alex landed on top of him and Alex was pulled up to his feet again by his t-shirt and pushed back towards the others.

The thinner man in front called to his accomplice abruptly, obviously telling him to leave Natasha alone. He hissed something back under his breath, and walked on muttering to himself.

The children were lead only a few yards to the right of where they had just been lying. The men stopped by two large boulders. They put their hands on the children's heads and pushed them down until they were sitting on the ground in a line. They then ordered Lorenzo at gunpoint, who was first in line, to shuffle forward to the opening of what seemed to be a low tunnel entrance in the ground between the two boulders. He inched reluctantly to the edge of the opening and hesitated. He turned back and tried to protest but the men yelled at him and pushed him down the slope, and out of view.

Gabriella shrieked at seeing her brother vanish. She began to cry hysterically. Before she knew it, she had been pushed down between the rocks herself. Alex and then Natasha followed into the hole, and slid down a slope of loose stones. They found themselves in complete darkness.

From the top of the slope, something was shouted down at them. A large boulder was pushed in front of the entrance, blocking the light out completely. The voices of the three men became faint and then, silence.

Chapter Twenty-Three

Huddled together in complete darkness, with their hands tied behind their backs, the four terrified children whispered to each other.

"Lorenzo, *dove se*? Where are you?" Gabriella called to her brother in Italian.

"Gabriella, *sono qui*, I am here. I will protect you. Try not cry, please, Gabriella."

She told him how scared she was. Lorenzo reassured her the best he could. He was pretty scared himself, but couldn't let his sister know. He had to stay calm, he had to think.

"Our parents will come for us, as soon as they return from Medinabad. They will see the note on the tent. Remember? We let them know we were coming up here?" Thank goodness we did, he thought, or they would never know where we were.

"Gabriella," he added, "we just have to be brave and patient for a couple of hours, that's all. Can you do that for me, Gabriella?"

"*Si*," she sniffed.

"If we could untie our hands, that would be a start," Alex said. "Lorenzo, you work on Gabriella's ropes and I'll try and undo Natasha's. Tash, turn round so that we're back to back. And keep still."

"Don't worry, I'm not going anywhere."

Natasha surprised herself by realizing that she had found a little inner strength. Hearing the fear in Gabriella's voice, made her feel stronger. It was weird, she thought, now that disgusting creep of a pig had left, she wasn't as scared as she ought to be.

"You must admit guys," she giggled, "this is a little far fetched. Do you think Marcello and our mother planned all this to get us to do a little family bonding?"

"How can you joke at a time like this, Natasha?" Gabriella snapped at her through her sniffs. My father would never do such a thing!"

"Shame," Natasha said under her breath. We might get out sooner if he had, she thought. "Well, life has been quite eventful recently for all of us, wouldn't you say? I actually asked myself a little while ago if anything else could happen to top the events of this holiday. And look! Bingo!"

She wished she had told Yanni where they were going; he would have been the first to the rescue. She sighed. Well at least there was the note pinned to Marcello's tent. They wouldn't be here long, she thought.

"Well next time you ask yourself something," Alex retorted from the darkness behind her, "ask for something useful, like a pair of scissors," he said. "And keep still!"

The boys continued working on untying their sister's ropes. It was harder than they thought, with their own hands bound tightly behind them as well. They had to feel the knots, and try to visualize what they were doing. All the time Lorenzo calmed his sister and kept telling her everything was going to be fine, just to be brave and patient.

"If I could get this backpack off, I could get the flashlight out," Alex said.

"What else do you have in there?" Lorenzo asked. "Gabriella, try to lift your hands a little for me, it is so hard to get at the knot underneath."

"Well, I have that chocolate spread," Alex continued, "and a couple of bread rolls, remember, from breakfast? Do you guys have anything useful in yours?"

"Only a drop of water, I think in mine," Natasha said. "We finished those pistachios."

"Lorenzo, it hurts," Gabriella whimpered. "Can you please hurry?"

Lorenzo was trying to be cheerful, but his heart was sinking. This was impossible, he was getting nowhere with the knot around Gabriella's wrists, it was tied too tight. He just couldn't do it with his own hands tied as well. He felt desperate.

Then he remembered.

"Oh! I have a knife!" he cried. "My Swiss Army Knife! It is in my jeans front pocket, I forgot. But I can't get it out. How can we get it out?"

"Where are you? Come here and stand behind me," Alex said. "I'll have a go."

Lorenzo stumbled around in the dark and managed to position himself behind Alex. Alex, with his hands still tightly tied behind his back, started to feel for the pocket in the front of Lorenzo's jeans.

"It is in my left pocket!" Lorenzo exclaimed. "Left… left… *MORE* left*!* Alex, I don't have a middle pocket… Thank you!"

"Sorry! Its not as easy as you think!" Alex said quickly. "OK, Lorenzo, listen. Bend your knees so you are a bit lower down. I'm not as tall as you so this is going to be tricky. I need to get my hands up and over the edge of the pocket." He struggled trying to get his hand in the right position. "It's just so awkward with my hands tied like this…" With his body contorted and Lorenzo awkwardly bent behind him, Alex eventually managed to get a hand into Lorenzo's jeans pocket.

"OK, I've got the knife in my fingers. Now, Lorenzo, slowly bend down lower, and I'll try to lift it out at the same time. It's hard because if I make a fist, my hand will be too big to get out of your pocket. So go down very slowly so I can sort of roll it up to the top of the pocket."

Lorenzo very slowly bent his knees, and went lower, an inch at a time, so that Alex could maneuver the penknife up and out of his pocket.

"Got it!"

"Good job you two," Natasha said. "I knew you could do it, Alex!"

"Good," Lorenzo said. "Now open it up, and work on my rope first. It's better this way, in case you accidentally cut me in the process; better that than one of the girls. Then my hands will be free to untie yours."

He thinks of everything, Alex thought.

So having turned back to back, Alex now worked on Lorenzo's rope, trying to feel and saw at the right place between his wrists. It was very difficult to tell what was rope and what wasn't. Even his own fingers didn't feel like his own when they were behind him and crossed over each other. He tried to feel the rope with one hand as he sawed through it with the other. It was difficult even deciphering whose fingers and hands were who's, and he jabbed himself as well as Lorenzo several times. A couple of times he dropped the knife, and each time he dropped it, he had to get down on to his knees and feel around for it, bending awkwardly backwards and sideways at the same time. The whole process was painfully slow, and Alex was dripping with sweat, but he continued to patiently cut away at the rope.

"I think I've done it," he said after a while.

The girls praised his efforts, and were encouraged. They couldn't wait to have their hands free.

Alex helped Lorenzo loosen his rope, and at last, Lorenzo's hands were free. He immediately felt for Alex's backpack and fumbled around for the flashlight.

Then they heard something; a noise from outside the cave.

"Somebody's coming!" Natasha whispered.

The joy of untying Lorenzo's hands turned to fear as they heard the stone being pushed to the side of the cave opening.

"Quick! Pick the rope up off the floor Lorenzo! Pretend you're hands are still tied behind you," Alex whispered.

Gabriella started whimpering quietly again. Her brother moved over to stand next to her. He quickly shoved the penknife into his back pocket, and stood with his hands behind his back. They waited.

A stream of light lit up the cave around them. It flickered and bounced from wall to wall as the hand that held it slid down the slope. The children could see for the first time since their capture, that they were in quite a large cave, which narrowed towards the back, and into the darkness beyond.

Two people had scrambled down the slope, kicking up dust and creating a miniature avalanche of pebbles and stones. The glare of the flashlight settled on the faces of the terrified children, obscuring the identity of the two people behind it.

A woman spoke.

"Where is Marcello?" she demanded. "When is he coming back?"

They didn't answer.

Who was she? Natasha wondered. What kind of woman would get involved in kidnapping? And she speaks good English too, she thought. How would she know Marcello's name?

"I *said*, where is *Marcello*?" the voice repeated louder, and loosing patience.

Natasha squinted and tried hard to look at her through the light. She caught glimpses of the woman's face. She knew that face.

"Oh. It's you!" Natasha couldn't help gasping out loud. "That makes perfect sense!"

The woman ignored Natasha's comment.

"I will ask you again. Where is Marcello? Where is your father?" She looked directly at Gabriella.

"They have gone to Medinabad," Lorenzo said quickly. "And he will be back with reinforcements very soon and arrest all of you criminals."

The woman said something to the man standing with her, and he disappeared back up the slope, kicking up more dirt and causing a few stones to tumble onto the cave floor.

"Where is the mask?" she demanded.

"Why should we tell you?" Natasha said. "If you think that by keeping us here will get you the mask, you're crazy."

"I assure you, keeping you here will get us the mask. This much is certain. And you will not be released until we have it. *That* I can promise you."

The man scrambled down the slope again, this time with the fatter man who was so disgusting to Natasha. He had another flashlight, and a knife in his mouth, which he handed to the woman when he had brushed the dust off himself.

"So it was you signaling from up here! Now I get it!" Alex said to the woman. "You were probably signaling to these idiots, weren't you! You had it was all planned!"

"Enough talking, you!" The woman threatened to hit Alex around the head with the back of her hand. She then waved the knife at Natasha.

"You, girl, come here. Turn around."

Natasha did what she was told, and wondered if she was going to have her hands untied, which surprised her since she had just threatened to hit her brother. She wanted to kick her, but daren't. She turned around with her back to the woman as asked. Perhaps Miss Unibrow has a conscience after all, Natasha thought.

But instead of undoing the rope around Natasha's wrists, the woman grabbed Natasha's plait, pulled her head right back, so that Natasha almost lost her balance and fell backwards. She then started to cut, scrape and saw through the top end of Natasha's plait with the knife. Natasha screamed, and struggled trying to get free, and the boys instinctively lunged forward to help her. Lorenzo, the only one with his hands free, went for the woman, taking her by surprise. He had her pinned against the cave wall within a second. He then felt a gun pressing in the back of his head. He froze, and backed off. The other man hit Alex in the face, and the force threw him to the floor.

"I wouldn't try to be a superhero again young man, or the lives of these young ladies will be on your hands," she said, panting and holding the knife to Natasha's neck.

"Hasim," she hissed. "Check his pockets."

He checked Lorenzo's pockets. He found the red pen-knife. Hasim examined it in the glare of the flashlight, opening and closing the sections, and enjoying the novelty. He obviously hadn't seen one like that before. Holding it by the round key ring attachment at the end, he dangled the knife in front of Lorenzo's nose.

"Velly good. I like, I keep, yes?"

"It was my grandfather's," Lorenzo protested. "You have no right to take it!"

He ignored Lorenzo and put it in his pocket.

"Now, that was very stupid behavior," the woman said to Lorenzo. "You do anything like that again you will be gagged for the night as well as tied. Now, as I said before," she said calmly, looking Natasha, "turn, please."

Slowly Natasha turned so that her long plait could be cut off. She cried silently to herself. Her tears stung as they rolled down her cheeks. She couldn't even wipe them away. She closed her eyes and bit her lip as she was pulled and tugged as the woman slowly started to saw through her plait.

Between sobs, Gabriella was trying to say the Hail Mary in Italian. She found it very difficult. She watched Natasha in the stream of light, and thought how brave her new sister was. How could any woman be so cruel?

Natasha was scared. It was like being in a terrible nightmare that she couldn't wake up from.

The cutting seemed to take ages, the woman sawed and pulled and Natasha yelped but it made no difference to the woman. She yanked it harder in order to make Natasha stay still. Alex felt helpless just standing there, unable to help his sister.

"You hurt her and I'll *kill* you!" Was the best he could come up with.

Hasim moved forward to strike him, but the woman stopped him. She told him to hold the flashlight.

"He is just a baby," she said in English. "Don't let him get to you so much. Tomorrow you can deal with him if he upsets you again, Hasim."

"And as for you," she calmly said to Gabriella, pointing the knife at Natasha's half severed plait, "this is to let your father know that we mean business. You think he will understand?"

Gabriela nodded. "Yes."

"I've almost finished. Now tie the boy's hands again," she ordered. "And tight! We can't afford another mistake."

Lorenzo was forced to put his hands behind his back again, and this time he tried to make sure that the rope wasn't so tight, and he pulled his wrists apart as much as he could while the man wound the rope round them.

At last the woman had severed Natasha's plait. She had over a foot of Natasha's hair in her hand. It looked horrible hanging there, like a limp, pale, dead snake.

She then walked over to Gabriella. She untied one of the ribbons in her hair. Gabriella froze, thinking that she was next, but the woman took the ribbon and put it in her pocket, and turned to go back up the slope.

Turning to the children, and said, almost as an afterthought, "oh, I think this belongs to you..."

She pulled something out of her back pocket.

It was a piece of paper. She unfolded it, and threw it on to the cave floor. She took the flashlight from Hasim and shone it on to the paper so the children could clearly see what it was.

The note that Natasha had pinned to Marcello's tent, telling him that they had gone up to the top of the ridge to watch the sunset, now lay at their feet.

Gabriella shrieked, realizing that her father would have no idea where they were upon his return.

"Good night," the woman said. "Oh, and young lady," she added, almost as an afterthought, shining her flashlight at Gabriella, "your wish is coming true. You *will* be sleeping the night up here on the ridge after all. I hope you enjoy it, you may be here some time."

CHAPTER TWENTY-FOUR

Julia and Marcello arrived back at the camp long after midnight. They'd enjoyed a lovely evening in a little restaurant on the outskirts of Medinabad in a small village that was popular with the few westerners that ventured outside the city.

Because of their late return, they didn't even contemplate waking the children to let them know that they were back. Julia knew she would see them in the morning at breakfast.

The following morning though, Marcello and Julia had a very early start, too early to wake her children for breakfast. They were busy from the get-go.

The palace site was a hub of activity. The international press, and several national dignitaries would all be arriving by lunchtime. A photograph of the priceless obsidian mask had been placed on every chair in front of the newly built platform, so that each person present would be able to see what an incredible mask it was that Marcello was talking so passionately about. The final preparations for the conference, and viewings of Queen Sorrea's tomb were almost finished.

Video cameras were being set up by the crew and shade had been created wherever possible with hundreds of yards of colorful fabric for the Prince, who had been taking a keen interest on the excavation and had been in contact with Marcello over the weeks for updates. To enable the visitors a better overview of the whole area, scaffolding had been erected near the Queen's tomb for those visitors and members of the press brave enough to climb it, so they could have an overview of the whole area. Marcello had even organized a red carpet to be placed around the tomb so the Prince could kneel down and look into the tomb to see the Queen. The whole team had thrown themselves into it wholeheartedly.

It was a very big day for Marcello, and he was coping well. His speech was very well rehearsed, but over all, his presentation on the mask and the Queen, he said, would come from the heart. Julia had advised him to keep to his script as much as he could, and not go off on a tangent, which he often did when he lectured on subjects that he was so passionate about. And this one, she knew, could possibly inspire a speech that could take days if he let it.

Despite his late night and early rise, the first thing he did when he got up was to go with Yanni over to the mosaic floor at the palace site.

The tiles were now cleaned up, completely excavated, and looking absolutely spectacular.

Completely excavated, that is, except for the head identifying the warrior in the middle of the design.

Marcello had told Yanni to purposely leave the head and face unexcavated and completely covered. Marcello was counting on the fact that the figure on horseback leading the charge was Queen Sorrea. He was ninety-nine percent sure it was her, with her long brown wavy hair quite visible flowing behind her as she galloped into battle, leading her army of foot soldiers and the infamous mounted archers behind them. Marcello had not wanted to reveal the image of the warrior Queen just yet; he wanted to keep the suspense and anticipation for everyone in the camp, and not just for the press and the dignitaries later on that day. He was the first to admit he liked nothing better than a drama.

He and Yanni squatted over this last remaining mound of dirt on the ancient mosaic floor. It was early dawn, and the morning sun hadn't yet absorbed the chill of the night.

They had come to have a sneak peek at her face, like two naughty schoolboys uncovering a secret. They couldn't resist it.

Inch by inch they gently removed the remaining section of packed sand that had covered and protected her face for so many centuries.

Within a few minutes, they had done it. The Queen was out in the open and set free again. Marcello gently swept her eyes, her forehead, her nose, in small, loving strokes, almost as if he was painting her.

There she was; His Warrior Queen. To Marcello, it was as if she had come alive; She could now breathe.

The two men marveled at the sight of the Queen's dramatic image. The colors in her face were as vibrant the day the ancient floor had been laid. The whites of her eyes, the pink in her cheeks, it was very rare that ancient portraits or likenesses were found in such perfect condition. With tears in his eyes, Marcello knelt back on the floor and looked at the vibrant face on the ground staring back at him. This was a very important find; it was the pinnacle of his career. He had found her, the Queen who had been forgotten and lost to the wind for centuries. The legend had at last come back to life.

The scene that spread across the vast floor was dramatic. The ancient artists had created a wonderful atmospheric picture of charging horses, the Queen's armor shining in the sunlight, and her blue and white robes billowing around her. Her famed mounted archers marched in unison behind her. The colors were exquisite and now Marcello would show it to the world.

"The craftsman who created this floor was truly a genius," Marcello said to Yanni, stroking the floor lovingly. "I wish I could let him know that his masterpiece would from now on be loved and looked after, and be famous throughout the world. I wish I knew his name to give him the credit he deserved."

Yanni looked at Marcello and smiled.

"How fantastic also," Yanni said, "to have the actual bones of the Queen in her tomb, and the portrait of her such as this, fully preserved for all the world to see."

"Yes, truly there is nothing else like it, Yanni. The 'Alexander' mosaic of the Battle of Issus at Pompeii springs to mind of course. While it is also marvelous in size, it does not compare, and nor is there a skeleton to go with the image, as we have here."

Marcello then confided in Yanni, and told him that he thought the image of Queen Sorrea was probably important enough for the country to have printed on the nation's coins and paper currency.

Yanni's heart thumped in his chest.

"Oh my goodness, unbelievable," he said softly, "unbelievable." He felt so proud to have been part of the team, to have been involved in unearthing such important finds. He thanked Marcello for his support and confidence in him. He told Marcello that working with him had been a privilege, and an experience of a lifetime. He told Marcello that he had definitely decided to change directions and study archaeology, and would be honored to work with him on the sunken ships in Pisa, if Marcello was still interested.

Marcello was very pleased to hear the news.

"Good. Young men like you, Yanni, with a love and passion for the past are hard to find." They shook hands and slapped each other on the back in a hard, macho way, as men did when they were feeling a bit emotional but it wasn't really appropriate to hug.

"I knew archaeology was in your blood, Yanni. It *is* our passion, no? We are two of a kind, you and I."

The two men absorbed the scene laid out across the floor before them for a couple more minutes. The warmth of the early morning sun was beginning to make its presence felt on their backs. It reminded Marcello of the big day ahead of him, and the last few things that needed to be done before his guests started to arrive.

"Come, now we must cover the Queen's face as before," Marcello chuckled, "to make it look untouched. You see, today, I am going to ask the Prince if he would like the honor of revealing the face of his ancient ancestor to the world. It will be a fitting gesture, don't you think, Yanni?"

Chapter Twenty-Five

Julia was a little surprised when none of the children had appeared for breakfast by eight-thirty. She had found time to stop what she was doing and go back to the canteen in the hope of seeing them. She finished her coffee and couldn't wait for them any longer; she had so much to do. She presumed that they too had had a pretty late evening the night before, probably chatting and getting to grips with the changes that were about to happen in their lives. She hoped her children had taken the news well, and she needed to sit down and spend time with them alone. Yesterday had been so hectic with all the preparations; there hadn't been a chance. She was hoping to see them this morning at breakfast, but it wasn't to be. She also wanted to remind them to wear something clean and tidy today.

Julia sighed; she really hadn't had any time alone with them at all. When today is over, things will calm down, she thought, and she'd be able to spend quality time with them. Perhaps she'd take Natasha and Alex to the coast for a couple of days to a nice hotel on the Gulf.

She waited a couple more minutes, and when there was still no sign of any of them, started to make tracks towards the palace site. Then she remembered she had to find her only dress that she had brought out here. She *should* wear a dress today, she thought, after all, she *was* meeting a Prince.

Julia decided to quickly go back to her tent and find the dress, straighten it out as best she could, and put it on, and be ready in case she ran out of time later on.

On her way to her tent, she passed that moody woman who had been so rude in trench Four the other day. Julia thought how odd she was, she still couldn't look Julia in the eye. Very odd indeed. She might mention it to Marcello and find out who she was. Something about her didn't seem right at all. She thought about the woman, and realized that she had never seen her in the canteen eating with the others, or socializing with any other team members in the evenings. It did seem odd; In fact she hadn't seen her around much at all, not even in the last two days or so, helping with the preparations for today's event. She noticed she had a bandage on her hand, and then realized that perhaps that was why she hadn't seen her around; she was probably injured and unable to do much.

Julia found her chiffon dress at the bottom of one of the boxes in her tent. She shook it, brushed the creases out the best she could, and put it on. She found her only pair of shoes with a slight heel, and put them on too.

She hobbled out of her tent, and called to her children as she walked past their tent.

No reply.

They must be tired, poor darlings, she thought. She was surprised at Alex sleeping in, though. She thought she should just pop her head in to check that they were OK. Julia didn't want them to miss breakfast completely. They had a long day ahead of them.

As she unzipped the flap to their tent, one of the volunteers called to her from a few yards away. It was Amanda, the young girl who had been working with the miserable woman the other day. She had been running and looked hot and flustered.

"Julia!" she called, "Marcello is asking for you. Can you come? They're in the tomb. They've found something! Come quickly!"

"Oh, OK," she whispered, so as to not wake her sleeping children after all. She zipped the flap closed after her.

She started to make her way to the site with Amanda, but after a few steps she hesitated and looked back at the tent. Were the children actually *in* the tent? She turned back to open the zip again.

"Julia, Marcello is waiting, and he hasn't much time before the guests start arriving, he did ask me to run and find you..."

"I'm sorry, Amanda, I'm coming."

She ran after Amanda.

"Amanda," she called as she caught up with her, "be an angel and check on the children, would you? I haven't seen any of them this morning. Have you?"

Amanda shook her head. "No, I don't think I have, sorry."

"Not even Marcello's children?"

"No, I haven't."

"What about at breakfast? Or in the bathrooms perhaps? Not anywhere?"

"No, but I have been rather busy, so that doesn't really mean anything. Why?"

"Oh, nothing," Julia smiled unconvincingly. "But do you think you could do me a favor when you're not rushed off your feet?"

"Sure, no problem, what?"

"If you could just go to their tents and wake them. Ensure they have breakfast, and remind them to wear something clean and tidy today, that would really help me. Could you do that? If they're not in their tents, they are around *somewhere*. I just haven't the time to look. But I think they're all probably still asleep after a late night."

"OK, no problem, consider it done! I'll be back." She turned to head back to the centre of the camp. "Oh, and by the way," she called to Julia, "congratulations!"

"Thank you, Amanda! News travels fast around here!" Julia grinned, and carried on towards the Queens tomb to find her fiancée.

Passing Marcello's tent, Julia noticed a box on the table by his door.

She thought it odd, and wondered if Marcello had seen it. It must have been left there after he had gone to the site with Yanni this morning. He never leaves anything out on the table unattended. It caught her attention because it was tied like a present with one of Gabriella's blue and white ribbons around it.

"How adorable!" she said, presuming Gabriella had left a present for her father at the start of his big day. "She's such a thoughtful child."

Julia decided to take the box over to Marcello, since he had obviously missed it. She picked it up. It was very light. She shook it close to her ear for a clue, but that revealed nothing. She smiled and felt a little more relaxed about the children. She pressed on towards the tomb to see what it was that Marcello had found.

CHAPTER TWENTY-SIX

The technicians had been in the tomb a few hours, and had already done three CAT-scans on the Queen's bones. Marcello patted his old friend Signor Muretti on the back and thanked him for convincing the sponsors to help pay for it and, even more importantly, for persuading them to let it be brought out into the desert. Any damage to the expensive equipment caused by sand getting inside it would be a major problem, not only for Marcello but also the sponsors. But Marcello had been convinced it would be worth the risk and expense. He had a gut feeling that his Queen wouldn't let him down.

This was the first time that Marcello had seen any type of scanning done 'in situ' in the field. Up until now he had always sent the bones, or samples, to the university back in the UK or the US to be X-rayed. He would then have waited for about three weeks for the results to come back. So having these instant results was very exciting for him and his team. Especially with a 3-D image, "which," he explained to his team when it had arrived at the camp, "can reveal the innermost secrets of a skeleton or mummy that the X-ray machine leaves hidden."

And Marcello was right. Already, the team had captured some incredible 3-D images, which to everyone's astonishment had revealed something about the Queen that nobody had expected, least of all Marcello.

The temperature in the chamber, generated by the team and the lamps in the extremely cramped space, was becoming very hot and sticky. Insects and flying bugs were being drawn into the tomb because of the lamps. However Marcello was totally oblivious to any discomfort at all. He was loving every minute of it, and was in deep discussion with the two paleopathologists about the incredible impact this portable technology was going to have from now on, for archaeology in the field. The Queen had given up her secret, and history books were going to be rewritten.

He looked up through the opening of the tomb when he heard Julia's voice. He called to her excitedly.

"Julia, my love, where have you been? Come down quickly and see this!"

She put the cardboard box down on a small pile of Marcello's files and papers that he had left beside the tomb opening. She took her shoes off, put them beside the box and papers, and climbed down barefoot into the chamber.

* * * * *

The previous night, when they were absolutely sure their captors had left, the children had after a long time, managed to untie their hands. It had been frustrating and difficult, but they had persevered, and eventually all their hands were free again. They immediately found the flashlight in the backpack and scrambled up the steep slope to the boulder blocking their exit. But it was no good; they heaved and pushed, but realized that they were never going to move it from the inside.

They sat down in the dark at the bottom of the slope, saving what was left of the flashlight's battery. They spent a couple of hours discussing their situation, sometimes despairingly, especially in Gabriella's case, and other times with logic and confidence.

In the dark though, Natasha did cry silently to herself, feeling her head and the uneven clumps of hair that now hung untidily around her face. She felt abused and hated the woman that had done it to her.

Alex sensed she was upset.

"Your hair will grow back, Natasha," he reassured his sister, "and when it has, just think, that woman will still be rotting in jail."

Natasha smiled and nodded, and her strength returned. After a little while, she felt OK. Gabriella was the most afraid, wondering what the kidnappers would do next, and took a lot of convincing by the other three that things would be all right. She tried not to whimper and clung to Lorenzo's arm in the dark. Much of her anguish though, was as much for her father as for herself, as she knew how desperate he would be when he realized they were missing. All the children were particularly upset about the note never reaching Marcello, and again the subject came up that if they had cut off Natasha's plait today, what would they do to them tomorrow? They had already hinted that Alex would be next.

"Do you think she meant it?" Natasha whispered to Lorenzo, "about Alex being next?"

"Well I intend to be out of here by then," Alex injected, "so I don't have to find out! And if I'm not out of here by then, I'll fight her to the death before she has a chance to lay a finger on me."

"Well, if we have a fight ahead of us," Lorenzo said, "I suggest we all get some rest. We should stop speculating, and save our energy. We will be able to think more clearly if could manage to sleep a little. Come Gabriella, lie next to me."

Natasha felt that same old respect feeling come over her again, like the time in the car with her mother. This time Lorenzo was the recipient. He was a calm, steady influence on everyone around him, and she liked many things about him. She especially liked the way he took care of his sister.

Natasha lay on her back and thought about everything that had happened over the last few days. Who would have known when she had said goodbye to her father at Heathrow, that she was going be tied up and shoved in a dark cave for the Easter holidays with her hair cut off with a bread knife? The fear of that woman's return ran through her veins, and she thought about her father, and what he would do or say in a situation like this. He was so practical and down to earth. One thing was for sure, she thought, he would be thinking of a way to get out.

What would he suggest at a time like this? Natasha asked herself. She knew the answer; he would probably tell them all to think, assess the situation, and deal with it. 'Don't get emotional or distracted, as that would loose you the battle,' She could almost hear him saying it. She wished he were here to do the thinking for her. The more she thought about their situation, and her hair, more she felt like crying.

She listened in the dark to Lorenzo talking softly in Italian to his sister, reassuring her the best he could. He was very thoughtful to the needs of others, always trying to do the right thing. He seemed to be there whenever help was needed. Natasha remembered how he appeared from nowhere to help her when she slipped and grazed her hand on the path their first time they ventured up to the ridge. Or when he was totally prepared to take all blame for their actions when they went gallivanting off to explore the pass without telling their parents. Natasha was glad Lorenzo was in the cave with them. He made her feel safe. He was definitely a calming influence.

"Lorenzo," she quietly said to him in the darkness.

"Yes?"

"I'm glad you're going to be my brother." She didn't care if it sounded soppy; it was the truth.

There was silence for a while, and she wondered if he had heard her.

"Me too," came the reply. "And Natasha," he whispered, "I will get us out of here, please do not worry."

"So will I," Alex's voice added. "Don't forget I'm here!"

CHAPTER TWENTY-SEVEN

Lorenzo was the first to wake. He opened his eyes. Absolute darkness.

He was unsure how long he had been asleep. Whether an hour had passed, or the whole night, he couldn't tell. The others were still asleep. He could hear Alex and Natasha breathing heavily.

He looked at his watch, but the illumination on the hands was too faint to read.

He lifted his head, and scoured the dark cave. To his surprise, it wasn't pitch black after all. He could just make out the outline of the cave and the huddled bodies lying around him. He thought it must be morning, as he saw tiny spots of brightness around the cracks of the boulder at the top of the slope. The white spots of light weren't enough to make any difference to the light in the cave though, and he was confused, because when he looked to the end of the cave on the other side, he noticed he could definitely make out the outline of the cave walls.

He lay there thinking for a while and came to the conclusion that there must be another light source. He scanned his eyes to the far end of the cave. Sure enough, it really did seem a little lighter that end; it wasn't his imagination.

He gently lifted his arm away from under Gabriella's head, trying his best not to wake her. She had quietly cried herself to sleep, and Lorenzo had held his sister close. Again, he had felt responsible for this mess they were in. But he wasn't going to dwell on that now. He knew what he had to do. He had to get them out of there.

He got up, and carefully followed the rough wall of the cave with his fingers as a guide and made his way slowly around towards the end of the cave that seemed a bit lighter on the opposite side to the slope. He noticed that the walls veered in a slight but steady curve, and he presumed he would eventually end up where he had started. But the side he was following carried on, still curving slightly, but he still didn't seem to be going back to where he started; the wall went round and then seemed to follow an almost straight line to the right. He had left the main chamber of the cave completely. The extraordinary thing was, the further he walked, the lighter it became. He realized he was now in a narrow passageway to the side of the cave.

The passage seemed to narrow further, and after walking a few feet, he could touch and see both walls each side of him with his out-stretched arms. The passage turned a gentle bend to the right, and then straight ahead of him, he could see he was at a dead end. Low, bright shafts of sunlight streamed through gaps in the rock wall in front of him. He walked towards the light, and gave out a yelp as he scraped and bumped his head on the cave roof. He realized the passage was becoming lower and narrower with every step.

Lorenzo was now forced to continue bent over, and then he had to crawl the last yard or so on his hands and knees until he reached the end of the passage and the source of light. Once at the end, he knelt down and felt the rock wall that blocked the sunlight from the passage.

It was solid. He ran his fingers down to where the sun streamed through the cracks at his knees. Some of the rocks at that level were a little loose, and crumbled away in a couple of areas as he touched it. He picked at it with his fingers. More pieces broke loose and came away. Then he started to hit at it with a small stone, and when he had some success and more stones broke loose, he then started to pound it, hacking it harder and harder. He thought of the man who had stolen his grandfather's penknife from him; it was worthless to the man, but meant so much to him as it had been a gift from his father on his thirteenth birthday, as it had been to his father on his thirteenth birthday from Lorenzo's grandfather. He hammered away at the rock wall even harder, thinking of the kidnappers who had so easily infiltrated his father's camp. The audacity of just taking prisoners at will, tying them up, cutting of Natasha's plait, infuriated him. He hit the rock harder and harder, thinking of his father's reaction towards him when he would eventually find out how irresponsible he had been letting all this happen. And, he thought, if they ever got out of this alive, how he would have to hang his head in shame for putting Gabriella's life in danger. All he wanted was his father to come home, to love him, and for them to be a family again. He didn't want to have to act the man, to be brave, to hold it all together anymore. He thought and prayed for his mother every morning and night, he missed her beyond words and ached inside whenever he thought of her. Why did she have to die? Why did she have to leave them? He hit the rock again and again, over and over, letting go of his frustration and pain, until finally he ran out of strength. His hand was bleeding, he was covered in sweat and dirt and he was mentally exhausted. He stopped, and crumbled in a heap on the floor, and sobbed his heart out for his mother.

Lorenzo hadn't noticed through the dust and his tears, that his hacking at the rocks and stones had actually made a sizable hole. Light was now pouring into the dusty passage, and the fresh, clean air eventually began to clear the thick stale air he had been breathing. After a few minutes, he began to realize this, and he opened his eyes. He wiped them, and squinted. He could actually see the rough walls of the passageway around him. He sat up, wiped his face on his shirt, and ran his fingers through his filthy hair to get it back off his face. He sat facing the light source, took some deep breaths and mustered his strength. Leaning back on his elbows, he drew both knees into his chest and then with all the force he could muster, he kicked at the rock, using his heels to ram it over and over.

It only took three very hard kicks to loosen the rock wall, and on the fourth thrust, a small part of the wall gave way completely, creating small rock-fall into the passage, but more importantly to Lorenzo, there was now an opening which almost looked large enough to squeeze through. Sunlight now streamed into the passage, lighting up his surroundings completely.

Lorenzo sat back coughing from the dust. After it had settled, he crawled forward to the opening, clearing the debris out of his way, and managed to stick his head and one shoulder out into the fresh air. He breathed in the clean air, opened his eyes, and was shocked to see how high up he was. He had forgotten that they were on the top of the ridge, and he was taken completely by surprise by the drop down into the pass below him.

Directly in front of him was the opposite cliff face of the gorge. He pushed and tried to wriggle himself through the hole a little further so he could to get a better look, and leant his one arm on a flat slab of rock that protruded from the cliff on the other side of the hole, which made a small ledge. He gasped; he realized that the slab was precariously sticking out of the cliff face with nothing beneath it but thin air. He took a precautionary shuffle backwards into the cave, feeling a bit sick as he did so. He carefully leant one hand on the stone slab again, gently pressing his weight down onto it, to test that it was safe. It seemed solid enough, he thought.

He then felt something sticky under his forearm. He looked, and on closer examination, saw that lying near his arm on the outcrop were small white bones and piles of droppings with feathers and fur amongst it. To his disgust, his hand and forearm were covered in the slimy bird mess. Lorenzo realized that he had come out on the falcon's ledge.

Scraping the worst of the slimy paste off his hand, he peered down again over the ledge.

He examined his position, and noted that the cliff had shed small chips of rocks and stones over the years, creating a sloping pile of loose scree, and these small, loose stones, which were only about twenty feet below the ledge, could be their saving grace, he thought.

If he had a rope, perhaps Alex, who was a bit smaller than he was, he could squeeze through the hole and be lowered down from the ledge onto the loose stones. He could then slide down towards the lip of the cliff-face, which dropped down to the pass. He reckoned Alex could climb down the cliff easy enough. It was their only way out, and he needed to get Alex.

He maneuvered his shoulder back through the hole, and retraced his tracks along the passageway back to the cave to wake the others.

CHAPTER TWENTY-EIGHT

"Look at this, Julia!" Marcello helped her down the last two rungs of the ladder in order to hurry her into the tomb. He was very excited and couldn't wait to share the latest development that he and the two technicians had discovered examining the Queen's bones.

"Look, look, see there?" He guided her around the top end of the skeleton, then bent down and gently touched it.

"Julia, just look at this! There is an arrowhead imbedded deep in her spine at the top of her neck. We could never have seen it so easily!"

He helped her around the cramped area to the imaging machine that showed sections of the Queen's skeleton. He pointed to the section that showed the underside of the Queen's neck, not easily visible on the skeleton itself.

"And look here, her ribs are cracked!"

"Marcello..." Julia said softly, wanting to gently change the subject. She couldn't focus on what he was saying. She needed to talk to him about the children. But Marcello didn't pick up the worry in her tone.

"You see," he continued happily, "the small arrowhead that is lodged in there, do you see, Julia? We could have missed it completely without this equipment. This is marvelous. Truly marvelous!"

Julia examined the image. She frowned and didn't say any anything.

"You know what this means, don't you, Julia?" he said. "This is very big. It means that we now know how the Queen died." Marcello looked at her eagerly for some kind of response.

"Marcello, can I have a word in private," she said quietly, "I need to talk to you. Something isn't right."

"I know, I know, this changes many things. Either she was not as popular as the writings say," he chuckled, looking down at the skeleton, "or more likely she was brave and strong and really did charge into battle with her army, as the mosaic floor depicts; even to the death. This is truly fantastic!" He shook his head.

"Marcello," Julia said softly again. She pulled his arm to get his attention. "Have you seen the children this morning?"

"Children? No, no I haven't, but they can see this later, there will be plenty of time for them to see the images."

He looked at his fiancé. He realized by her expression that that wasn't what she was talking about.

"Julia, what is it?"

"Oh, Marcello, I'm not sure, but …"

She was interrupted by a voice calling down from the top of the ladder.

"Signor, there are cars arriving, I think you may want to come up now."

"Thank you, I'm coming," he called. He turned back to Julia.

"What is it Julia? Tell me. Why do you ask about the children, is there something wrong?"

The voice from above called down again. "We are clearing the area around the top of the tomb, would you like this small box put in your office along with these papers, Signor?" the helpful voice asked.

"What? Box? Yes, yes, please put everything away… oh, no, no leave my papers, I am coming up now." He was distracted and could only focus on one thing at a time.

"The children, Julia, what is it?"

"I don't know, but I have a feeling something isn't right. It seems that none of them have made an appearance yet this morning, except perhaps Gabriella, she left you a little something outside your tent. Can they *all* be tired and oversleeping? They know what a big day this is, do you think they could have gone off somewhere without telling us?"

"No, no, Lorenzo knows better than that, I know him, he is not irresponsible. Come, Julia, I am sure they are all in the canteen. They probably had a very late night, having fun without us. They are young! Let them enjoy a little! I am sure they are all in the canteen bothering Claudio for a late breakfast."

He turned towards the ladder.

She took his arm and stopped him. She shook her head. "No, Marcello, they're not," she said.

"And you checked both tents?"

"Well, no, not exactly," she admitted, "but I sent Amanda to check for me. She should be here soon."

They climbed up the ladder and into the fresh air. Immediately a cameraman and a reporter approached Marcello, introduced themselves, and ask for an interview.

"All in good time, all in good time. Later, I promise, after the talk." He wiped the sweat from his brow and smiled. He greeted the reporters warmly, and pointed them to the area where the conference was to be held. He told them to walk around and get their bearings, and to save a good seat for themselves in front of the platform.

"Signor Muretti will be with you shortly," he called after them, then turned back to concentrate on Julia. Her face told him that she wasn't convinced the children had overslept.

Amanda was approaching, and Julia walked quickly towards her, eager to find out what she had learned. She instinctively knew the answer by the look on Amanda's face.

"Julia, none of the children are in their tents, she puffed, "I went to Gabriella's and Lorenzo's tent too; it's empty. They're not in the canteen either, and I'm afraid Claudio said he hadn't seen them this morning at all. He said he had looked out for them as he had found something that Alex had asked him to get for breakfast. But none of them showed up for breakfast; He is absolutely sure of it."

Marcello overheard Amanda's report. He stared at Julia in disbelief.

"But what does this mean? Where are they?"

More guests were approaching up the hill towards them. He glanced around for his right-hand man to take over, but Signor Muretti, already had a group of dignitaries with him over by the trenches.

Marcello was about to explode with frustration not knowing what to do next. He looked back at Julia almost hyperventilating at the thought of what could have happened.

"Darling, you deal with these people, it's OK," she reassured him, "I'll sort out the children, you carry on and greet the parties as they arrive. The children must be about *somewhere*, because, look! I almost forgot, this was left outside your tent earlier; it's obviously a little gift from Gabriella, don't you think?"

Marcello's anguish melted from his face when he recognized his daughters ribbon around the box.

"Definitely."

He relaxed, untied the bow, and grinned at Julia as he struggled to slide the tight cardboard lid off.

"It is so sweet of her," he said, relieved. "I know what it is! It is a little good luck gift from her, or maybe it's a gift from both the girls, a way of congratulating the two of us." He nodded knowingly, and kissed his bride to be. Smiling, he said, "the children are fine, Julia, what was I thinking? Lorenzo is with them, he would never do anything irrational!"

"Signor, please excuse me." A young student volunteer had approached him. "Your presence is needed at the reception area, cars are arriving. The Prince will be here very soon."

"*O Dio*. Yes of course, yes, thank you." He turned to Julia, "Take this box, I cannot open it now. Could you look after it until I have a moment? I'll open it after I've made the welcoming speech. Perhaps you could leave it over by my chair on the platform for me with my papers," he said, and winked at her. "*Ti amo*," he said, "love you…" He handed the unopened box and Gabriella's ribbon back to her. He kissed her on the cheek, and happily went to greet a small party of reporters.

His big day had begun.

Chapter Twenty-Nine

"Wow! I see what you mean, Lorenzo." Alex's head was through the hole and he was straining his neck trying to look over the falcon's ledge. "It is a bit of a long drop down, but you know what? With that slope of loose stones under here, it'll make a soft landing; I think it's just about do-able. If we could make some kind of rope, you could just lower me down onto them from this ledge. I could then slide down those loose stones until I reach the edge of the cliff. Then all I have to do is climb down the last bit of cliff and I'll be in the pass in no time. It can't be that hard!"

"That's exactly what I thought we could do," Lorenzo said. "But do you think you'll be able to get through the hole? You're wider than I thought you were."

"Sure!" Alex tried to show him, and pushed himself inch by inch further through the hole, but his shoulders were just too broad to get through the gap.

"This is ridiculous! I just can't get my..." He had one arm and shoulder through, but that was as far as he could go. Lorenzo suggested he came back in and tried his other shoulder first, but it was still no good. Alex, like Lorenzo was just too broad to squeeze all the way through.

In desperation the boys tried to enlarge the opening, kicking and hacking at the rock. Lorenzo had already kicked out the loose pieces earlier, but what now remained wasn't going to budge no matter how hard they kicked.

They were exhausted and very frustrated, and sat back in silence, and the girls joined them in the narrow passageway. No one said anything; they couldn't believe they had come this far only to be stumped by the size of the boys' shoulders. The warm sun streamed through the opening, tantalizing them. They tried to think up a plan 'B'.

In turn, Gabriella and Natasha looked out of the opening, and gagged that at their high position in the cliff face. They worried about Alex falling when he did eventually manage to squeeze through the hole.

"Well, it doesn't really matter how high we are," he snapped. "Neither Lorenzo or I can get through the stupid hole so you girls can stop worrying about it."

"Well now we have a window and fresh air!" Gabriella tried to make light of the situation.

"It's the rugby, Alex," Natasha said, ignoring Gabriella and feeling irritated with her brother. "Why do you have to do rugby instead of football? That's why your shoulders are too wide, you should have done football, like Dad wanted you to."

"It's not the rugby that makes you broad, you dork! They pick *broader* players to play because they're broad in the *first* place."

"No they don't."

"What do you know about rugby or football anyway?"

"Obviously more than you, dork!"

"OK, OK you two," Lorenzo cut in. "It does not matter what came first, the broad shoulders or the rugby, it is not important now, it's like the chicken and the egg, shall we move on, please." He was frustrated. He needed to think. How was he going to get them out?

There was silence for a few minutes.

"And anyway Alex, your face looks like it's swelling up," Natasha retorted.

"I know, Natasha, so would *yours* if you had been walloped in the chops by 'psycho-woman'. Of *course* it's swelling. It hurts too."

"I will do it," Gabriella said, looking at Alex's ballooning jaw. "I think I can fit through the hole, I will climb down."

"No Gabriella, you certainly can not," her brother said automatically. "It is not an option. It is too dangerous. I could never let you do it."

"*Oh*, so now you are my keeper? Why do we have to obey you?"

He looked surprised.

"I may be your younger sister," she continued, "but I have an opinion, whether you like it or not, Lorenzo."

"Gabriella! I cannot allow you to risk your life!" he protested.

"But you would risk yours! That is discrimination!" she said. "Natasha can not do it, she is wider than me. So I have to."

Natasha and Alex had never heard her be so forthright. Natasha looked at her. Would she really offer to climb down a cliff face for them?"

"So, you would let me stay here and wait for that woman to come back, and let her cut off what ever she feels like?" she continued, "is that what you want Lorenzo? For her to cut my hair off, like Natasha's? For you to be beaten? Look at Alex's face, Lorenzo! Has he not had enough punishment?"

"Wow!" Natasha said. She was amazed.

"Gabriella, that is not fair…" Lorenzo pleaded. He sat with his head in his hands and closed his eyes. He should never have agreed to come up here. It was all his fault. He had no more ideas; his plan for escape had failed already. He had failed his father and his sister, and put everyone's life at risk.

"Just because I am a girl does not mean…" Gabriella was still protesting.

"Shh. Listen, "Alex interrupted her. "I can hear something!" Alex scrambled over to the hole and stuck his head and one arm through as far as he could. He tried to get a good look to the pass below.

"It's a car! No, it's three cars in convoy… Actually there are more! I can see them. They must be starting to arrive for the press conference. I forgot; it's the big announcement today!"

"Throw something down, Alex; shout! Anything! Get their attention!" Natasha said.

Alex desperately threw a handful of small stones as far out as he could, but it wasn't very effective since he had to throw with the same arm that he was leaning on. The stones landed very short, bounced down the slope and stopped short of the cliff edge. He called out to them, but the cars drove on obliviously with their windows closed. His echo bounced off the cliffs, and it worried him.

"It's no good, their car windows are closed, they can't hear anything. But even if they did, our kidnappers would probably hear it too from the top of the ridge. Pull me back in."

"I told you, I will climb down," Gabriella carried on where she had left off. "I will fit through the hole, you are all too big. I will do it, Lorenzo. It is our only hope."

Gabriella sounded determined. Seeing her brother deflated and despondent gave her courage. Now she wanted to do something useful.

"Lorenzo, let's go back in to the cave and find all the ropes that they used to tie our hands. We tie them together, and make it as long as possible. I will hang down and you can lower me to the… how do you call the little loose stones?"

"Shingle," Alex said, happy to help Gabriella out.

"Scree, you dork," Natasha corrected him.

"And then I can get down, as you would have done, Alex, if you had played football instead of Rugby."

Natasha laughed at Gabriella's joke.

Gabriella didn't respond. It wasn't a joke.

Using the fading flashlight, they managed to find several pieces of rope on the cave floor. The children were in a hurry, because they knew that at any time their captors might return to check on them, or to do more damage with the knife. Lorenzo had given up protesting over Gabriella's offer. He didn't really have a choice anymore, so he agreed to let his little sister scale the cliff to get help, and prayed she wouldn't be hurt.

The children weren't sure if the arrival of the guests to the site was a good thing for the kidnappers or a bad thing. It could help or hinder their cause. For all they knew, this could have been planned around this day intentionally. But whichever way they looked at it, it now made little difference to them in the cave; the quicker one of them escaped to get help, the better. They had discussed waiting it out, in the hope that they would be rescued soon, but that could be days before they were found. And they dared not think what the kidnappers would do to them if things didn't go their way. Also, as Gabriella pointed out, without having seen the note, perhaps their parents were so busy preparing for the event that they might not have even noticed they were even missing yet. And even if they did, they wouldn't know where to start looking. The cave was so well hidden they might never be found and they would all die! Whatever way it was looked at, it was clear, even to Lorenzo, that Gabriella had to make her way out and get help.

While the boys tied the ropes together, Alex was reminded of prisoners of war he had read about, who were held at Colditz during the Second World War. He mentioned it to Lorenzo, but to his surprise, Lorenzo hadn't heard of Colditz.

"Colditz was a medieval castle in Saxony, complete with a moat, dungeons, underground chambers and secret passageways. It was more like a fortress than a castle, with gruesome stories that go back hundreds of years."

"Was it pretty from the outside?" Gabriella asked, "like a trick? Only when you went inside it was horrible?"

"No. I think it's pretty ugly from the outside too."

"But all castles are pretty," Gabriella insisted.

"Well this one isn't. And that's beside the point."

"What made you think of it?" Lorenzo asked him.

"Well, being in this cave and tying these ropes together. During the Second World War, it was used as prison camp by the Nazis for captured Allied soldiers and officers; it was considered absolutely escape-proof, like our captors think this cave is. It's famous for all the escapes and attempted escapes made by the soldiers sent there. They are even films and documentaries about it."

"Oh, that is fascinating, Alex," Gabriella said with genuine interest. "So we are like them! Will they make a film about us, do you think?"

They laughed.

"I doubt that Gabriella!" Natasha said.

"But these prisoners made it their mission to escape, rather than sit there and do nothing. They made homemade ropes made from anything they could get their hands on," Alex explained. "That's what made me think of it, tying this rope together."

"How brave," Gabriella said.

"They made all sorts of escape plans, like tunneling under the castle, dressing as German guards..."

"Where did they get the uniforms from?" Natasha asked.

"They made them. They even forged papers, passports and train tickets. They drove the Germans crazy trying to keep up with them. Sometimes the most obvious escapes done under the guards noses were the ones that were never discovered."

Lorenzo was fascinated. It raised his spirits entirely.

"Well then we shall do it," he announced. "Are you sure you can hang on to the rope, Gabriella?" Lorenzo asked hopefully, looking at it.

"Well, I will try, Lorenzo believe me!"

Alex looked at Gabriella; wow, he thought, the wimp has left us! What happened to her? She's made of tougher stuff than either he or Natasha had imagined. But smiling reminded him of his swollen face; it throbbed, and he was getting really thirsty. He could feel a headache coming too, which always happened when he didn't drink enough.

At last the ropes were securely tied together, and the children laid out the finished product on the ground and straightened it out to see how long it was. They felt they had accomplished something. Their spirits were high. It was a positive step in the right direction.

They looked down at the rope. Then the reality struck them.

There was complete silence. No one wanted to be the one to say it. But is was obvious; it was short; much too short.

If Gabriella let go of that, Natasha thought, she would drop down over eight feet onto the shingled slope, and fall and tumble the rest of the way over the cliff. She would probably roll to her death.

They were all thinking the same thing, but still no one actually one dared say it.

Gabriella was the first to speak.

"I think we have to make it a little longer," she said, hardly audible. "I don't think it's quite long enough, Lorenzo."

He said nothing.

He bent down, picked up the rope, and threw it across the cave into the darkness. He disappeared around the corner to be alone.

Alex and Natasha looked at each other not knowing what to say. They hadn't seen him behave like that before. They looked at Gabriella.

"He will be all right. He is upset," she explained quietly. "It is because he feels responsible for all of us. If we leave him for a while, he will be OK."

Alex and the two girls sat down on the cave floor in silence.

"We've got to somehow make it longer," Natasha said. "It's the only way out of here."

"Yes, I know, but how? What can we use?" Gabriella asked. "There is no more rope."

"I know!" Alex announced, standing up. He had a brain wave. He started to undo his jeans. "Natasha, take your jeans off!"

"Alex, are you *crazy*?"

"No, no he's not," Gabriella said, and stood up. "He is not crazy. Alex, it is an excellent idea!" She was thinking exactly along the same lines as him.

"We tie our jeans together, leg to leg!" she said to Natasha. "Like the men in Colditz!"

"They didn't have jeans," Natasha said dryly.

"But if they had, they would have done just this. It will work! Alex, you are fantastic!" Gabriella said as she unzipped her jeans, and to Natasha's horror, she proceeded to undress.

Natasha saw Lorenzo in the corner of her eye appear from the shadows. He came over and looked at Gabriella in utter disbelief. He sat on the floor next to Natasha. Nothing was said, but Natasha and Lorenzo were wracking their brains trying to think of a better, less embarrassing solution while the younger two stood there in their underwear.

For the older two, removing their jeans was not an option either of them relished.

They sat for a minute or so in silence, searching for an alternative solution, but neither of them could think of one.

Eventually, sighing reluctantly, Lorenzo and then Natasha stood up, turned their backs to each other, and took off their jeans.

CHAPTER THIRTY

"Your Royal Highness, Ladies and Gentlemen, honorable Ministers, members of the press, welcome! I thank you for all for coming here today." Marcello bowed at the Prince, who in return acknowledged Marcello with a nod and a smile.

"It is a *very* special honor for me to have you all here, you have no idea! This was always a dream of mine, since my early twenties, to find evidence of the true existence of the legendary Queen Sorrea. And now today, I can finally share her with you all." He grinned from ear to ear, and the audience clapped.

"You see," Marcello continued, "it was always thought in the academic world, that this Warrior Queen was a myth, not considered to be worth any time or money spent looking for her. It was simply presumed she had not really existed.

Admittedly, there had never been any concrete evidence of her existence. Hearsay and local legends were all we knew. But I spent a lot of time thinking about her over the years, and I researched and looked for anything that mentioned her by name, or indeed any anonymous Queen that perhaps could have been her. Local legend always talked of her as a just and fair Warrior Queen, who gave to her people as a river gives to the land, and that she had been loved and respected by all who came close to her. Folk tales say that the prosperous city she ruled, disappeared beneath the sands of time when the rains never returned. There was not much to go on, except that she was in Mesopotamia, around five thousand years ago, and that her city was well positioned. With no money for research, even I had to admit it was a wild, how do you say, 'goose' chase?" Marcello chuckled to himself. "But oh, I do so love a challenge!"

The audience laughed, and he looked down at Julia and smiled.

"Well, gradually, over the years because of other commitments and projects that consumed my time, I had put my search for this mystery Queen on hold. Years passed, and I continued working on other exciting things that kept me busy. But always, always, at the back of my mind, I felt a little disappointed that I was unable to prove the existence of the 'just' Queen, who disappeared beneath the sands of time.

That is, until five years ago, when something extraordinary happened! I was at the time in Sri Lanka, researching ancient medical instruments; a subject totally unrelated to Queen Sorrea, of course. My research had taken me from China to Egypt and Timbuktu in Mali, and then, to a dusty showcase in the backroom of a small museum in Sri Lanka. It was here that I saw these torn, ancient inscriptions. The museum labels describing the old scripts were vague, to say the least, saying they had been found in India in 1823 by a German archaeologist. I looked closer through the glass cabinet, and amongst these dusty scripts that mentioned surgical instruments, which is what I had initially gone there to see, one of the labels describing the parchment exhibits jumped out at me as if my magic! The words, *Queen Sorreah* and *Land of Ashookeh*, were staring at me. I checked and re checked my translations, but it was absolutely right! Then on another piece, I deciphered the words for '*kind Queen*' and '*drought*'. A lot of it was too badly damaged and torn for me to even try to read or understand, but this was like a gift from heaven! Unbelievable! There was maybe half a page of complete script, but those few words were all I needed. It was the lead I had always longed for that would ultimately guide me to this exact spot where we are today. I had stumbled across the best evidence of my ancient Queen, all the way in a museum backroom in Sri Lanka!"

The audience clapped, and Marcello looked down at his adoring Julia. He was a happy man.

"In my euphoria," he continued, "I asked the museum director what he knew about the fragmented pieces of manuscript, and he told me that his predecessor had said that they were remnants of a document, about four to five thousand years old, that described the travels of a group of Indian surgeons who were revolutionizing the then known methods of plastic surgery. How they came to be in Sri Lanka is a mystery, but I obtained permission to study the parchments, and with the help of an expert in ancient Indian script, we worked out that these inscriptions talked mostly about skin grafting for facial injuries and malformations. It seemed that this surgical team had toured all the major cities along the trade routes of the Middle East, the highways of the ancient world, for over a period of three years, over four and a half thousand years ago. There was even a diagram showing the route they had taken, and another showing something of the methods they were teaching, where a strip of skin was stretched from the patient's shoulder to the reconstructed nose. But what is fascinating, is that this technique is still widely used today. From what I understand it is to do with the blood supply of the grafted skin not being completely severed from the original donor area…I do not understand it exactly, to for me, it is…it is…."

He grimaced jokingly, showing disgust, shaking his hands in the air as if he had to dismiss it and changed the subject. His audience laughed at his feigned discomfort and squeamishness.

"However, my point is, is that these Indian surgeons came to Ashook, here, in the land we now call Iraq. The manuscript mentions that these doctors were housed in the palace, and that their hostess, the Mesopotamian Queen, had gained a reputation throughout the region for leniency and fairness. Can you imagine my joy! This was it! It was her! The soft- hearted character was one of the things about Queen Sorrea that made the legend so interesting. And here they had named her and her city, and where it was! They even described the city as being at the foot of a large split rock, between two rivers. It also said how these physicians were impressed by the fact that clean water ran into every household from large underground holding tanks."

Marcello took a deep breath and smiled.

"You see, for me, that did it. She was real! My search was on!"

Signor Muretti cleared his throat to get Marcello's attention, and when Marcello glanced at him, he tapped his watch. He nodded back.

"To cut a long story short, after having found the large 'rock with the split'," he continued, "it was not hard to find her city. He looked at Signor Muretti and smiled at his good friend, "and now better still, I have found her, the Queen herself. *We* have found her."

The audience applauded, and Marcello waited for it to die down, smiling at his friend. They looked at each other the way friends do when no words need to be said. They had become very close, and it was obvious to all that these two men had experienced a lot together.

"We have also found in her palace, an incredible floor, with detail and color beyond description, which I will show you all later. We have also located the site of the temple over there to the west. There are also some very interesting artifacts, including several hundred pictographic tablets that seem to be of accounts or written receipts of trade. Not only that, my daughter Gabriella found, what I believe could be two of the instruments brought over from India by these surgeons themselves! We will have to do further research, of course, but it is very exciting! You can see these with the other finds in the tent over there."

He glanced at where he thought Gabriella might be sitting, hoping to applaud her, but couldn't immediately see her, so he quickly carried on. Signor Muretti cleared his throat again, tapping his watch with a grin.

"And beyond the temple, beyond the walls of the city, there is something quite remarkable; an enormous underground water tank, perhaps even two, constructed in brick with what looks like a filtration system built into it; Absolutely incredible."

"This water tank has yet to be excavated, of course, but what is certain is this; it was strewn with arrow heads, especially in and around these water tanks. We have found the legendary Queen Sorrea's city. And it is real. Welcome everyone to Ashook!"

The audience clapped again, and Marcello put his hands up to tell them to wait.

"And of course, as well as the assortment of skeletons and artifacts, there is the 'piece de resistance'. A mask! The Queen's priceless, stunning, obsidian death mask."

And so continued Marcello's passionate speech about his moving discovery, about his Queen, and her mask. He told his audience about the mosaic they would be seeing later on, how it was his intention to work with the Iraqi Government and Minister of Culture, to build a permanent museum on the site to house the artifacts and protect them. He explained that now in the twenty first century treasures no longer had to be removed from their sites, they could stay where they were, in their own countries, and people could come to see *them* rather than taking the pieces away to museums around the world. Archaeologists were not adventurers and plunderers anymore, feeding the hungry museums of the world upon demand; they were scientists and scholars, wanting to preserve and restore the ancient sights and treasures.

Marcello waited for the applause to quieten down again, and then he explained his mission, which was so close to his heart; the hundreds of clay tablets, the surviving fragments of armor and jewelry found would remain on site where it belonged, and everything else that would be unearthed from the site in years to come. Marcello explained how he was setting up a trust to protect the site, which would enable future archaeologists to work here, so that students could come to Medinabad and the site at Ashook to study for as long as it took to finish the project. The trust would continue to provide all the necessary and latest equipment needed to create a library, offices, and an administrative building on site. After all, he said, there was a city under their feet, with all its secrets yet to be unearthed; there were years of work to be done here. It was an archaeological gold mine.

His passionate speech was interrupted several times by applause.

Marcello was a happy man. He was fulfilling his dream, he had proved her existence, and in a way, was giving the lost Queen back to her country.

He stood on the platform, and looked out to the one hundred and sixty people who had flown in and made the journey in the heat across the desert to hear about his momentous find. He was in his element. His career had reached a point far beyond anything he had dreamed of, the mask would be housed and protected with the Queen and her entourage where it belonged. He had found his Queen and, most importantly, he was to marry the woman who had brought him back to life.

He took a deep breath and smiled to himself as he waited for the applause to die down.

He looked out at the faces looking up at him, smiling at him. He thought how lucky he was. There was his fiancé, sitting in the second row looking so beautiful. In the front row, sat His Royal Highness, Prince Farouk, dignified and proud, dressed in his traditional finery, and next to him sat several dignitaries and members of his government. It was an important day for the country, finding their lost warrior Queen.

Marcello glanced back at his fiancé. She seemed distracted, he thought. He noticed she was hiding her mouth with her hand, and whispering surreptitiously to Yanni who was leaning forward from the row behind. Yanni looked worried, and was whispering into Julia's ear. Marcello quickly glanced along the row of seats.

The four places he had saved for the children, had reporters sitting in them; the children weren't there! None of them! He carefully checked the row again, but they were nowhere to be seen.

He flushed. His eyes quickly scanned all the rows of chairs, but there was no sign of any of them. The applause had died down and the pause in his speech had been too long. The rows of faces looking up at him were now wondering if he had finished, or forgotten the rest of what he was going to say. He cleared his throat to buy time while his mind raced. Where are the children?

His eyes flashed to Julia. His worried face said it all. The conversation they had had earlier outside the tomb sprang to mind. He stared down at her, his eyes showing the panic that was inside him. She nodded and smiled at him as if to tell him to carry on, it was OK. He could feel the sweat tickling his temples, and his pale blue linen shirt sticking to his back. His mind was a blur. He had to continue. He had to focus.

"Here in Southern Mesopotamia, almost five thousand years ago, on this very spot, in an ornate bed chamber in a palace that consisted of over two hundred rooms, with elaborate mosaic floors and inner courtyards and fountains and vistas that looked out over the valley towards the Gulf, which of course was much closer then, than it is today," Marcello indicated with a sweep of his arm the direction of the sea, still looking at Julia, "a powerful and deeply respected Queen lay dying. Whether the last battle had been won, we have yet to decipher, but legend says not. But what we do know for sure is this: Imbedded so deep in the Queen's neck was an arrow tip. It is this arrow tip that I hold in my hand. It is this arrow tip that killed the Queen."

There was a stir from the audience. This information was totally unexpected, and the press wrote feverishly on their ipads and laptops. He held up the arrow tip between his fingers for the photographers, and looked down at Julia trying to read her face for any information as to what was going on. She was whispering to Yanni again.

"...The arrow had entered from behind." He turned with his back to his audience and demonstrated the point at which the arrow had entered her body at the base of her neck.

"This was the cause of her death. Queen Sorrea was shot in the back."

Yanni was still bent forward whispering to Julia when Marcello turned to face his audience again. Julia was nodding sideways to Yanni, who then quietly rose from his chair and started to squeeze apologetically past the dozens of knees blocking his way to the end of his row. He then disappeared behind the colorful sheeting that had been erected for shade, and out of Marcello's view.

Marcello was so distracted, that he had trouble remembering where he was in his lecture.

He turned to his right, where his good friend sat, looking at him little perplexed, and Marcello cleverly introduced Signor Muretti to the audience, and handed the arrow tip and the lecture over to him.

Understanding that something was very wrong, his experienced friend smiled and bowed, and took the stage. He continued to talk about the Queen's death, and the conclusions drawn about the sad fate of the city. Marcello sat back in his chair wiping his brow, staring at Julia.

"The children, where are the children?" he mouthed to her.

Julia was trying to tell him something, making a shape with her hands, a square, perhaps. She kept pointing down at his feet. He couldn't understand what she meant. She was mouthing something to him over and over and surreptitiously pointing to his shoes.

"Oh! The box!" he said to himself, realizing at last. "The box under the chair! The box! She wants me to open the box!" he said to himself.

He very slowly bent down so as not to draw attention away from Signor Muretti, and felt for Gabriella's gift under his chair. He picked it up and put it on his lap.

Chapter Thirty-One

"Promise, Lorenzo that you will not let me drop?"

"Gabriella, upon my life, I will not let go. Of that you can be sure."

He looked at his sister.

"You do not have to do this, Gabriella."

"I do. We have no choice. Come on, let's do it before I change my mind."

She turned and hugged Alex and Natasha, who were both in the narrow passage to see her off. They gave her words of encouragement, and then they were silent. The four children understood the danger in what Gabriella was about to undertake.

"You know Gabriella, you are as brave as any prisoner in Colditz," Alex said.

"I know," she said honestly.

Secretly, Natasha feared for Gabriella's safety, but she didn't really want her to know.

"Gabriella, you will be careful, won't you," was all she could come out with.

She wanted to tell Gabriella that she admired her, despite the two years between them. She wished she could tell her that she was very brave and selfless. She wanted to tell Gabriella how sorry she was about her loosing her mother, and that she would try to be a good friend that she could always rely on. She wanted to say she was glad that they were going to be sisters. All this was bottled up inside

Natasha, and she couldn't say it. What if Gabriella died trying to save them? She would never know how she felt.

Gabriella kissed Alex and Natasha on the cheeks, then she hugged her brother.

Natasha felt frustrated as she watched her wriggle through the hole. She had to say something before she completely disappeared.

"Gabriella… you will be very careful..." she called.

"I intend to!" came the reply. "But thank you, Natasha."

"Yeah, good luck!" Alex said. "Come back with lots of soda and chocolate and anything else you can get your hands on!"

"OK! I will try."

Lorenzo, desperately unhappy about the situation, pretended not to be. He had no choice.

"*Buona Fortuna*!" he said, smiling the best he could. "Good luck."

Three pairs of jeans had been tied tightly together, leg to leg, plus Lorenzo's belt and the extended rope which was tied to the last jeans leg, to give that extra few feet. They had all decided that Gabriella had better put her jeans back on, in case she was scratched or hurt on the way down. And anyway, none of them liked the thought of her walking into the camp in front of all those people, in her underwear!

Gabriella had maneuvered herself through the hole and was sitting on the falcon's ledge, leaning against the side of the cliff for a few minutes before she dared look down. She sat there, gripping tightly to Lorenzo's arm. His head and nearest shoulder were through the hole as far as he could go.

She took a deep breath, looked down and tried to gage the situation. Beneath the falcon's ledge there was nothing except the big drop down to the unstable loose stones and rock chippings that had, over thousands of years, created the steep slope leading towards the edge of the cliff. Lorenzo told her that kind of loose, pebbly surface was a nightmare for climbers of all calibers whenever they came across it, as they couldn't get a proper grip and sink with every step. But that, he told her, was if you were climbing up it; she was going down it, so he didn't think she would have any trouble.

Gabriella's main concern was coming to a stop as she slid down it before it came to an abrupt end at the lip of the cliff. She felt sick when she looked down. So she looked up instead. The falcon was flying high above the cliffs, and seemed to be circling over her, watching her. She was trembling, and knew she had get off the ledge soon or she wouldn't go at all. She heard Lorenzo talking to her but she couldn't take in a word he was saying.

"OK Lorenzo, I'm going now. I love you."

She rolled onto her stomach and let her feet dangle. She let go of his arm with one hand and grabbed the belt. It was tied in a loop through the knot of the last jeans leg. She shuffled to the side of the ledge nearest the cliff so that she could feel it on her way down, psychologically giving her a sense of security. She didn't quite understand Lorenzo when he tried to tell her to use the rock to 'walk down', and she got flustered.

"I cant! I don't understand! Let me just be lowered down. Then I can close my eyes. Lorenzo, I'm beginning to change my mind."

Her body was shaking with fear.

"You will be OK, Gabriella," her brother smiled assuredly. "I know you can do it! Hold on to the belt with all your strength and I will lower you down as gently as I can. If you twist and turn in the air, wait until you are facing the cliff before you plant your feet and let go. Try not to land facing downhill or you may fall forward. You need to keep your eyes open! You need to see which way you are facing."

"OK," was all she could manage. She was trembling so much, her jaw was chattering. But her eyes were shut tight.

"Gabriella, open your eyes!"

She opened them, a little at a time, and when she could just see what she needed to see, she pushed herself further and further over the ledge until her whole body was hanging over the side. The only part of her left on the ledge now was her arms and chin. She was at the point of no return. One hand at a time, she let go of the falcon's ledge and hung on to Lorenzo's belt with her little dainty fingers for all she was worth. She squeezed her eyes shut again.

Lorenzo loosened his grip on the belt to lower her down, and the jeans and rope immediately slid four feet through his hands and she was gone.

"Ayeee!" he yelled out loud. The burn hurt his hands so much, that his immediate instinct was to let go. He fought the reaction and tightened his grip again, clenching his teeth. The rope stopped. He let out the last three feet and hung on to the knot at the end with all his strength.

"Are you OK, Gabriella? I can't see you!" Lorenzo called desperately. Hold on!"

He was frantic. His voice echoed around the cliffs… "*hold on… hold on… hold on…*"

His elbows were forced hard into the stone ledge and taking the brunt of Gabriella's weight. He couldn't believe how much it hurt. His hands were trembling with the strain and his knuckles had turned white with squeezing the rope so hard. Gabriella was heavier than he had imagined. The jeans seemed to be stretching, but the knots were holding. He was frustrated enough not being able to see his sister, now he couldn't hear her either.

Gabriella opened her eyes, and realized she was slowly turning round. She looked down, and saw that the steep slope of loose stones below her.

"Lorenzo let me down! Hurry, my arms can't hold on any longer, please, let the rope down more!"

"Gabriella, there is no more, you'll have to j..."

And to his horror the rope in his hands suddenly went slack. The pressure on his elbows was released; She was no longer holding the other end.

Gabriella landed facing the cliff as her brother had told her to, but she had immediately lost her footing and fell, slipping and rolling down about thirty feet, scraping and cutting herself as she tried to grab anything as she went. Finally she came to a stop as her back thumped into a rock. She lay there stunned and frightened. She was so close to the edge of the cliff, that she dared not move in case she rolled over the edge.

She spat out the grit in her mouth and wiped her lips, and realized her bottom lip was bleeding.

She looked up the cliff to the falcon's ledge. She couldn't believe where she had just come from, it was such a long way up. She had rolled quite a distance, and saw that half way up the slope, she had lost her shoe. There was no way of retrieving it now, she thought.

She saw the jeans being pulled back in from behind the ledge, and smiled to herself at Lorenzo, knowing that his main priority would now to be to untie the knots and get his jeans back on. She was grateful she had been able to keep hers on; or her legs would have been in a very bad way.

"Gabriella, are you OK?" she could hear her brother's voice calling from above.

"Lorenzo! *Sto bene*!" she called up to the ledge to let him know she was OK. But she didn't feel OK. She had been knocked about and she ached all over.

"*Brava*, Gabriella! *Brava*! *Buona fortuna*!" came the distant reply that echoed around the pass. She hoped the kidnappers at the top hadn't heard the echo.

She looked up at the sky beyond the top of the cliffs. It was so blue and clean; it felt good to be out of that cave, she thought, despite the cuts and bruises, and the state of her torn and filthy blouse. She hated being dirty. She brushed off the worst of the dust and dirt, and noticed the scrapes on the underside of her arms. It hurt when she tried to wipe the blood away from her lip, so she left the blood to dry up on its own. She wiped her face with her blouse and realized her forehead and the bridge of her nose were cut too.

She hadn't realized though, that she was bleeding at the back of her head.

"Well, I can not lie here all day nursing myself," she said to herself, "and it's getting hotter by the minute. I've got to get down somehow; only half way there..." She looked up to the top of the cliff to check if the kidnappers were watching, but she couldn't see anyone.

She slowly got up and looked over the edge below. It was still a long drop down to the pass below. The rock that she had rolled into had definitely saved her from falling all the way. She gingerly leant over the rock to examine the side of the cliff, looking for the easiest way down. This was a lot more frightening than going over the falcon's ledge. This was different; she didn't have any rope, and Lorenzo wasn't there to give her reassurance. She wasn't sure how to get down. It hadn't looked this bad from up there on the ledge, she thought.

She felt like crying. She really didn't want to do it. True enough, she had been the smallest, and was able to squeeze through the opening that Lorenzo had created, but she wasn't the sporty kind, and she was scared of heights, and she certainly wasn't a rock climber. The tears rolled down her face leaving clean channels on her dirty cheeks. She wiped them away and her face became a smeared mixture of blood, tears and dirt.

She was miserable, and felt stuck, and alone.

Then she remembered how brave Natasha had been when that awful woman had cut her hair off, and Alex, when he had been punched by that man, and she thought of Lorenzo trying to always do the right thing, protecting her; The thought of all three of them still in the cave relying on her gave Gabriella strength. She thought of the men escaping from that castle during the war that Alex had told her about.

Then she thought of that horrible woman coming back into the cave. She had to get help. She had to do it.

She carefully peered over the edge again, picked her route down, turned onto her stomach and slowly put her legs over the edge and felt for holes or indents in the rock for her feet. Very carefully, she slowly began to climb down. It wasn't easy with one shoe missing. At one point she got stuck and had to climb back up a few feet and take a different route. Her arms and thighs were shaking with fatigue but she kept moving down, telling herself that every move was closer to her father.

At last Gabriella's feet touched the ground. But as she turned away from the cliff wall, her trembling legs gave way beneath her. Her whole body shook, and it scared her a little, so she sat down on the ground to rest. She was thankful to be down in one piece, and thankful for the shade. Her hands, legs and jaw were trembling, and she didn't feel too good at all. Her back ached. She looked back up the cliff face and again, could hardly believe what she had done. She felt a bit dizzy. But she knew she shouldn't waste any time as she had a long walk ahead of her. She put her head between her legs for a few minutes.

Feeling a bit better, she then slowly got to her feet and started walking towards the far end of the pass. A few minutes later she had turned the bend, out of the pass and the cool of the shaded cliffs. Facing the desert, and blinded by the brightness, she stood still for a few moments and waited for her eyes to adjust to the glare.

The heat was oppressive, and the ground burned the sole of her shoeless foot. After walking a few yards, the hot air burned her nostrils when she breathed in. The heat pounded her head. Her arms were burning, and her lips were throbbing. She did her best to see through her squinting eyes.

With her eyes almost shut, Gabriella stumbled and staggered on for ten minutes or more, keeping the cliff wall close to her left. A couple of times she drifted away and found herself heading into the desert. When she had realized her dangerous predicament, she was jolted into concentrating harder and tried to focus. This drifting scared her, and she talked to herself out loud, and pushed herself on, making a point of focusing, keeping the cliff wall close to her. She wondered why it wobbled the way it did, it didn't look very strong at all. She would have to tell her father to do something about it.

The relentless sun continued to pound on Gabriella's frail body, and with her mind starting to play tricks, her steps became slower and heavier. She pushed herself on, telling herself that soon she would reach the outskirts of the camp. Funny, she thought, she didn't remember putting her ski boots on; but she could feel them. She looked around for her poles.

"Lorenzo has picked them up for me," she smiled, and she pressed on.

She began to limp as the bare foot could hardly touch the hot sand. Eventually she couldn't walk another step, she felt dizzy and she found that her legs wouldn't do what she wanted them to do. The left foot now hurt so badly under the stones and the hot sand that the sole of her foot had began to blister. She stood still for a moment, dehydrated, confused, and exhausted. Her swollen eyes closed. She swayed and tried to stay upright as the sun beat down on her head.

"My hat, my hat…" she muttered to herself over and over. "Papa said I must wear my hat…."

"Gabriella!" she heard her name being called, but she couldn't respond. The voice was echoing in her head. It was a distant dream.

"Gabriella!"

She collapsed onto the ground and the world went blank.

CHAPTER THIRTY-TWO

A few minutes after Marcello had started his speech, Julia had explained to Yanni about the children not being up for breakfast, and now with the seats that they had saved for them occupied by other people, Yanni was as concerned as Julia.

Sitting next to Amanda in the row behind Julia, Yanni leaned forward and whispered that he thought very it odd too, that he didn't remember seeing them last night at dinner either.

"Natasha and I had a chat earlier yesterday afternoon," he told her. "She seemed fine and didn't mention anything about going off anywhere. But Julia, we must not panic. Be calm, and try to think logically."

He had glanced up at Marcello, who was receiving his first round of applause from the audience, oblivious to the possibility that the children were missing.

"Do you think they are upset with Marcello and me?" Julia asked him. "We announced our engagement to them yesterday, you see, and I wondered if Natasha had confided in you about it?"

"She did mention it, yes, but she was OK with it. I think you can rest assured that Natasha's absence has nothing to do with the engagement. In fact," he added, "she left me yesterday evening in very high spirits."

He leant back in his chair and thought about it. He was now worried and his mind raced as to what could have happened to all four of them. He had to wait for another round of applause before he could talk to Julia again, but when they had their chance, Julia asked Yanni what he knew about the unfriendly woman who had been working with Amanda in trench four.

"I know who she is," he said, "but I don't know her, I only know that she keeps to herself and doesn't mix with any of the other workers. Amanda had mentioned to me that she is not much fun to be with. She told me she had been glad when the woman took a few afternoons off."

"*Off*?" Julia whispered back over her shoulder in disbelief. "We don't just take afternoons *off*. Didn't the supervisor say anything?"

"I don't know," he whispered back, "it is only what Amanda told me, and she was happy the lady was sometimes gone. She didn't want to mention anything in case..." he hesitated, hoping he didn't get Amanda into trouble, "well, in case it somehow got back to Amanda in a negative way. The woman is not the friendliest of people, and keeping the peace in this camp is essential to everyone's well being!"

"Oh Yanni, I'm afraid. My gut tells me something bad is afoot here. It's just not right that the children have completely disappeared."

Julia wanted Marcello to look inside the box that was still sitting under his chair on the podium, but she could see it wasn't going to be easy for him to open it in front of everyone. She realized she would have to wait until after he had finished his introduction, and Signor Muretti had taken the stage. Or should she stop the show, she wondered? She sighed. Perhaps she was just an overreacting, worried mother. Was she justified in disrupting the day by interrupting Marcello's speech? She decided she needed him to open the box as soon as possible, and she needed to prompt him to do it.

Yanni leant forward again.

"Try to get him to open it immediately. Julia, I think the children's absence is very suspicious," he whispered. "I am wondering if that small box is… is maybe not a present from Gabriella after all. Perhaps it has something to do with the hold-up in the pass the other day."

"Oh Yanni, I hope you're wrong."

Julia felt desperate. If he felt it too then she knew she wasn't being over reactive. She tried to think straight.

"I am going to look for them. I cannot sit here," Yanni whispered.

"OK, how about going to the pass? Start looking where we know the children have been before. They may have gone back there."

"Good idea."

"And if they aren't there," she added, "and they haven't made an appearance by the time you get back, then I will have to interrupt the program and tell Marcello that they are definitely missing. We can call the authorities, and get a full-blown search going."

He nodded in agreement.

"Thank you Yanni, I don't know what I'd do if you weren't here…" She turned around to him, but he had already gone.

Julia had to wait until Marcello had at last introduced Signor Muretti to the audience, and was sitting down behind him before she could get him to open the little box under his chair. She tried to point to the box and mime opening it.

Marcello had finally understood what Julia was trying to get him to do.

He put it on his lap and grappled with it for a few minutes. It was a square, cardboard box, about six inches by six, one of hundreds that they use to store shards and artifacts in. The lid was as deep as the box itself and fitted tightly over the sides. Marcello had to use his nails to ease each side up inch by inch. He was trying not to draw attention away from Signor Muretti, who was standing in front of him describing the exquisite craftsmanship of the mask, and explaining how it had been taken, for the time being, to Medinabad where it would say for safe keeping.

Seeing the stress in Julia's face made Marcello realize that something was definitely wrong, and the box had something to do with her anxiety. He inched the lid further and further, one side at a time, until at last he had got it off.

Placing the lid carefully on the floor beside him, he stared into the box.

It took him a moment to register, or to believe that what he saw in the box was really what he thought it was.

He didn't move. He didn't blink. He was in shock. He stared at it while the blood drained from his handsome, weathered face. His stomach churned.

He just continued to stare into the box.

From where she was sitting, Julia was desperately trying to tell from Marcello's expression what was inside. The fact that Marcello didn't look up at her, smile or make the slightest grin, made Julia panic inside. She knew it wasn't good news, she could tell. She just knew it. The box wasn't from Gabriella at all; it had her ribbon tied around it, but it wasn't from her.

Marcello stared at Natasha's unmistakable plait curled in a coil. There was a note tucked beside it. The curly grey hairs on the back of his neck prickled. He couldn't believe what he was seeing.

He slowly put his hand in the box and adjusted the note so that it faced him the right way round. He could now read it without lifting it out. He knew Julia was watching, and he didn't want her to see it. He took a deep breath and reluctantly began to read the chilling words.

WE HAVE THE 4 CHILDREN.
LEAVE THE MASK AT THE ROCK WHERE THE PASS IS NARROWEST. TONIGHT AT 9.00 PM.
COME ALONE, ON FOOT.
NO POLICE. NO LIGHTS.

ANY TROUBLE AND YOU WILL NOT SEE THEM AGAIN.
WE ARE WATCHING FROM ABOVE.

Marcello stared at the note. It was like a nightmare. Was this a joke?

We have the 4 children, he read again and again. It was no joke.

Very slowly he lifted his eyes from the note, and stared over at his fiancé. His pale, expressionless face said it all.

Julia immediately stood up and started to make her way down her row to get to him. She was oblivious to the legs and knees she knocked and jolted as she struggled to get through.

Marcello put the lid back on the box, stood up and walked across the platform to his friend. He gently put his hand on his shoulder to interrupt Signor Muretti's lecture as politely as he could.

"Alberto, my friend," he said softly in Italian. "Would you be so kind as to help me off the platform? There has been an incident involving the children. I think I need a drink of water… could you... help…"

Alberto Muretti was stunned. He saw in Marcello's eyes that he was in shock. He turned to the audience, smiling politely.

"Excuse us your Highness, Ladies and Gentlemen, please do not be alarmed, but there has been a turn of events that needs our immediate attention. Please bear with us for a few minutes, if you would. We will take a ten-minute water break, and we shall show you around the site. Thank you."

He took his friends arm and supported him off the platform.

CHAPTER THIRTY-THREE

On the outskirts of the camp was the designated parking area for the guest's cars, which Yanni had to walk past to get to the pass. As he neared the cars, he was surprised to see two men standing by a stretch limousine; in fact he heard them before he could actually see them, as they seemed to be having a heated discussion. He was curious as to who they were, as everyone invited was already at the site for the presentation. He approached them with caution, not knowing if they could have any involvement in the children's disappearance. On closer inspection, to his relief, he realized that they were dressed in crisp black suits and were two of the Prince's chauffeurs from his entourage. They obviously had to stay with the cars until they received the call to pick the Prince up. But the men were extremely agitated, pacing back and forth around the parking area. They still hadn't noticed Yanni running towards them. Yanni looked around to see if the children were with them, but quickly realized they weren't.

He ran up to the two men, calling and demanding their attention. He soon realized by their disinterest in him, that they were frantically trying to sort out problems of their own. He eventually got their attention, and managed to get across to them in broken English that there were four missing children from the camp, and he needed to know if they had seen them. The chauffeurs were shocked to hear this, even more so when they understood that two of the children were those of the famous archaeologist. They said they hadn't seen anyone at all. They added that they probably wouldn't have noticed though, because while they were watching a video in one of the cars of the fleet, one of the Prince's other cars had been stolen from under their noses. It had happened sometime within the last hour, and they hadn't realized it was gone until a few minutes ago. They had no idea who had taken it, or where it had gone. They were just in the process of working out how to explain it to the Prince's officials when Yanni had approached them.

"I understand that the stolen car must be very important to you, a great concern, but," Yanni said, a little frustrated, "we have four missing children and ..."

But then he stopped in his tracks. Was the stolen car and the children's disappearance in some way linked?

He shared his thoughts with the two men, and they then walked over to where the stolen car had been parked, and followed the tire marks for a few yards; It was obvious the car had been driven into the desert, and there was no sign of it anywhere now.

"You had better quickly go back and let the Prince, his entourage, and the director of the dig know about the car. This is very serious! It must be connected to the children in some way!"

The chauffeurs agreed and ran towards the camp.

Yanni pressed on towards the pass, and every pace he took in the oppressive heat made him more worried for the children's safety. He went over the conversation in his mind that he had had with Natasha the previous afternoon, trying to find a clue, or something he had possibly missed. But he couldn't think of anything that suggested anything was wrong. What worried him most was that Natasha hadn't been there for the conference. She knew that the Prince was uncovering the last part of the mosaic, and she had said that she wouldn't have missed it for the world. She was now about to miss the whole thing, and he knew by just this point alone, that something was very wrong.

The thought of something happening to Natasha made him feel sick inside. He realized how fond he was of her. For some reason he felt protective towards her. Sure, he thought Amanda was gorgeous, and there had been a mutual attraction between them straight away, but she was going back to the States in a few weeks, so he didn't feel there was any point in starting anything that would never last. They had even discussed it. It wouldn't have been fair to her or him. Wow, he thought, this puts it all into perspective! He hadn't realized how much he cared for Natasha. The more he thought of something happening to her the more he quickened his pace. He wasn't sure if it was because she was becoming like a sister he never had, or something else. He quickly dismissed the latter; that was crazy, she wasn't even sixteen yet, but nonetheless, he was surprised it had entered his mind.

He quickened his pace and wiped his brow. The heat was burning his shoulders through his t-shirt, and his mind now raced. He focused back on the task at hand, and thought up all sorts of scenarios as to what could have happened to the four of them; the fact that it wasn't exactly hard to keep the ridge in full view, cut out any possibility of them getting lost in the desert, but this only made him feel more worried.

Then his heart almost missed a beat! He saw someone about two hundred yards in front of him. But he couldn't tell exactly who it was, as the shimmering image was like a mirage, giving the impression that the person was almost liquid; quivering, and hovering above the ground.

He ran towards it, hoping it was one of the children, and half hoping it wasn't; a lone figure out here in the heat had to be bad news, he thought, especially if the other three were not close by.

As he approached, he saw that the person was standing still, swaying in the heat. Yanni ran towards the form, and his fears were realized when he was close enough to see who it was.

"Gabriella!" he called.

He called out her name again, but she didn't respond. He called out again, and she collapsed to the ground as he reached her.

She was listless and unconscious. Yanni was shocked at her condition. He stroked her filthy hair back off her face and saw how swollen her lips and eyes were. There was dried blood on her face and he realized when he lifted her that she had cut the back of the back of her head. What on earth had happened? Where had she been? He desperately looked around and at the direction she had come from to see if the others were there, but there was definitely no one else with her.

Yanni gently picked her up.

He ran back towards the camp with Gabriella in his arms, talking to her as much as he could when he found the breath, begging her to wake up, and to stay with him.

She was unresponsive, but whimpered every now and again, which Yanni hoped was a good sign. He ran as fast as he could, pressing her bouncing head against his shoulder and telling her she as going to be fine, and she would soon be with her father. A million scenarios went through his head as to what could have happened to them. Whatever had happened to Gabriella might only be a hint of what state the others were in; otherwise wouldn't the elder brother be taking care of her and getting help himself? He passed the parked cars, and wished he had his car keys on him so he could have driven the rest of the way. He pushed on, and by the time the tents came into view he was exhausted. He continued to run until he was out of breath, then he walked a little until he could start running again, though his pace was becoming slower each time and he had to force his feet to keep going. All the time, he kept talking to Gabriella, telling her how brave she was and how she would have a drink of water soon.

The girl whimpered quietly, and Yanni pressed on.

All kinds of thoughts kept racing through his mind as he ran into the camp, passing the neat rows of empty tents, calling for someone, anyone to help. But no one was around.

"Of course," he thought out loud, "they were all still over at the site. Not to worry, Gabriella, I know where everyone is, we will be there soon."

He ran on through the camp, and out towards the hills of the excavation site, thinking, wracking his brains trying to work out what could have happened to this child. He pushed himself on, and by the time he reached the site he was close to collapsing himself.

As he approached he could tell that Marcello's talk was obviously over; all the chairs facing the platform were now empty and the area abandoned. Instead, there was a lot of commotion over by Marcello's black tent on the hill. Yanni staggered towards it, stumbling and trying not to trip as he reached the large group of people gathered around it. His feet could hardly move another step, and his arms were about to drop Gabriella. He couldn't see what was happening immediately outside the tent because of the crowd, but he could hear Marcello and Signor Muretti addressing them. He could see reporters taking photos, and could now hear the questions being asked. However, it wasn't the Queen or the Mask they were asking about; it was the children. Everyone was firing questions, interrupting Signor Muretti as he tried to explain very calmly and precisely that the police and military were on their way. Yanni could hear him saying that no one was allowed to leave the camp until they had arrived He was politely telling them to make their way to the refreshment tent.

"Marcello!" Yanni called into the crowd. "Marcello!" he gasped. "I have Gabriella!"

The crowd turned and saw the young man carrying one of the teenagers in his arms; a dirty, bloodied and unconscious young girl. Yanni was exhausted and barely able to stand. He carefully laid Gabriella on the ground and then collapsed beside her, panting, and telling someone to get Gabriella some water. Photographers started snapping their cameras at him and Gabriella and Marcello rushed forward to his daughter.

"O Dio, *O Dio*!" Marcello exclaimed, clutching her, "what has happened? Gabriella, what happened?"

CHAPTER THIRTY-FOUR

"Gabriella," Marcello said quietly in her ear. "Darling, it is Papa, can you hear me?"

He stroked his daughter's forehead, whispering to her, encouraging her to wake up. At last she groaned and moved her head a little, showing signs of coming around.

She had been placed on his bed almost an hour ago, and had been changed and cleaned and was hooked up to a drip. The wounds to her head and foot had been dressed by the nurse, but her frail body still looked like she had been badly beaten. It killed Marcello to see his daughter like this. It had taken him great strength to keep his composure in front of the press and stay calm. He and Julia sat at her bedside, talking softly to her, stroking her hand, waiting for her to wake.

They were confused as to how Gabriella was free of the kidnappers. The note hadn't in any way indicated that a child would be released. Marcello couldn't imagine what had happened to his daughter for her to be found alone, without the others, and in this terrible condition. He now worried that the criminals had left in the stolen car with Lorenzo, Alex and Natasha. He patted her hand desperately trying to revive her and to find out where the others were.

Yanni was standing by the entrance to the tent, also impatiently waiting for Gabriella to come round so he could get on with locating Natasha and the boys. After he had carried Gabriella back to the site, and had been reassured by the nurse that she was going to be all right, Yanni was then taken aside by Signor Muretti, away from the prying eyes of the press, and shown the box and its contents. It had taken Yanni a couple of seconds to compose himself after he had realized what it was curled up inside the box; he was absolutely horrified. It made him feel a little nauseous and he had had to sit down in the shade for a few minutes. He was in shock. He couldn't believe anyone could do this. The exhaustion he felt from running back from the pass with Gabriella had almost completely disappeared, and was now replaced by anguish, anger and fear for the children's safety. Seeing the same blonde plait that he had pulled and teased, completely hacked and separated from her, was unbelievable. It was like a nightmare. He couldn't imagine the circumstances in which it had been removed from her head.

He had a long, cold drink, composed himself, and tried to think straight. He gathered his strength, and then he stood up, determined to find the people who were holding the children. He wasn't waiting for the police to arrive. He had to find them; he had to rescue them.

He went to Marcello's tent to tell him and Julia what he intended to do.

He had found Julia pacing up and down outside on the verge of tears while she waited for the nurse to finish washing and examining Gabriella. She was understandably under great stress. Yanni had told her that he was going to immediately gather a small party together and meet back outside Marcello's tent with medical supplies and water. He reassured Julia that he would search for them, and not stop until the children were found, regardless of the orders given by the Chief of Police to stay in the camp until he arrived.

In order to console Julia, Yanni had told her that he believed, even in the little time he had known them, that her children would be fine. He also told her that he believed they were still in the area, for if the kidnappers had taken the car with the other three in tow, the children would probably have made some kind of noise that would have got the chauffeurs attention; there's no way they would have gone with them without a fight and a struggle.

"Natasha is very strong-minded," he consoled Julia. "And Alex is brave, Julia. They are with Lorenzo, who I know is very sensible. Together they make a good team. These are the best qualifications to have in a situation like this."

Julia looked down at the ground shaking her head unable to even think straight. His reassuring words had little effect.

"Listen to me, Julia," he said firmly, almost as an order. He put his hands on her shoulders and forced her to look up at him.

"Listen!" He shook her. "I learnt this during my military service in Poland. It is the mind over the matter that is important. You understand what I am saying, Julia? They are all strong kids!"

She nodded like a helpless child, wanting to believe.

"You can have the toughest, fittest man, with muscles bigger than, than… Hercules. But if he is not strong minded, he crumbles like a cookie when put under pressure. Your children are not weak minded, Julia. They both have strong characters."

"But her hair… in a box..."

"I know, I know, it is horrible. But it is only hair." He was thinking how Natasha got off lightly, but didn't tell her that. "Come on, be strong for them!"

His reassuring words helped Julia a little, and she hoped what Yanni said about the children's state of mind was true. She took a deep breath and managed a smile for this intuitive young man who was so concerned for her children's safety.

Marcello, Julia and Yanni all had their suspicions that the children were somewhere up on the ridge, but there were of course two ridges divided by the pass, and to go up either on a whim wasting time was futile and dangerous, especially if they stormed ahead without thinking first. So Yanni decided to wait until Gabriella came round to see if she had an exact location before they went rushing around and wasting valuable time.

The camp's nurse found Yanni pacing outside the tent and informed him that Gabriella was beginning to wake up.

"But why was my baby free?" Marcello was asking himself over and over again. He was sitting on the edge of her bed, trying to hold it together. "What could have happened to Gabriella that caused her to become separated from the others? Why was she alone? Where was Lorenzo?"

Marcello was now becoming impatient, and he wiped Gabriella's forehead with a very wet, cold flannel hoping that would wake her quicker.

"Gabriella, come on darling, can you hear me? It is me, Papa. Wake up. Please!"

At last Gabriella moved her head, indicating that she could hear him. He looked up at Julia when he saw her respond. Gabriella licked her dry lips and her father put a cup of water to them. She took a sip.

"Darling, you are safe now," he said. "You don't need to worry. But we need to know where the others are. Can you tell us? Are Natasha and the boys all right?" He tried to sound as calm as he could. But he was fidgeting with impatience.

"Can you tell us where to find them, Gabriella?" he said a little louder, and patting her hand a little harder. "Are they somewhere in the pass? Or on the other side of the ridge, perhaps? Or were they taken in the car?"

Julia stood looking at Gabriella with her hand covering her mouth in anticipation of the answer. Gabriella tried to open her eyes, but there was something cold and damp covering them. She whimpered and shook her head to try to get it off. Marcello quickly removed the cold compress that he had placed over them. She opened her eyes and looked at her father sitting beside her, then at her surroundings.

"Darling, you are safe now. You are in the Nurse's tent. I am here, Julia is here too," he reassured her. "But do you know what happened to the others, can you remember? We need to know."

"Yes," she nodded.

Julia put her hand over her mouth again to prepare herself for the awful information she was about to hear; they could be miles away by now.

"They are in a cave, Papa," she said quietly. "At the top of the ridge, at the end that overlooks the pass."

Marcello stood up, almost relieved, looking over to Yanni who was standing just inside the door.

"It is covered by a large stone," she continued, "It is hard to find," she whimpered. "The lady, she cut Natasha's hair off, and they hit Alex."

Julia gasped, and turned her back to Gabriella, unable to hide her emotions. Gabriella's burned face crumpled and she tried not to cry. The thought of the whole ordeal and the others waiting for help in the cave while she was safe in her father's bed was too much for her.

"They? How many Gabriella?" Marcello pressed her.

"Three. The lady, and two men I think… you must go up there now to get them, Papa."

"Lady?" Julia said. "That woman!"

Marcello was stunned, but tried to stay composed. At least they were still in the area, he thought.

"Please go Papa…" Gabriella started to cry.

"Shhh, it's OK, it's OK, we will, we will," he said, calming his daughter. She wanted to tell them more.

"They tied our hands behind our backs and they pushed us down into the dark cave. It was the lady from the trench with messy hair, and the men who searched Natasha and Alex's car. They both recognized the men."

"They had guns?" Marcelo asked.

"Yes."

Marcello looked at Julia, stood up, then sat down again. He was beside himself. He was doing everything within his power to stay calm and collected for his daughter. Julia shook her head in disbelief, and before he could say anything, Gabriella continued, "we managed to untie our hands, and then this morning Lorenzo lowered me out on a rope that we made from all our clothes to get help. They are still there Papa, in the dark cave."

She tried to hold back the tears but couldn't.

Julia was overcome with anguish. The thought of Alex and Natasha with their hands tied behind their backs in a cave made her frantic. And Alex had been hit in the face! She wasn't going to wait for the authorities to arrive. She had to do something *now*.

"OK, OK," Marcello said soothingly to Gabriella as she cried quietly to herself.

"Is it the nearest ridge, the one you went up before to see the sunset from?"

She nodded.

Marcello looked over his shoulder at Yanni. He now had the information he needed. Yanni nodded back to him, and was gone.

"I'm going up with Yanni," Julia immediately announced.

"No! Julia, wait!" Marcello called. He was going to stop her, but the look in her eyes when she glanced back made him think twice.

"Take water and a first aid box," he said. "Be careful…"

She was gone.

The tent was quiet again. Marcello looked at his daughter. Her eyes were swollen, her face was burnt and her head bandaged. Her frail little body reminded him of a wounded sparrow.

He leant on the edge of the bed and covered his face with his hands.

"*O Dio*, what have I done? What have I done?" he whispered to himself. "It was selfish of me to have the children come out here. It was so stupid, so stupid."

He shook his head in despair. He had been so wrapped up in his work and with Julia, that he didn't see the clues in front of his eyes. He thought that he would never forgive himself. Ever.

"How could I have let this happen to the children?" he whispered. He wondered if Julia would ever forgive him.

He sat for a while going over and over the situation. Despite the fact that he had been given strict instructions by the Chief of Police not to act until he arrived, Marcello wanted desperately to go up to the ridge and find the children with Julia. He knew the kidnappers would be weak now that their plan was breaking apart at the seams. An escaped hostage would have changed everything for them. They probably knew they were finished. The police would flush them out in no time, that is, if they were still in the area. But it sounded to him like they had gone already.

Marcello was now torn. He needed to go and find the children, but he couldn't leave his daughter's side. He shook his head in his hands wondering how he had let it all happen.

"I am a bad father Gabriella, forgive me," he whispered. "Look what I have done to you. God knows how sorry I am. And dear Lorenzo; always trying to please me, and I give him such little credit. I don't think he really knows how much I love him. How could he, I have practically ignored the boy since his mother… since…"

Marcello sighed a deep, painful sigh. He turned his head away.

A frail little hand stretched out and held her father's arm.

"Papa, he knows you love him. Lorenzo will be OK. He is strong. But you must go. Lorenzo would want you too find him. Please Papa, just go. You do not have to stay here with me. I will be fine."

Marcello wiped his eyes, and looked at his daughter. She was so brave; so selfless. He lifted the cup of water to her lips to give her a sip. She finished the cup.

"I will leave you in good hands," he promised. "The nurse is here, and Amanda, you remember her? The nice girl from America? They will sit with you until I return."

He beckoned the nurse and Amanda to come into the tent and sit down next to the bed.

There was an awkward moment while Marcello hesitated to leave his daughter.

"Papa, ... *go*!" Gabriella's split, swollen lips broke into a smile.

Marcello kissed her hand, put his hat on, and left the tent.

Chapter Thirty-Five

The authorities were on their way from Medinabad, and Signor Muretti was left in charge of the very full camp until the police arrived. He had taken care of the press, giving them a long statement with as much detail as he could. The hot, noisy cafeteria was now the communications room where everyone, including the students, archaeologists, guests and the press converged, speculating and pulling together all the facts they had. The press were having a field day, in their wildest imagination they couldn't have hoped for so many choices for their front page stories; *Archaeologist's Children Kidnapped for Ancient Mask, A Severed Plait And A Ransom Note, Child Hostage Escapes Kidnappers;* Their imagination ran wild, and the volume in the tent was tremendous; Claudio's iced tea was being consumed as fast as perspiration was being shed, despite the old, noisy overworked fans that blew the hot air around.

When his embarrassed chauffeurs had returned to the camp and relayed the news of the stolen car, Prince Farouk had been advised by his aids to make a hasty departure from the area. He had refused at first, finding the whole drama rather exciting; a novelty in his well organized, protected life. But more than that, he was genuinely concerned for the safety of the missing children. He felt personally responsible for their safety and wanted to stay until they were found. He was ashamed and humiliated that such an event could take place in his country and he also made a statement to the local television station, saying how despicable this whole episode was, and when the kidnappers were caught, they would be severely dealt with. He also told Signor Muretti that he would find a way to make it right to the families once it was all over. Eventually, however, he had to submit to the advice of his aides who were pressing him to leave, and accepted that his presence was a tremendous security risk and adding to the turmoil. He was disappointed that he hadn't even seen the Queen's tomb, or the face on the mosaic floor but he realized that today wasn't the day for it. He could always return.

So despite the orders of the Chief of Police to Marcello over the phone of a complete lockdown of the archaeological site until he arrived, a second group now ignored the order, and the Royal entourage prepared to leave immediately, albeit in one car short. The entourage was to take the long route back to Medinabad, in the opposite direction from the narrow pass, therefore avoiding any risk of an ambush.

The camp almost sighed with relief after the Prince had left. Although charming, and absolute honor to have his presence, the liability of having him and his stressed guards on site was nerve-wracking for everyone; Anyone could have taken a shot at him from the top of the ridge had they wanted to. Now that he had left, however, the focus was wholly on the kidnappers and the three missing children.

The canteen was buzzing with people speculating and sharing their opinions as to who the kidnappers were. They discussed and swapped what snippets of information they had on the young girl's escape from the cave, and the latest news; the stolen car, and whether or not it was the kidnappers who had taken it and fled because of the young girls escape. Then, over and above the noise and commotion, the sound of someone banging something loud and hard on a table was heard over by the door, making glasses and plates rattle and even fall over. Slowly people stopped talking, and turned.

"Will everybody please *sit* and be *quiet!*" the voice bellowed. "I will need absolute silence, everybody's full attention and co-operation! Please!"

The room hushed.

The Chief of Police had arrived.

CHAPTER THIRTY-SIX

Yanni led the way up the steep climb to the summit of the ridge.

Julia and Marcello followed close behind, and despite being a little apprehensive as to who would greet them at the top, especially as the kidnappers were armed, they were ready for the worst. In fact Yanni was almost looking forward to confronting the woman who had cut Natasha's plait off. He hoped she hadn't fled in the car, so he could deal with her himself.

He was trying to remember anything about the woman that he could. The few times he remembered seeing the her, other than when she was working in the trench with Amanda, she had always been on her own. She rarely ate in the canteen, as far as he could recall, and she never mixed with anyone in the evenings. As he lead the way up the path, Yanni racked his brains trying to think of anything over the last few days that might have been a warning or a hint of the foul play that was looming on he horizon. But he couldn't think of anything. He had been so wrapped up in the incredible mosaic floor he was unearthing, he probably wouldn't have noticed had it hit him on the head, he thought.

He quickened his pace up the side of the cliff, and all he could do was see in his mind's eye was Natasha's long blond plait curled inside the box. It infuriated him. He could picture her twiddling the end of it around her finger, as she did when she was pensive or a little shy in his presence. It warmed his heart, and hurt him to think of her being abused.

He quickened his pace again, and thought of the boys. What would the woman do to them? He widened the gap between himself, Julia and Marcello.

At the top of the ridge, he looked around the uneven plateau strewn with rocks and boulders, but there was no one there. He was almost disappointed. No movement or sound at all. He was so geared up and ready for a fight, he couldn't believe no one was there to greet him with a gun at his temple.

He examined the plateau while he waited for Marcello and Julia. It was still and lifeless.

"There is no sign of anyone, anywhere," he said quietly to Marcello, offering him his hand as he climbed the last few feet of the pathway. "Absolutely no one up here at all."

Even Marcello admitted that he had almost expected to be jumped upon by the kidnappers. After all, he wasn't exactly following their demands written in the ransom note by coming up here to face them.

"But we must still be careful," Marcello quietly pointed out. "Just because there is no sign of them, Yanni, it does not mean they are not here, we cannot presume they have all left in the stolen car. There could be one or two of them hiding."

This didn't seem to faze Julia who, not wanting to waste any time, started to walk defiantly along the plateau towards the western side of the ridge where Gabriella had said the cave was. But it was Yanni, who only a few minutes later, beckoned her to come over to where he was.

"I think I've found it!" he whispered.

He was standing beside a mound of rocks. One rock in particular looked a bit odd because it seemed larger than the rest, and was leaning against them at an unnatural angle, he thought it could be blocking an entrance. Marcello rushed over and discarded the smaller rocks out of the way, and helped Yanni move it to one side. Julia immediately started to scramble down the small cave opening and called out into the darkness to her children.

"Julia, wait," Marcello tried to stop her, but she had disappeared.

Marcello slid down the slope after her, followed by Yanni. They stood close to each other, and Marcello shone his flashlight around the cave.

"It's empty," Julia whispered, looking around the cave. "I can't believe it. They're not here, Marcello."

But there was evidence that someone had been there. There were water bottles, dirty plates that had obviously taken from the camp, two lamps and a couple of blankets, and an old mattress against the wall. Strewn around the floor of the cave were loose papers. Marcello picked one up and showed it to Yanni. It was one of the photocopies he had printed out for the conference. It was a picture of the Queen's obsidian mask.

He shone is flashlight on to the paper. There was writing all over the perimeter of the photograph, with circles and numbers around some of the stones that were imbedded in the mask. From what Marcello could make out with his basic knowledge of Arabic, these stones had been identified by name, approximate size and value, with some form of mathematical calculations in brackets beside them.

Marcello folded the paper and put it in his pocket. He kicked one of the water bottles on the ground in anger and without a word, he scrambled up the slope, leaving Julia and Yanni behind in the dim light of the cave. There was an awkward silence for a moment.

"Would they really have taken the children with them, Yanni?" she asked.

"I don't know. But this is not the cave where they were being held, of this I am certain. Look; food, blankets and see here…" he bent down on his haunches. "Cigarettes. The smell of the cigarettes is still strong in the air. This is not where the children were. But I think there is hope that they may still be nearby."

"Is there, Yanni?" Julia asked hopefully. "Why?"

"Well, why would anyone drag three children along with them when they were in a hurry to go? Remember, their plan has completely crumbled since Gabriella's escape. She knows who they are. It's over for them. Believe me, they won't want two strong boys and a girl slowing them down. See here, they even left a pair of sunglasses behind by this blanket, and look; unopened water bottles. They left very quickly. Maybe they watched me picking up Gabriella from up here, and knew that it was over for them."

Julia shuddered and couldn't get out of the cave fast enough. She needed fresh air. She needed to press on and find the children.

Chapter Thirty-Seven

"Do you think we'll ever get out of here?" Natasha asked Lorenzo. "I mean, where *are* they? Wouldn't they have been here by now? What could be taking so long? It wouldn't be so bad if we knew they were coming; I could wait a week if I knew they would be here for sure."

Natasha was beginning to wonder if Gabriella had made it back. She worried that something must have happened to her. Natasha and Alex had both tried to reassure Lorenzo that she must have reached the camp, but now Natasha secretly had her doubts. The whole thing was dragging on far too long. Too much time was ticking by; they should have been rescued hours ago. They knew Gabriella had slid down to the lip of the cliff, as she had called up that she was OK. But after that, no one knew what had happened. She could have slipped and fallen while climbing down the cliff. It didn't bear thinking about. But no one mentioned their fears. No one dared say what they were really thinking.

They sat on the floor by the small stream of light in the passageway, for the most part lost in their own thoughts, or dozing off to sleep, if they were lucky. Alex at one point had tried to cheer up his sister and Lorenzo by talking about all the things they were going to do when they got out. He had seen people do that in films and it had kept the captives's spirits up, but Natasha just barked at him to shut up, and Lorenzo ignored him. Natasha and Lorenzo preferred to lose themselves in their own thoughts. Neither had the energy to talk or think coherently any more.

Because of his headache and his throbbing jaw, Alex was the only one of the three who seemed unable to rest. He decided to feel his way back in the darkness, along the corridor to the main chamber of the cave. He climbed up the slope to the entrance to listen for voices beyond the large stone that blocked them in.

He came back twenty minutes later and reported to Lorenzo that he had heard absolutely nothing outside the cave.

"I think we've been abandoned to rot here forever. There's no sound at all of anyone outside. I listened for some time. No one's there. Not even your leering friend with the golden tooth, Natasha."

"Well don't sound so cheerful about it, Alex," Natasha snapped. "I don't know what's worse; being guarded by violent, creepy, kidnappers or being abandoned."

"You two are so boring! I'm almost wishing they'd come back just for some better entertainment!"

Gabriella had left only a couple of hours previously, yet seemed more like ten hours. Time went so slowly with nothing to do but wait. Before Gabriella's escape, the stream of light that hit their legs at the ground level of the passage had given them encouragement that they would soon be out of their confinement. But now, playing the waiting game was beginning to drain their energy, and the sunlight was frustrating them. The euphoria of Gabriella's escape had now dissipated, and the endless waiting was taking its toll.

The thought of their captors returning at any moment and discovering that Gabriella had escaped, secretly frightened Natasha and she dreaded hearing the noise of that large stone being moved at the cave entrance more than ever. The anticipation of the woman coming down the slope again and grabbing her to harm her in some other way in revenge for Gabriella's escape, almost made her feel sick with fear. She also feared the fat man, and hoped he wouldn't come down on his own. She began to look on the ground in the hope of finding a sharp stone to put in her pocket.

"I wish they hadn't stolen your penknife from you, Lorenzo. We could do with it for protection," she said.

"Yes. I am sorry also. It was my father's. It had a lot of sentimental value attached to it. My father will be upset too when he learns of it."

That wasn't what she meant, but she let it go.

The boys took it in turns to stick their heads out of the hole and try to see or hear any cars go by, but none had passed since the streams of cars had driven by that morning.

They were now very thirsty and becoming irritable when they spoke to each other. The small amount of water they had with them had been finished the previous night, and the chocolate spread that Alex had brought was shared out between them long before Gabriella had left.

The three captives waited, deep in their own thoughts, sometimes drifting off to sleep, but mostly waiting, listening.

"So what's the big deal about this mask then?" Alex broke the monotonous silence. The question was addressed to anyone who was awake. He was lying on the floor, covering his eyes with his arm because of the headache. He was finding it hard to grasp the importance of the stupid mask that had got them into this situation in the first place.

"OK," he continued, since no one had responded, "I get that it must be valuable, that's obvious; we've seen photos of it, with all those stones stuck in it. But is it really worth kidnapping and holding hostages for? Personally, I actually think it's an ugly-looking thing."

"Well it *must* be worth kidnapping for, *derr-brain*, look at *us*!" Natasha said. "And they're not *just* stones, idiot, they're priceless jewels and gems. And a piece of obsidian like that doesn't just appear from nowhere, you know. Even without the jewels on it, it's pretty amazing to find a piece of volcanic glass that big, *and* carved in the shape of a face, *and* still in one piece after thousands of years. *And* it belonged to an ancient Queen! Surely you would know the difference between precious jewels and ordinary stones, Alex."

"Whatever." He didn't know the difference and he didn't really care anymore.

"I saw the mask, as you know, before it was taken to Medinabad," Lorenzo offered. "In all honesty Alex, to my untrained eyes it did not look so wonderful to me, either. But from my father's euphoria at finding it, I know it must be a momentous find. And look at the interest surrounding it, the Prince, the government, the press from around the world. It must be something…"

"Well when I get out of here I intend to see the thing," Natasha said. "If I have to be shoved in a cave and have all my hair chopped off by a bunch of criminals, I want to at least see what it's all about. It obviously means a lot to these people, or they wouldn't go to such lengths to get it."

Alex sat up.

"Do you think these people want to sell it, you know, I mean on the black market to overseas collectors, or a museum, like in the films? Or do you think they want to keep it for themselves?" He was now imagining himself tangled up in some large undercover international art heist.

"Oh, I don't know, all I want is to get out of here!" Natasha snapped. "The novelty of being trapped in here, not knowing if we'll ever get out has actually worn off and I don't know about you, but I'm so thirsty and hungry. What I want to know is where on earth our parents are. They're taking their time aren't they?" She kicked the side of the cave. Gabriella left *hours* ago! I just want to get out of here."

"Natasha, we're all in the same boat, you know."

"Well, I'm the one who has had their hair hacked off!"

"And I'm the one with a knuckle sandwich! My face is throbbing! Your hair is nothing!"

Lorenzo could see a situation brewing. He tried to calm them both down a little, and he started to apologize for the dire situation they were in.

Natasha immediately snapped at him.

"Lorenzo, you're not responsible for me, you know, I have a mind of my own. I'm here because I chose to come up here, not because you let me!"

He looked at her. He said nothing. He quietly got up and went down the corridor into the darkness of the cave.

"That was pretty mean of you Natasha, well done!" her brother whispered when Lorenzo was out of earshot. "He was only trying to be nice, you know. Why do you have to be so mean?"

"He always has to take the blame for everything. Doesn't he realize we have minds too? I make my own decisions; He doesn't make them for me. He doesn't *always* have to be so nice. I can't stand it!"

Natasha put her face in her hands. She started to cry to herself. She was scared and she didn't have it in her to be brave any more. She had given up. She quietly sobbed, and wished her mother were there.

Alex sidled up to her; he wasn't sure what to say. He knew she was frightened, but what could he tell her? He wasn't sure what was going to happen either.

"Alex," she sniffed, wiping her nose on her knee, "what if they saw Gabriella escaping? What if they caught her? Gabriella will be alone. We should have kept her here with us and all taken the consequences together."

"Natasha, don't say that," Alex whispered. "It'll make Lorenzo will feel even worse!" He glanced towards the dark end of the cave. "No, I think it was the right decision. Had either Lorenzo or I been able to fit through that hole, one of us would have gone. We can't risk staying here indefinitely without anything to drink, we'll all go mad! We'll have to start drinking our own blood or pee or something if we don't get out soon."

Natasha smiled. She was so glad Alex was there with her.

"What if the gang was caught by the police," he continued, "but they refused to say where they were holding us? It could take *days*, and the cave isn't that easy to find. *We* missed it, and we were practically sitting right next to it, remember?" He poked at the ground. "We made the right decision, Natasha. Gabriella had to go to get help. She'll be OK. She will. She's tougher than even she thinks she is."

He put his hand on his sister's knee to comfort her, but withdrew it when he realized he had touched a wet patch. He wasn't sure if it was wet from her tears or from her runny nose.

"Thank you Alex," Lorenzo's voice came from the back of the cave. "You put my doubts to rest. It *was* the right decision, no?" Lorenzo came back into the passage to join them and sat next to Natasha. He put his arm around her and gave her a hug.

"Natasha, I am sorry to have been arrogant. I only want to protect you. Please forgive me if it came out the wrong way. I am soon to be your brother, and I will protect you as I would Gabriella. Can you be brave a little while longer?"

He gave her a squeeze that made her feel better. "We will get out soon, I can feel it. After all, we are not in a Verdi opera!"

"Thank our lucky stars for that!" Alex said under his breath. "The only opera I've heard of is *Aida*, the one where three people get sealed up in an Egyptian tomb and are left to sing themselves to death." It all seemed a bit close to home for his liking.

Natasha smiled at her brother. She felt a bit better.

"Sorry I was rude, Lorenzo. And Alex, sorry," she said, wiping her eyes. "I'm so glad you are both here with me. I'm just so frightened of that woman coming back, and the creepy man." She wiped her nose on her knee again. "I'm so thirsty. I suppose I'm just scared. I didn't mean to snap at either of you. Sorry."

"Shhh!" Lorenzo put his hand up. He thought he heard something.

"Didn't you hear that?"

"What?" Natasha's heart almost missed a beat. The fear of that woman returning took over again.

"Voices! Listen!" he whispered. "I think I heard voices!"

CHAPTER THIRTY-EIGHT

It didn't take long before Marcello, Julia and Yanni found another boulder that looked like it could be covering the low entrance to a cave. Smaller stones and rocks had been placed at the base of it, just like the other one, to stop it from being pushed or forced open from the inside. There were footprints and cigarette butts on the ground all around the boulder.

"This has to be it; there must be a cave behind here," Marcello whispered. He indicated with his finger to his mouth that they should be silent. The kidnappers could be in the cave with the children, waiting for them.

"I will go in first to check the situation," he whispered, "and you two wait and listen here outside. I will call out to you when the coast is clear. If I do not come out, or if I do not call, for whatever reason, you will know that there is a problem, and Julia, you are not to come down into the cave after me. Go quickly back to the camp to report to Signor Muretti and wait for the Police. Is it clear?"

"But Mar..." she was cut short.

"Julia, this is dangerous," he insisted. "And the children's wellbeing is at stake here. Please, do not come down unless I say it is clear."

"All right Marcello, but please be careful," she whispered.

The large stone was quietly heaved aside. They stepped to the side of the entrance, out of the view of anyone who would be looking out from inside the cave. They waited and listened.

Nothing.

"I'm going in," Marcello whispered. He took his hat off and handed it to Julia. Cautiously and as quietly as he could, he slid down the slope, breaking the silence with the crunching of loose stones under his boots, then he disappeared from sight. Yanni and Julia held their breath, straining their ears to listen.

Marcello braced himself for what might meet him at the bottom of the slope. It was dark and he reached for his flashlight. But no one grabbed him, nor was he struck over the head with a blunt instrument, which he was half expecting.

He switched his flashlight on and shone it around the cave. It was large, and it was empty. He looked around. No sign of anyone. He could see a couple of very short lengths of rope on the floor of the cave, which looked as if they had been severed, confirming to him that this was the right place. The children had been here, but it was empty. His heart sank. They had been taken to another location, probably in the stolen car, after all. He waited a few minutes before he had the courage to call up the slope with the bad news.

"Julia…"

"Yes, Marcello?" She held her breath.

"It's safe to come down!" he called up quietly. "But…"

Julia scrambled down the slope, not waiting for him to finish his sentence. She was followed by Yanni. She stood next to Marcello following the beam of his flashlight as it lit up different areas of the cave. She saw the rope on the ground, and her heart sank. The children had gone. They were too late. Julia's legs felt weak, and she leaned against the cave wall for support. She was stunned. It was too hard to take in. Her children were gone.

Yanni bent down and picked up the short length of rope at his feet.

"The children could be miles away by now," he said quietly to Marcello. "Now what do we do?"

"I... I… the police... we must…" Marcello was crushed. All his hopes of finding them had vanished. His son was taken, and Julia's two. It was all too much. He turned to Julia and took her in his arms, not knowing what else to do.

Yanni dared not say anything, and the silence was deafening. They started to climb their way back up the slope. Then they heard something move from the other end of the cave. They stopped in their tracks to listen.

"Mum?" a quiet, frightened voice called out.

They heard the voice, but they couldn't see where it was coming from.

Marcello immediately shone his flashlight around the cave walls again, but still saw nothing.

"Natasha?" Julia called out. "Natasha, is that you? Where are you?"

Three figures slowly emerged at the far end of the cave, as if by magic from behind a solid wall of rock.

"Mum, we're over here!"

CHAPTER THIRTY-NINE

"Sir, please excuse me, but there is a man, a peasant in fact, waiting outside with his wife. He says he would like to see you."

"*What*?" The Chief of Police looked up from his paperwork at his assistant. "Please send them away, Gamil! I told you I am not to be disturbed. I have more things to worry about than a runaway daughter or a stolen donkey. Can you not see I am busy with this kidnapping case? The airport is on high alert and the borders backed up for miles because of the added security. How am I going to find any leads when I keep getting interrupted?"

"But sir…"

The Chief of Police looked at his watch. "Gamil, I really don't have time..."

"But sir, I think…"

The phone rang and the Chief of Police answered it instantly, cutting the young man off. He indicated to him with a wave of his hand to leave the room and close the door behind him. But he hesitated, and nervously stood his ground and waited for his boss to finish his call.

Since the reward had been offered for information leading to the capture of the kidnappers, the phone had not stopped ringing. Every call had to be taken seriously, but it was extremely time consuming, with false leads that had all come to nothing. The overstretched Chief of Police had little to work on, and he was frustrated.

He finished the call and put the phone down.

"For Heaven's sake, Gamil, are you still here? They are trying to turn anyone in; from their noisy neighbors to their nagging wives. What people will do for money. And now, you tell me they are even outside the Police station itself? It's a total mess. I do not have time for games, Gamil. What I need is a lead!"

He thumped his fist on the desk in frustration.

The jolt to the desk made Gamil jump and a decade-old, black and white photograph of him shaking hands with three dignitaries, fall to the floor.

The young assistant bent down to pick it up. He dusted it with his cuff and gently placed it back on the desk, the wrong way round.

"I'm sorry Gamil, I'm just under pressure. I really wanted this all wrapped up by tonight. But it is clearly not going to happen. Please leave me for a few minutes to think."

He put head down and massaged his temples.

"But sir," Gamil said softly. "He has come all the way from the village of Saramuk, and I really believe he has something for you."

"Where? *What*?" the Chief looked up at him.

"Saramuk, sir, it is a small village on the Alwassi road not far from where the excavations are taking place at the ridge. You know, sir, the place where…"

The Chief slowly looked up at him.

"I am fully aware where the excavations are taking place, thank you Gamil. If you remember, I was there only two days ago. This is where all the trouble began in the first place! But continue, please, go on, go on."

"The peasant, he wishes… well…"

"Gamil, spit it out! What does this honest peasant want of me, apart from the reward? A new, younger wife perhaps? I am only up to my eyeballs in paperwork here, and you mean to give me more! Come on, so tell me about your man from the village of Saramuk..."

"He asks that you meet him outside, sir," Gamil blurted out before he could be interrupted again. "What he has, he says is too difficult to bring in, sir."

The Chief of Police sighed and put his pen down.

"Ok, Ok, you win," he said. He reluctantly followed his young assistant out of the building and into the street.

Parked outside the police station, at the bottom of the steps, was a two-wheeled wooden donkey cart. A tired, thin man was standing at the side of the busy road next to the donkey, and a plump, wrinkled lady was sitting in the back, to one side.

"Is this what he has for me, Gamil, his wife? Is he trying to tell me that this is the female kidnapper from the ridge?" he asked sarcastically.

The peasant bowed humbly as the Chief of Police approached him, and thanked him profusely for his time in coming out to see him.

"What is it? What do you have for me, old man?" He tried not to sound too impatient, but it was difficult.

"There is rumor in the village that your Excellency is looking for three men and a woman."

"Yes, it is a 'rumor' that just happens to be in all the papers and on the radio every hour," he said. "Now let me guess; your sister, or is it your wife, has been acting strangely, or perhaps inexplicably disappearing for a day or two at a time…" He waited for the peasant to condemn the woman sitting in the back.

"No sir, my wife has been with me all the time," he replied honestly. He looked confused. "But I think we may have something your Excellency would like to investigate, sir."

"Oh *really*?"

The Chief forced a smile, and followed the old man to the back of his cart. He told his wife to lift her feet and uncover the cargo lying under them.

"Is this them, sir? The kidnappers that you are looking for?"

The cover was pulled back and there, lying at the wife's feet were three men and a woman, sedated, tied up and gagged.

The Chief stood there for a moment, absolutely astonished.

The peasant handed him three wallets and a duffle bag. His assistant helped him examine the papers in the wallets. It was them! Unbelievable!

"But... how... how did…"

"They have been using our house, sir, against our will, of course, for a while now. We were bound not to report them as our lives were at risk. Then they left, taking two of our donkeys, and we were still too frightened to report it in case they, or their boss, would come for us. We went to my sister's house a few miles away while we discussed what to do. We were too afraid to tell the police in case they…" he pointed to the bodies lying there, "returned and killed us, sir."

"So how did you…" he stopped, and thought better of discussing it in the street. "Please come into my office. We cannot discuss this outside. Gamil, you and the others take these sleeping beauties down to the cells. And you," he said to another Policeman, who had come out to see what the commotion was, "see to it that his donkey is watered and taken care of round the back."

The peasant and his wife were led into the Police station and through to his office, where they sat down at the large desk opposite the Chief. He made an urgent phone call while the old couple sat quietly and waited.

The wife looked at the black and white photograph on the desk. She nudged her husband to look at it too. He stared at it, and his eyes grew larger with fear. The couple became uneasy, and when the Chief had finished his phone call, they politely informed him that they wanted to leave.

"There is no hurry, Mr…?"

"Saiidi, sir."

"Mr. Saiidi, we have the details to take down, your statement of course is very important evidence. And then when this is done we have to discuss the reward..."

"Sir, I must go," he said. "They have really done me no harm and I am sorry for the bother."

He and his wife got up to leave.

"No, we need a statement and the details. Perhaps you do not realize the importance of what you…" he hesitated to find the word, "have *delivered* to me this evening. Whether you and your wife like it or not, you are now involved in this multi-million dollar kidnapping ring. So for the time being, please sit, Mr. Saiidi."

They sat down again. They felt doomed. They hung their heads and expected the worst.

"Then, you should have this, sir," the wife said.

She awkwardly placed the heavy bundle that was at her feet, onto the desk, and a small automatic weapon slid out of the opening and onto the Chief's papers in front of him.

The Chief couldn't believe his eyes. He opened the bag and saw an assortment of handguns and two more automatic weapons.

"It is all here, sir," the man said. "And these are, I believe, portable telephones."

He emptied his pockets of four mobile phones onto the desk.

"They have been ringing and making noises in my pockets all the way here, sir."

The Chief took one of the phones and opened it.

"Unbelievable," he muttered, as he read the screen. "Unbelievable!"

"Our house is now clean of these people," the farmer was saying. "Now will you let us go, sir? We want nothing more to do with them. Their car is still outside my house in our village. Please come and take it as soon as you can, I do not want any more trouble."

"Do you not want your reward, Mr. Saiidi?"

"No sir, we have a long journey, sir. We must go."

The Chief of Police looked at them. Something had scared him. Outside the station he had been quite forthcoming with information, now he was clamming up. Something had frightened them since they had sat down in the office.

The Chief rose from his chair, and slowly walked round to the other side of his desk, and stood behind the couple, thinking.

Then he looked at the photograph on the desk in front of them. He bent down between the couple and said quietly in their ears. "Mr. Saiidi, is it someone in the photograph? You said correctly that I now have the four of the kidnappers, but that implies that you know there are more, perhaps. You mentioned the boss. Did you see him? Was he at your house too?"

The man trembled and wouldn't look up.

"What is it that has scared you so much that you wouldn't want to stay to collect your reward?"

He slowly leant forward between the couple and picked up the photo frame. He held it in front of them so they had no choice but to look at it.

"This photograph is about ten years old. This was the Minister of Agriculture, as you may know, being a farmer," he said pointing to the man on the left in the photograph. "And this man, standing beside the Minister of Agriculture, was the Minister of Trade and Commerce. They are now both retired, as you no doubt also know. Or perhaps not," he added, wondering if politics was interesting to village people.

"Then this is me, standing beside The Minister of Agriculture, and this man, standing to the right of me, is Mr. Habibi. He is… he is the…" The Chief of Police went quiet for a few moments, lost in thought.

He eventually stood up and walked back to his chair and faced the couple. He looked at the old man.

"Is there someone in the photograph, Mr. Saiidi, other than myself of course, that you recognize? Someone who you have seen recently perhaps, in person?"

The old man looked down, and shook his head.

"Mr. Saiidi, these are not friends of mine, you understand, I met them on official business. It is very important that you tell me, even for your own safety." He looked at the man, and smiled reassuringly. "So I will ask you again, Mr. Saiidi; is there anyone you would like to point to in the photograph, that you may have seen recently in connection with these kidnappers?"

The peasant shook his head again.

"It is this man," the wife announced, quite clearly pointing to the one the Chief had called Habibi.

"He arrived at our house with a bodyguard and a driver," she said. "And he sat for only ten minutes in my house. He threatened the three men with torture if they did not deliver a mask. Then he left. As quickly as that. It seemed they had had a chance to do something and had failed. I was cooking in the kitchen for them, and overheard everything."

The Chief of Police was dumbfounded.

"Mrs. Saiidi, can you remember if this man mentioned anyone else, any other names that might be of interest to us? A client, or a partner perhaps?"

"A South American, I think," she glanced at her husband for confirmation.

He nodded.

"Yes, they didn't want to upset a South American," she confirmed.

"I see, I see. So these people that you just brought in, they were living in your house?"

"Yes, well the men were, sort of off and on. Sometimes two of them sometimes just one," the wife said. "Not the woman. I don't know where she came from. I wish she had been there; she could have done the cooking for them. I was forced to, you see, they threatened to kill me if I did not. They made my husband kill one of the four sheep for meat…"

"Yes, yes, I see. And did this boss come back again?"

"We did not see him again. He caused these men anguish. They were very afraid of him. He threatened them with torture I believe."

The Chief of Police said nothing for a while. He stared back at the photo.

"Are you absolutely sure it was this man? The photograph is old, after all. We have all changed in a decade."

"Yes sir. We are sure," the wife said. "I would be sure even with my eyes closed. His voice is very deep and he smelled of cigars and flowers."

"Aftershave, dear," the husband corrected her.

"What is the difference?" she retorted. "Flowers, aftershave! Because of him, we are two donkeys, a sheep and a good mattress short!"

"Have you told anyone about this man? Friends, family, anyone other than your sister?" The Chief interrupted quickly, sensing a domestic row brewing.

"No sir, no one. We do not know who he is," she said honestly.

"Now, please tell me, how in the world did you manage to capture these four criminals, and bring them here?"

"Sir, we must go," the husband tried again.

"You may go, in due time. But first tell me the rest of the story. We need the whole report. You mentioned that you went to stay with your sister. You need to tell me what happened. You are safe with me, I assure you." He picked up his pen. "Now, what happened, Mr. Saiidi?"

"We returned home. We had to feed the animals, you see. As we approached our house, a car passed by us, coming from the direction of our house, with dark windows, driving very fast and I had to swerve the cart into the ditch at the side of the road. But when we returned home, there was another very long car outside our house, longer than the house..." he indicated how long it was with his arms stretched out wide.

"We were afraid. We didn't know if the same men had returned, or if it was other dangerous people. I was about to turn the cart round to return to my sister's house, but my wife insisted we should ask them for some of our belongings from the bedroom, and for our livestock and chickens; my sister cannot feed us indefinitely. I was going to tell them they could stay the house if they would let us go with our necessities. I knocked on the door, many times, and no one answered. I went in, and listened. It was empty, but their guns were on the floor next to their shoes, where they usually put them; there was the long car outside, but no one was there."

His wife whispered something in his ear and the old man stopped talking.

"Mr. Saiidi, please carry on."

"Sir, my wife is worried that what she did to capture these people was a crime."

"I assure you, your wife will not be prosecuted, Mr. Saiidi. If anything, she may be commended. Please, carry on."

"My wife was in the kitchen quickly collecting some things to take back with us. We knew they could not be far, as their shoes were still by the door, next to the guns…"

"Yes, yes, go on..."

"We heard noises from outside, from the direction of the back yard. I thought perhaps one of the goats was ill, as I did not recognize the noise."

He stopped, and looked down at the floor.

"It was very bad, sir."

"Go on. You followed the noise..."

"I went to my back yard, and still saw nothing unusual. The goats were fine, and the sheep, only a little hungry. I fed and watered them, and heard nothing for a few minutes. But as I was going back inside there it was again! I followed the noise, beyond my yard, and kept walking to a small sand dune. Then I saw the footsteps in the sand, and I followed them over the dune, and then I saw them."

"You saw who? Your goats?"

"No sir. There were four people tied to the wooden posts of my old donkey shelter. The posts had been hammered into the sand. Three of the people were the men who had taken over my home, and the other was a woman, who we had not seen before. They were alive, and moaning, blistering in the sun."

"My wife and I removed the tape from their mouths, and put cold wet cloth over their eyes, which were swelling very badly. It was not a pretty sight. They were all half dead. We kept them tied while we decided what to do. At this point, we knew we had to come to Medinabad and report everything to you. But my wife did not want to leave them tied up in the sun, in case they died and their deaths would be on our hands. We could not let them go either, for fear of what they would do to us if they caught up with us; We knew we had to come to the police but we could never get to you fast enough in the cart if we released them. So my wife suggested we should bring them with us to you directly."

"Very good, very good idea. Commendable, Mrs. Saiidi. But tell me, how on earth did you do it?"

The old wife looked down in shame.

"Mrs. Saiidi, what did you do?" The Chief was intrigued, and insisted she told him. But she would say nothing more.

"She made a very strong tea," her husband announced with a grin on his face, "with herbs that we use on the goats during the birthing season. It calms them down in times of difficulty. We let the tea cool, and because they were very thirsty, the four of them drank it effortlessly. We held their heads up for them as they drank it, as we had not untied them. Very soon they were asleep like babies. We were then able to untie them, one by one, from the posts, and drag them across the sand to the cart."

There was silence in the room. The Chief of Police sat back and shook his head in astonishment. He sat for a while and thought everything through. He stared at the black and white photo, drumming his fingers on the desk. The couple fidgeted uneasily in their chairs.

The Chief eventually called for his assistant. He wrote a note on a piece of paper, signing it with a flamboyant swoop of the pen, and told his assistant to go to the bank and see the manager directly with the note. He then turned his attention back to the humble couple.

"Mr. Saiidi, you and your wife are now free to go. You have both been very courageous. My assistant has gone to pick up two thousand dinars for you from the bank, which should hold you over for the time being until the rest of the reward is released. We will have you escorted back to your village where we will also collect the abandoned car outside your house, and any other evidence. Your home is a crime scene until we have collected evidence and taken all the photographs we need. You will, I am afraid, have to stay with your sister for a couple of days. There will be a twenty-four hour watch over you and your sister's house until further notice. For your information, the car parked outside your house belongs to Prince Farouk; it was stolen from the ridge a few miles from your house. So you see, you have been more helpful than you can imagine. These are ruthless thieves, that you brought into custody, that had kidnapped the four children in exchange for a priceless ancient mask that was excavated there behind the ridge."

They nodded, but were not surprised.

"You have done a great justice. Enjoy the first installment of the reward, Mr. Mrs. Saiidi. We are very grateful to you and your wife. If you could please wait a few moments on the chairs outside my office while I make some phone calls, we will then arrange for your escort and transportation back to your village. I will have tea and refreshments brought out to you."

"Thank you, Excellency, tea would be appreciated. And the two thousand dinars; it is a fortune, thank you," the husband said. "We must decline the offer of transportation and escort; we need our cart and donkey, and couldn't possible leave it here."

"I understand, I understand. You are free to ride the cart back. However, you must be escorted by the police, I am afraid, and have the twenty-four hour police protection. It will be a very slow journey for my police officers, I grant you, but a necessary one." He grinned to himself imagining the officers driving that distance at five miles an hour.

"You will be hearing from me again soon with the balance of the reward. You do have a bank account, don't you, Mr. Saiidi?"

"Yes, sir, my son opened…"

"Perfect. Perfect. I must now make some calls. I will leave you for a few minutes in the capable hands of another officer who is now waiting to take down all the necessary details from you. Thank you again for all your help. Both of you have been very courageous."

They got up to shake hands.

"Thank you, sir…"

They were ushered out of the office to sit in the chairs outside. The Chief of Police closed his office door. He sat on the corner of his desk, and picked up the photograph.

"Well, well! Who would have guessed?" he mused out loud. "Who would have guessed indeed? This is even bigger than I had imagined."

He stroked his moustache pensively. He had to plan this with care; one mistake would ruin everything. There is no rush, he thought, he would wait a little longer to see what transpires.

He reached for the phone, then hesitated. He took a deep breath, picked it up and dialed.

CHAPTER FORTY

"Ready everyone?" Julia asked. "Here we are! You're going to be celebrities in there, so remember to smile!"

The white limousine pulled up outside the entrance to the International Bank of Medinabad, perfectly aligning the passenger door to the red carpet and the ropes that kept the press and onlookers back. There were flowers, the national flag, and hundreds of yards of gold fabric draped over and around the grand entrance of the building.

"Wow, that's an impressive building for a bank!" Alex said.

"That's because it was a palace for almost four hundred years," Julia told him. "It's even more amazing inside, just wait and see. Come on, ready?" She smiled at the four young adults sitting with her. "Good luck everyone! And smile Natasha, don't look so worried, it's all in honor of you guys!"

Photographers and passers-by crowded behind the barriers to get a closer look at the four children who had been all over the Internet and newspapers for the last week. The world was buzzing with the news of the newly excavated national treasure and the kidnapping, and it seemed the world had come to Medinabad.

Above the massive ornate double doors of the old palace, hung a large horizontal banner commemorating the discovery of the mask. Natasha looked up at it through the car window. On the banner, in full color, was an enormous image of the obsidian mask looking down at her through its hollow eyes.

She stared back at it. Natasha wondered what the person who had created the mask all those thousands of years ago would have said had they known the fuss and media coverage it was going to cause. She wondered if this exposure and hype over it was really right; It had after all, been sealed with the Queen to be hidden safely underground for eternity, now it was going to be on display to the world for eternity instead. It didn't seem right, somehow. She was dying to see it, but at the same time, she wanted to protect it.

"Natasha, come on, *move*!" Alex's voice jerked her back into the present, and she realized the car door had been opened and a doorman was waiting to help her out.

One by one, the four self-conscious celebrities stepped out of the car, the girls looking like Princesses in their long dresses, and Alex and Lorenzo proud and handsome in black-tie. They were escorted by two doormen, with neatly shaped beards, dressed in elaborate red, yellow and white silk Ali Baba-style clothes, and silk scarves wrapped round their heads. Their soft shoes curved upward like those in a fairytale, and their curved golden swords hung at their sides in ornate sheaths.

The crowd across the road clapped as the young celebrities walked the red carpet, through a gauntlet of flashing cameras into the sanctuary of the lofty building.

Marcello's car pulled up as theirs pulled away, and Julia waited for him and his closest friend, Signor Muretti. With a hand on each of their arms, Julia was escorted into the bank. This was an evening none of them would forget, held in honor of Marcello by the Prime Minister to show the gratitude the Nation for discovering their priceless national treasure. It was also a celebration of the mask itself, and of the warrior Queen, who could now be put firmly into the history books as a Queen who had really lived. And lastly, the evening was in honor of the two young men and women who had suffered at the hands of criminals because of the remarkable discovery.

Over a week had passed since their ordeal in the cave, and each day the children had gained a little more of their confidence and strength back. Natasha, who seemed to have been the most psychologically effected, still feared that the kidnappers would seek them out and recapture her. It took a lot of convincing by Marcello and Signor Muretti, and even a special written conformation by the Chief of Police to her personally, that their captors were definitely in custody behind bars and couldn't harm them any more.

One by one Lorenzo, Natasha and Alex had been discharged from the hospital in Medinabad. But because Gabriella had suffered the worst physical injuries, she had stayed in hospital a few days longer. Her foot was badly scorched from the sand after her escape, and because of her concussion, and the small gash at the back of her head, she had to be monitored a little longer. But she was recovering fast, and the swelling on her sun burnt face was almost gone completely. Her spirits were surprisingly high, and though she wasn't supposed to walk on the foot until it was completely healed, she had been given a pair of crutches for the occasion.

The swelling from the blow Alex had received to the side of his face had almost disappeared too, but the bruise it left behind seemed to be going through an interesting metamorphosis of all the colors of the rainbow. He promised it looked worse than it felt, and he declined his sister's kind offer to cover it up with make-up for the evening.

Natasha and Gabriella had both been to the hairdresser in the hotel where they had been staying the last week, and Natasha had had her severed hair cut to a proper style; a style that Yanni had told her looked very elegant. His comment made her feel a lot more confident, and although she missed her long plait, she was getting used to this new look; and it made her feel a lot more mature.

"Perhaps that woman did me a favor, cutting my plait off," she had told Gabriella before they left their hotel room.

"Yes, I think she did, Natasha. Yanni was right. I think you should write to that woman in her prison cell and thank her for what she did."

They were led through the beautifully ornate marble hallway of the bank, past statues and an ornamental fishpond in the inner courtyard, to the base of the main staircase, where about twenty people were waiting for them. The bank Manager approached Natasha and Gabriella and presented them each with a bouquet of flowers, while the officials and other guests applauded. The girls curtseyed gracefully as they had practiced in their hotel room, which Gabriella managed to do without crutches and without wobbling over.

Alex and Lorenzo, both looking dashing in their new dinner jackets, stood beside their sisters as photographers took dozens of shots for the papers.

Marcello, Julia, and Signor Muretti were officially introduced to the Prime Minister, the Bank Manager, and the Director Arts and Culture. More photographs were taken of them shaking hands in front of the sweeping staircase. Photographs were then taken with the children being introduced to the Director of the Museum of Antiquities, and many other dignitaries, who all became a blur to the children after a while. The four young celebrities bowed, smiled, curtsied, and shook hands over and over until Natasha's smile began to wane. After fifteen minutes, thankfully, the whole party was ushered up the sweeping circular staircase through an enormous, intricately carved wooden doorway. It was a ballroom, beautifully elaborate, which was a sharp reminder of the building's origins; a Sultan's palace.

"This is amazing," Natasha whispered to Gabriella. "It's just how I imagined a real Sultan's palace would be!"

"I know, Natasha, look at the chandeliers and the amazing vaulted ceiling, and the mosaics on the floor, it is just wonderful! It really feels like we've stepped into a fairy tale!"

Aside from the richly colored tiles, which seemed to engulf the room in elaborate geometric patterns, the room was decorated with dozens of onion-shaped mirrors around the walls, mounted in lattice plasterwork and intricate fretwork. In the centre of the room were twenty round dining tables, decorated with gold, white and silver tablecloths. A tall arrangement of cascading flowers stood in the centre of each table.

"This is like a dream," Gabriella whispered. "And look, your mother looks like a Princess! And my father is so proud of her, Natasha. It is so obvious!"

Natasha looked at her mother. Gabriella was right; she did look lovely. She moved over to her.

"Mum, you look stunning in your dress," she whispered.

"Thank you, darling, you look lovely too, Natasha. And have you noticed, there's a young man over there who can't take his eyes off you?"

Natasha followed the direction of her mother's eyes. Across the room, beyond two groups of people by the far wall, was Yanni. He looked so handsome in his suit and crisp, white shirt and a pale blue bow tie to match his cummerbund. His hair was combed back off his forehead and he looked very different from the Yanni she had first seen sitting outside his tent, drinking squeezed lime juice from a jam-jar. He was in a group with three other men, but he seemed distracted from the conversation, and was smiling directly at Natasha.

She flushed.

"Oh my God, oh my God, oh my God…" she kept whispering to herself. "He's gorgeous!" She turned quickly away before he or anyone else noticed how red she had become. She then thought how rude that must have seemed to him, to turn away. She took a deep breath, and composed herself before she was ready to turn around and smile back at him. But when she turned, he had gone. The people he was talking to were still there, but he wasn't. She looked around, but couldn't see him anywhere in the crowded room.

"Natasha," a voice whispered in her ear. She turned.

It was Marcello.

"Natasha, come with me. Let me show you something," he said, smiling at her. "This is what it is all about. Come with me, my dear."

He politely excused himself from Julia, gave her his Champagne glass to look after, and gently took Natasha by the arm, leading her towards the far end of the room. Weaving her through the crowd of inquisitive onlookers and well-wishers, but shaking hands politely with them when he was stopped, Marcello eventually reached the little platform at the end of the great room where he was to make a short speech. A group of guests were gathered at the foot of the platform, with their backs to them, and when they realized Marcello was approaching, the guests respectfully turned and stepped aside, making a space for Natasha and Marcello to step forward.

And there it was, poised on a marble pedestal, Natasha found herself face to face with The Obsidian Mask.

No glass, no screen, no barrier between them, just her and the mask.

Jet-black, shiny and beautiful, gazing directly at her, its inlaid precious stones and gems shone and glittered under the light of the chandeliers, its ancient majesty took Natasha's breath away.

"Marcello, it is absolutely beautiful," she whispered. "It's absolutely beautiful beyond words! It's more than I had ever imagined it would be."

He looked at her and smiled, nodding in agreement.

"You are one of the only people who would truly understand. You are the only person I can tell."

"Tell what?" she asked, still gazing at it.

He glanced to his side to check no one could overhear before he told Natasha his secret.

"It is talking to me, Natasha," he said as quietly as he could. He clutched his chest, half smiling, but half frowning at the same time. "The mask is *telling* me something; something very important, Natasha!"

"What?" she was totally drawn in. She stepped closer to him and leant forward so as to hear.

"It tells me it has to stay here. I cannot ever let it leave its home. It belongs with the Queen. I think I was given the honor of discovering it for a reason, and that reason is to protect it. I will make sure it does not leave its resting place, here. My duty is to take it back to the site, and make sure it is secure and safe, and that it stays with the Queen, forever."

Natasha grinned. She knew he was joking about the mask 'talking' to him, but she understood his point.

"Marcello, I know what you mean," she nodded. "I was thinking something along those lines when I saw its image on the banner above the door outside. It has to stay with the Queen, you're right. It wasn't created to roam the world away from her. It is a part of her. But how can you guarantee that will happen? The ministers will never agree. There must be money in it for them, if it went on tour."

"Yes, millions. But they will agree to keep it here, with the help of Prince Farouk." He winked at her.

"Good," she said. "I'm glad he is on your side." They looked at each other and smiled. There was a pause, and Marcello put his arm on her shoulder.

"You know, Natasha," he said, "I could not have wished for a more understanding and lovely step-daughter. We have much in common, no? If we were not in such a public arena as we are now I would have liked to have hugged you."

She looked down, a little embarrassed.

"The feeling's mutual," she said shyly. It was hard to admit, but it was true. And she was glad she had said it. She wanted him to know.

A gentleman approached Marcello.

"Excuse me, Dr. Milanese, are you ready to give your presentation? It is time, dinner will be served in fifteen minutes."

"Absolutely! I am ready, thank you."

He followed the gentleman up the steps of the platform, and glanced back at Natasha. "Thank you," he said with a smile. "our kind words have touched my heart. You have made my evening even more beautiful."

He put his hand over his heart and smiled at her.

"Ladies and Gentlemen, please take to your places at your tables. Dr. Marcello Bonamici-Milanese will be giving a short presentation on the Queen of Ashook and her incredible Obsidian Mask."

CHAPTER FORTY-ONE

After Marcello had finished his presentation and the applause had died down, the lavish six course dinner was served. Natasha was happier than she had felt in a long time. She finally began to feel the weight lift from her shoulders for the first time since the day they had been abducted outside the cave.

She was now very fond of Marcello and tonight she had virtually told so him in person. It was a feeling of release. The kidnappers were behind bars, and now after ten days, she finally felt confident that she was safe and the whole ordeal was behind her. To top it all, to complete this feeling of contentment, Yanni was sitting at her table only two seats away.

It was as if the tightness in her chest had lifted, and she could finally relax, knowing she was in safe company. Even her mother commented on how relaxed she looked.

"I know, I think it's the first time I have felt out of danger for a while. It's a nice feeling!" she said, beaming.

Not only that, she thought, she knew Yanni was going to be working for Marcello in Pisa on his next project, and she and Alex had been invited to Italy to stay with Gabriella and Lorenzo for the Summer holidays. It will be strange, she thought, having them as stepsister and stepbrother, but she felt mature enough to cope with all the changes happening in her life. At the moment though, she thought, as she watched Yanni talking to Alex, things just couldn't get better.

She tried very hard not to look at Yanni too much, in case it was too obvious to him or anyone just how handsome she thought he was. Only when he turned slightly sideways in conversation with her mother or Signor Muretti, did Natasha feel it was safe enough to gaze at him and absorb every inch of his face with her eyes.

"It's so nice to be clean and uncrumpled," Alex was saying. "We must have got pretty stinky in that cave."

"That's funny coming from you," Natasha said laughing at her brother. "The boy who until only recently had a soap-phobia!"

"I never, Natasha! I'm just saying how nice it is not to have sand getting into places you never thought sand could get into."

"*Alex*, we're *eating*!" she protested.

"I'll agree with that, Alex!" Yanni agreed, laughing.

"Me too!" Marcello said, and he raised his glass to make a toast.

"Here is to the absence of sand in all the wrong places!" he said, and they all raised their glasses.

"To the absence of sand in all the wrong places!" they all announced, and everyone laughed at the silly toast.

Marcello was still very much the centre of attention of the room, and even after having sat down to eat dinner, guests from other tables occasionally came over to introduce themselves to him, shake his hand, or merely congratulate him on his find and meet his family.

One of these guests who came over as they finished their second course, was a gentleman who the children had already been introduced to downstairs in front of the press. He was the country's Minister of Arts and Culture, and had become quite a dominant figure since the discovery of the Queen's tomb and the mask. Marcello had met him on several occasions over the last few months, as he had visited the site often, especially during the early days of the opening of the tomb. He had taken a great interest in it, and had even suggested putting his own security men at the site to protect the artifacts as they were excavated, which Marcello had politely declined to do.

The Minister congratulated Marcello on his interesting speech, and to Natasha's disappointment, Marcello invited him to join them for coffee, and had a chair pulled over for him to sit at their table. He was probably in his sixties, and a bit boring, Natasha thought. He had a thin, black moustache, shaved in a straight line across his plump upper lip, and jet-black, dyed, thinning hair, combed back with so much oil and spray that it made distinct, stiff tramlines over his head, making him look slimy and revolting. He stank of aftershave and Natasha could hardly look at him. She realized though, that he was important and involved in Marcello's work, so she tried to smile politely to this man, who she felt was intruding in on their enjoyable evening. He had taken Marcello's attention, and the atmosphere around the table had changed. She was annoyed too as she could no longer focus on Yanni, who was leaving the follow morning to go back to Poland to see his mother and to sort out the arrangements for changing his university degree. She squeezed her napkin under the table at the thought of it, hoping he really would come to London.

"I am so sorry your family was put through this terrible ordeal," the Minister was saying to Marcello, distracting Natasha from her thoughts. "It must have been very frightening for your children, to have been held up once in the narrow pass upon their arrival in our country, and then to have been taken by force and sealed in a cave only a few days later. These people are ruthless," he said with distain. "I am so glad it is over for you all. Now tell me," he said, looking across the table at Lorenzo and Alex, "which one of you brave young men was it who managed to escape from the cave to alert the authorities?"

"Neither of us, sir. It was actually my sister, Gabriella, Lorenzo said proudly. "She saved us all! Without her courage, we might not be here now."

"And she probably stopped the mask from getting into the wrong hands," Alex added. "If she hadn't escaped, who knows what might have happened. The mask might be half way across the world by now."

"Indeed, indeed. Who knows?" the Minister mused pensively. "I expect your parents would have paid anything to get you all back safely. *Anything* at all, is it not true Doctor?"

He looked at Marcello, holding eye contact a little longer than was comfortable. Marcello nodded at him, and said nothing. There was something in his tone Natasha didn't like; an undercurrent behind his words. They held their gaze on each other, and Gabriella broke the atmosphere.

"Really, I was just the only one who was small enough to fit through the hole," she admitted. "I was not so brave. It was Lorenzo who made the hole! And Alex's idea to make a rope from our jeans."

"Oh, I see. But it was you, young lady, who escaped, then."

The Minister held his attention on Gabriella, stared at her, smiled politely, and then turned back to Marcello and Signor Muretti.

"Now that all this excitement is over and you have the four adventurers back safely, and the perpetrators behind bars, the mask will be able to start its official tour of duty, of course."

He lit his cigar and took a couple of puffs to get it going.

"I have been in contact with several museums around the world to start the arrangements for the tour immediately," he continued. "From the response I am receiving, I predict that the magnificent mask will be on tour for at least two years. What do you think, Doctor? London, Philadelphia, Boston, Montreal for the first year, and Los Angeles, Tokyo, Sydney for the second? The international interest in the mask has already been quite overwhelming, has it not?"

Marcello shuffled uncomfortably in his chair, and smiled while he composed himself.

"Minister, with all due respect, I believe you know already that is Prince Farouk's wish that the mask is to be kept safely in this country, at least for the time being. As I tried to put across in my presentation just now, obviously not quite well enough, it seems, it is no longer necessary for *any* priceless artifacts to leave their country of origin for months or years at a time; if at all. The museums of the world are overcrowded with monuments and treasures belonging to other nations, while those nations are left with nothing but holes in the ground. Surely you, in your lofty position, Minister, would understand this reasoning. I cannot quite understand your haste to have the mask leave your country. I am working with your nation's interest at heart here, Minister." Marcello paused and looked at him in the eye, "And," he continued, "I wonder Minister, whose interest it is that *you* are working with at heart?"

This was blunt. Even Gabriella, the youngest around the table, sensed the atmosphere. Julia flushed, and was about to change the subject when the Minister answered Marcello. He started with a fake laugh.

"My dear Doctor, what are you suggesting? We cannot deprive the thousands of people over the world, who are willing to pay to see the magnificent mask! The Americans, for example, you cannot deprive the Americans of having a glimpse …"

"The Americans who are that interested," Signor Muretti injected, "will, I am sure, be more than happy to come and see the mask here, where it belongs, by the tomb, the Queen and her artifacts. Surely, Minister you must agree it will boost your country's economy no end to have the mask permanently housed here in a 'state of the art' museum at the site. Visitors will be able to see work in progress as the excavation of the palace continues, which will generate more interest in archaeology, and increase enrollment at the university here in Medinabad. The Prince himself was even quoted in the paper this week saying he is giving his go-ahead for the plans for the visitor center at the site and the paving of the desert road. Surely you read the paper?"

The minister said nothing, and smiled into his coffee cup.

Marcello concluded, "so for now, Minister, the Mask will remain here in Medinabad Museum until the site to house it is completed. The kidnapping of my children, surely, is a warning to us all, that there is almost *too* much interest in the mask, and it should be kept safely in one place where its security is guaranteed. Taking it out of the country, and from city to city is for now, a security nightmare. If these criminals have tried once, what is to stop others from trying again?"

"If I was a thief," Alex offered, "I would make an exact copy of it in a sort of plastic resin and switch it over in transit. It would be easy. No one would know, because so few people have seen it. It would make a good film too!"

The Minister of Arts and Culture glared at Alex, and his eyes narrowed. He was about to say something when Marcello suddenly stood up.

"Ah, my friend, please join us for coffee and chocolates!"

He greeted the Chief of Police who had just entered the room and was heading over to his table, "I am so glad you were able to come."

They shook hands warmly, and Marcello was relieved to see a fresh smiling face.

"Please join us, pull up a chair next to the Minister, who I believe you have met already."

"Yes, many moons ago," he said to him. "In fact, Mr. Habibi, I am very glad to find you here at Dr. Milanese's table."

Marcello added a chair for the Chief of Police to join the party.

"Thank you, it would be an honor to join you and your family." He smiled politely.

"May I introduce you to Lorenzo, my son, Natasha, my daughter," Marcello said, "my son Alex, and Gabriella my youngest daughter. My fiancé, Julia, you already met at the site, and Signor Muretti, you know of course. This is Maric Janowski, my first assistant, affectionately known as Yanni. This," he said, addressing the children, "is Mr. Azzam, the Chief of Police, who has done such a good job in finding the abductors and getting them behind bars."

Lorenzo stood up and reached out to shake his hand, as did Yanni. Alex proudly followed suit, looking very serious, feeling older than his thirteen years, and enjoying it.

"Thank goodness we meet tonight under much happier circumstances, than when we were last together at the camp," Marcello said. "Thanks to you and your Police Force's tireless efforts and detective work."

"Doctor, you flatter me, however I am glad you are all safe."

The Chief smiled at the girls and Natasha thought he had a kind, open face.

He was poured a coffee and offered chocolates from a plate on the table.

"Thank you, you are too kind, Dr. Milanese. You must forgive me for being late, I have actually been crossing the remaining 'T's and dotting the 'I's, as they say in English, trying to bring the case to a close."

"Oh, I thought it was already completely wrapped up!" Julia exclaimed. She smiled but there was worry in her tone.

"Wow! You mean there is more to the case?" Alex asked. "Can you tell us what you're working on now?"

"Alex! I don't think the Chief of Police is at liberty to discuss his work..." Julia tried to cover for her son's forwardness. "But everything is all right now, isn't it?" she asked.

"No, no, it is fine, Madam, he is young and impulsive, and asks what he feels," he said, smiling at Alex. But the Chief didn't answer the second part of Julia's question.

"Thank you," Julia said. "But is this case completely closed now? You do have everyone involved in the ordeal behind bars, don't you?"

"Yes, everything is under control." He looked at Marcello and Signor Muretti. "To be precise, we are ninety-nine point nine percent there. There is just one more little piece to the puzzle; one other person we have to detain; the mastermind of the operation, in fact."

"Wow! The mastermind?" Alex liked the sound of it. "So cool to be involved with a mastermind of an operation!"

Natasha began to feel that old feeling of fear return. She wished the minister of Arts wasn't there with them, so they could talk about it more freely and put everyone's mind at rest. She glanced at the Minister. He was shifting on his chair. He was fumbling in his trouser pocket for a handkerchief to wipe his brow. As he did so, something fell out of his pocket and slid under the table, across the polished floor towards Natasha's chair.

Natasha bent down to pick it up for him. She hesitated. Curiously, she examined it, and slowly looked at Lorenzo, who was oblivious to what had just happened.

"Do you know who the mastermind is?" Alex was asking the Chief.

The Chief of Police half smiled and half frowned, then looked at Marcello. "Well actually we do. Doctor, it turns out," he said pensively, "that your first suspicions were right that evening at the camp. I admit I was wrong to dismiss it. I had a hard time accepting the evidence, but I can now tell you that we know who it is. We have all the evidence we need to convict him."

The Chief of Police and Marcello held their gaze at each other. Marcello seemed a little stunned.

"I didn't realize there was a mastermind behind it, other than those four brought in by the old couple that we read about in the papers," Yanni said. "And I had no idea the Doctor had his suspicions on who it was…"

Marcello shifted uncomfortably in his chair.

"Nor did I," Julia said dryly, looking at her fiancée. "Are you close to capturing him, Mr. Azzam?" she asked

"I am very close, Madam. Very close indeed."

The Chief of Police looked at the Minister, who was tapping his upper lip with his handkerchief.

"What was it that you dropped from your pocket, Mr. Habibi?" The Chief asked. "A pair of sunglasses perhaps? You wouldn't want to lose those, and have your eyes unprotected in the bright sunlight, would you? As you know, Minister, the sun can be quite torturous if one is out in it for too long…"

"No, no, it is, er, not sunglasses," he said uncomfortably. He looked over to Natasha to retrieve the object from her. "Just a small thing… a trinket."

Natasha nudged Lorenzo, and showed him what she had in the palm of her hand. He looked down and saw what had slid across the floor. It was a red penknife, just like his own. Lorenzo took it from Natasha, and turned it over, examining it with curiosity. He could see the agitated Minister across the table waiting for it to be handed back to him. Lorenzo carefully placed it on the table by his father. He looked up at the Minister, who was now sweating profusely.

"May I ask, Minister, where you got such a fine penknife as this?" Lorenzo asked.

Marcello picked it up. He pulled out one of the blades and examined the bent tip.

"I had one just like this," Lorenzo continued, "but it was stolen from me when we were held in the cave."

Lorenzo was confused. He knew it couldn't be his, but it was. "I am sorry Papa, I did not tell you, I..."

Marcello shook his head, indicating for his son not to be concerned. His frown, though, as he examined the penknife, showed he was deep in thought. He glanced up at the Chief. They surreptitiously gave each other a nod.

The Minister wiped his brow again, and tried to answer Lorenzo's question.

"It was a small gift from an employee, it is nothing; a cheap souvenir from Europe. Switzerland I believe. May I have it please?"

He reached across the able to take it, and as he did so, the Chief of Police stood up and clamped a handcuff round his wrist.

"I think we will be leaving now, Minister," he whispered in his ear. "We can do this discreetly, so as not to cause a disturbance in front of the guests, or my men at the door can make a show of it. It is entirely up to you. Ladies, gentlemen..." he addressed the shocked table, "would you please all excuse us? Please enjoy the rest of your evening."

CHAPTER FORTY-TWO

That night, Natasha was feeling very relieved. She had been shocked and upset at what happened at the dining table, as had everyone else. But now she was absolutely sure she had nothing more to fear. It was all over. She and Alex were flying back to London with her mother in the morning. There was so much more to think about than the silly Minister. Arrangements had already been made for the four to spend time together during the summer holidays in Italy. But still, Natasha couldn't sleep. She wasn't thinking about the Minister, or staying with Gabriella and Lorenzo. She was thinking about something else.

"Gabriella, are you awake?" she whispered.

"Mmmm," came the mumbled reply from Gabriella's bed.

"Where is your house again? I forgot what you told me. Where exactly is it we're going to be staying for the summer?"

"In a valley, near Piacenza," she replied quietly. "Go to sleep, Natasha."

"So how far is that from Pisa, you know, from where your Dad will be working on those sunken ships?"

There was a long pause, and Natasha thought Gabriella had fallen back to sleep again.

"You will see Yanni, Natasha, no matter how far it is. Now go to sleep. Please. Good night."

"Night," she whispered, grinning. She turned over and closed her eyes. Only three months until the summer holidays. That wasn't *too* long to wait.

Printed in Great Britain
by Amazon